Pamela Taylor

Pestilence

Second Son Chronicles - Volume 3

Black Rose Writing | Texas

ISBN: 978-1-68433-481-0
PUBLISHED BY BLACK ROSE WRITING
www.blackrosewriting.com

Printed in the United States of America
Suggested Retail Price (SRP) $18.95

Pestilence is printed in Book Antiqua

*As a planet-friendly publisher, Black Rose Writing does its best to eliminate unnecessary waste to reduce paper usage and energy costs, while never compromising the reading experience. As a result, the final word count vs. page count may not meet common expectations.

This series is dedicated to the hope that thoughtfulness, compassion, respect, and rational dialogue can triumph over bigotry, greed, mistrust, and self-righteousness to create a world that is truly a better place for all of humankind.

I'm particularly grateful to Linda Kirwin for her help and guidance. Though her project started as a beta read with critique, she quickly grasped what I was trying to do in this series and became a valued editorial consultant. Thanks also to the members of the DFW Writers Workshop who listened to readings and offered their food for thought. And a very special thank you to Jeffrey — himself a second son — who was my first reader and who encouraged me in the early days, when I was unsure if my vision was worth pursuing.

Praise for The Second Son Chronicles

Second Son

"A fine-grained and emotionally satisfying medieval adventure."
— *Kirkus Reviews*

"In the genre of historically inspired fiction, Taylor has done a marvelous job of combining fact, fantasy, and fun."
— *Indie Reader*

"Historical fiction lovers will enjoy this tale of knightly adventure."
— *Sublime Book Review*

My Father, My King

"Written in elegant prose, with an intricate storyline that is woven together like a fine medieval tapestry."
— *Authors Reading*

"An absolutely sensational renaissance novel filled with dry humor, heartfelt moments, and exceptional characters."
— *Sublime Book Review*

"An intriguing… enchanting… fictional take on ancient ruling family, and its traditions."
— *Indie Reader*

2nd Place – Fantasy, 2019 PenCraft Awards

The Royal Family

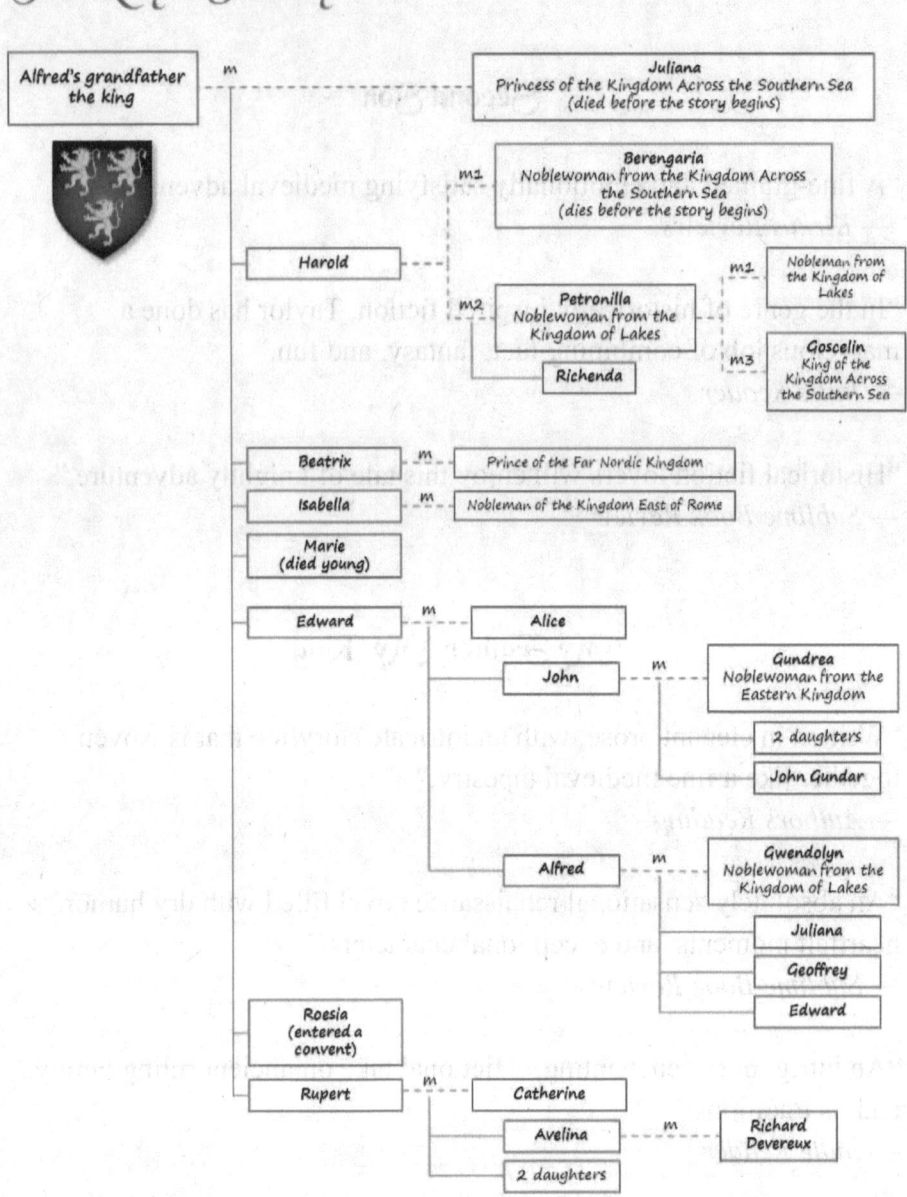

Alfred's grandfather the king — m — **Juliana** Princess of the Kingdom Across the Southern Sea (died before the story begins)

Harold
- m1 — **Berengaria** Noblewoman from the Kingdom Across the Southern Sea (dies before the story begins)
- m2 — **Petronilla** Noblewoman from the Kingdom of Lakes
  - **Richenda**
    - m1 — Nobleman from the Kingdom of Lakes
    - m3 — **Goscelin** King of the Kingdom Across the Southern Sea

Beatrix — m — Prince of the Far Nordic Kingdom

Isabella — m — Nobleman of the Kingdom East of Rome

Marie (died young)

Edward — m — **Alice**
- **John** — m — **Gundrea** Noblewoman from the Eastern Kingdom
  - 2 daughters
  - John Gundar
- **Alfred** — m — **Gwendolyn** Noblewoman from the Kingdom of Lakes
  - Juliana
  - Geoffrey
  - Edward

Roesia (entered a convent)

Rupert — m — **Catherine**
- **Avelina** — m — **Richard Devereux**
- 2 daughters

The Nobility

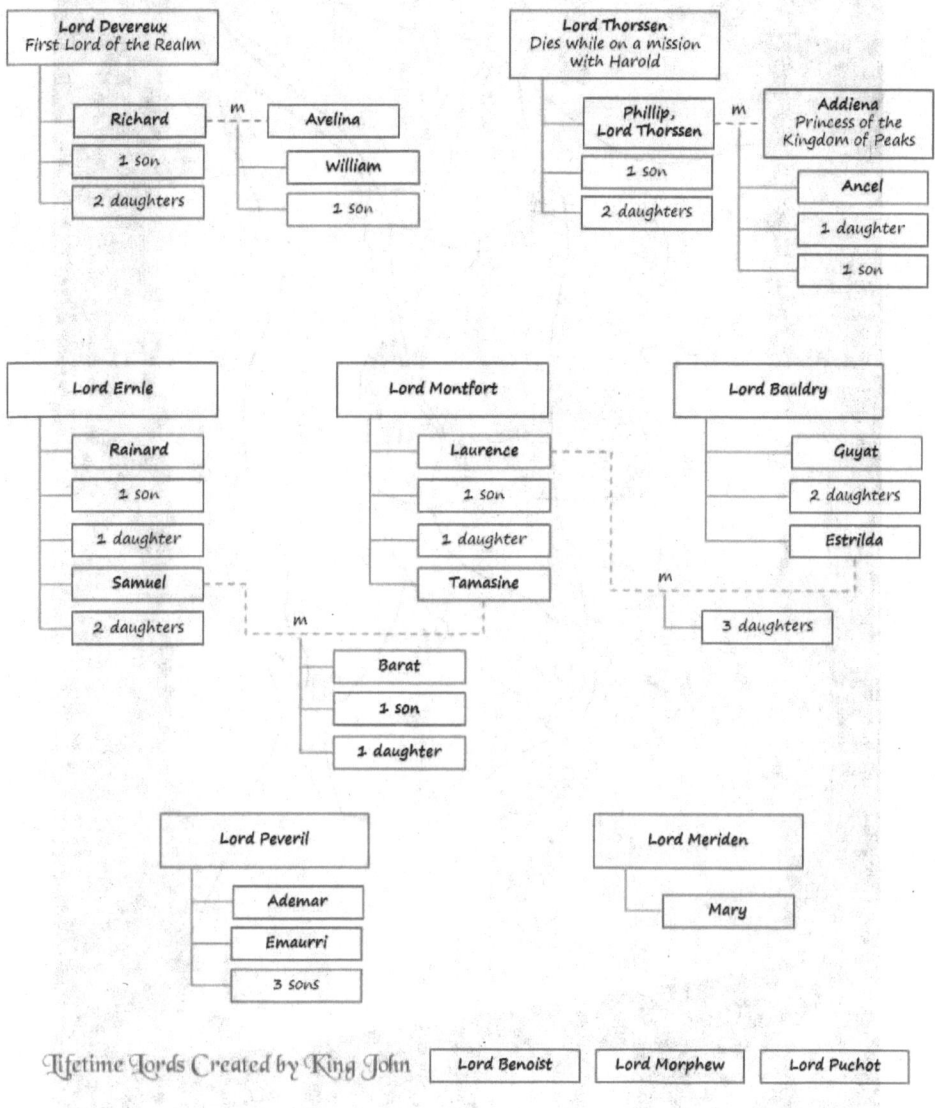

Lord Devereux
First Lord of the Realm

- Richard — m — Avelina
  - 1 son
  - 2 daughters
    - William
      - 1 son

Lord Thorssen
Dies while on a mission with Harold

- Phillip, Lord Thorssen — m — Addiena
  - 1 son   Princess of the Kingdom of Peaks
  - 2 daughters
    - Ancel
    - 1 daughter
    - 1 son

Lord Ernle

- Rainard
- 1 son
- 1 daughter
- Samuel
- 2 daughters

Lord Montfort

- Laurence
- 1 son
- 1 daughter
- Tamasine

m

- Barat
- 1 son
- 1 daughter

Lord Bauldry

- Guyat
- 2 daughters
- Estrilda

m

- 3 daughters

Lord Peveril

- Ademar
- Emaurri
- 3 sons

Lord Meriden

- Mary

Lifetime Lords Created by King John

| Lord Benoist | Lord Morphew | Lord Puchot |

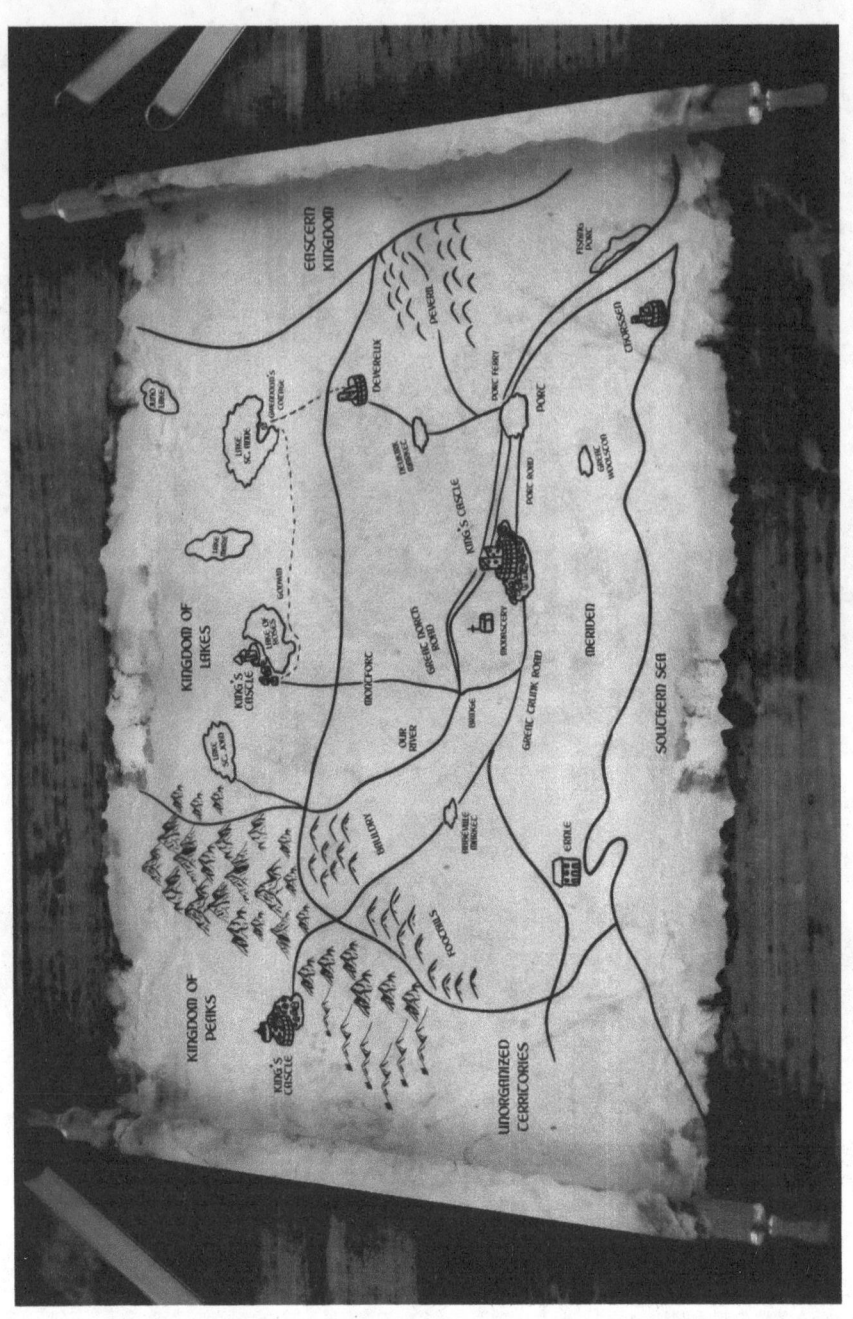

Pestilence

Pestilence

My beloved son,

If you are reading this, then you know that I have taken no steps to alter the succession. Whether that will be my conscious decision or whether fate will intervene to take that decision from my hands is unknown as I write this. Perhaps that is for the best, for it frees me to say the words that are in my heart and in my mind, unencumbered by any foreknowledge of what may transpire.

As I look at the familiar handwriting, tears well in my eyes, causing the words on the page to blur. No less a blur are the events of the past week. It's hard even to remember that a mere nine days ago I was enjoying a pleasant holiday with family and friends at my parents' country manor. It's still difficult to take in the fact that, despite all our efforts, Ralf has taken his vengeance by taking my father's life.

For one thing I'm grateful – that I was there at the end and that he knew I was holding his hand as he passed into the next world. After he took his last breath, the silence in the room seemed to last an eternity. No one moved for a very long time. Finally, the bishop had no choice. He stepped to the side of the chair where I sat next to my father's bedside. Placing his hand on my shoulder and looking across the bed at my uncle Rupert, he said very quietly, "I have no special instructions."

In our tradition, the king's will is lodged with the bishop for safekeeping in the vaults of the church. A king may specify the succession for two generations in his will. If he does so, he provides the bishop with a separate document of special instructions to be read and acted upon before the next king is declared. If he doesn't, the rules of primogeniture apply.

The bishop stepped back to the head of the bed and turned to address the room. Quietly, but with great authority, he intoned those dreadful words of transition. "The King is dead." Then, looking directly at my elder brother, John, "Long live the King." Rupert and I each made our way to the new king and delivered the ancient pledge of loyalty.

A state of affairs that so many had tried and so much had been done to forestall was now upon us. My brother is ill-suited by temperament, intellect, and attitude to be king – a fact of which we were all reminded as we watched his response to the bishop's words and our pledges. He held his head high, looking down his nose to accept our pledges rather than deigning to bend his neck. His chest puffed out like a peacock seeking a mate . . . so much that one could easily imagine the tail feathers fanned out in grandiose display behind him.

He then gave the bishop what seemed to me a rather menacing look. Undaunted, the bishop moved slowly to the door that exits into the private reception room where the lords of the kingdom were gathered. Opening the door, he once again intoned those fateful words, and John walked into the outer room, followed by the rest of us. At almost the same instant, the opposite door opened and Gwen, my wife, rushed to my side, followed by Richard, one of my four great friends since childhood, all sons of hereditary lords of the realm. Richard and Laurence are heirs to the Devereux and Montfort domains, respectively. Phillip has already become Lord Thorssen, his father having perished alongside King Harold when their party was mistaken for the advance guard of a rebel force during an unfortunate expedition in the Kingdom Across the Southern Sea. Alone among my mates, Samuel Ernle will never be a lord, being the third son in his father's large family; but he's distinguished himself in the knighthood, most recently as captain of the King's Own Guard.

The lords made their pledges, which John accepted with the same haughty demeanor he'd shown to me and our uncle. "Devereux," he addressed the first lord of the realm in a commanding tone. "We'll have the funeral two days hence and the coronation the day after."

Lord Devereux couldn't suppress his look of complete astonishment. "With all due respect, Your Grace," he began.

And then my mother completely lost her composure – something I don't believe I've ever seen in my entire life. "Nooooooooo," she wailed, running to John and beating on his chest with her palms. "No, no, no, no, no. You can't do that. He was your father. He was our king. He deserves your respect."

John couldn't even deign to offer comfort to the woman who gave him birth and who now was overcome with grief at the sudden loss of the man she loved. Rupert rushed to her and gently pulled her away from her son. She turned into his arms, tears flowing down her cheeks, and laid her head on his chest, sobbing. He led her back to where Gwen and I stood alongside his wife, Catherine, and the women did their best to console her. "Ignore him, Alice," said Rupert. "Devereux will see that it's done properly."

The bishop spoke up. "My son, your mother is right. This is not about you. It's about the people. They won't think well of you as their new king if you fail to allow them to grieve the passing of your father."

I was surprised how deftly the bishop managed to pander to John's self-importance while still telling him the funeral was not about his personal glory. I recall wondering at the time how much was his own insight and how much my father might have prepared him for what to expect from John. Undoubtedly, some of both. There's equally no doubt this was all about John. He wanted the crown firmly on his head before anyone could come up with a reason why it shouldn't be placed there.

"Very well, Bishop," he replied. "The funeral one week hence as usual. But the coronation will be on the following day."

Both Lord Devereux and the bishop were still dismayed. As first lord of the realm, it's Devereux's responsibility to organize both events. And tradition holds that the king's will is opened and read by the bishop on the day following the funeral. "Again with respect, Your Grace," Devereux began.

This time, he was interrupted by Gundrea, John's wife, our new queen. She walked straight to her husband, stood facing him with both fists clenched at her side, and said, "No."

Taken aback, John could only look at her and say, "What?"

"No," she repeated, even more firmly. "I want my father see me crowned."

When John brought Gundrea here from the Eastern Kingdom as his wife – disregarding royal protocol that the sovereign must approve marriages – she was just fifteen, illiterate, and from a culture where bathing was still considered a dangerous undertaking, so a nose-hair-curling stench wafted in her wake and that of her two companions. Since John had promised her father not to consummate the marriage until she was sixteen, my father could have had it annulled and found a more suitable match. He chose, instead, to use the situation to try to teach his heir some lessons of kingship. Sadly, as with most everything Father tried to teach John, the lessons were ignored.

Father insisted that Gundrea be prepared for her future role as queen. Brother Nicholas, a monk who grew up on our border with the Eastern Kingdom, was enlisted first as her translator and then as her tutor. Though she *has* improved, she still hasn't mastered our language. She was given no choice but to adopt our practices of cleanliness. At first, she would wear only black and only the shapeless style in which she'd arrived. She tried to resist my mother's insistence that her new gowns should be more fashionable, but in this matter, too, she was given no choice.

John kept her with child until she finally gave him an heir two years ago. Now that he feels the succession will never come to my line of the family, he has little use for her.

"You can be crowned anytime," John replied dismissively. "It's *my* coronation that's important."

But Gundrea was not to be swayed. "No," she said again, this time with a little stamp of one foot. "I want my father see you crowned then see me crowned. I want my father proud of my husband and proud of me. Must send message. He must travel. We wait."

"And what if I don't agree?"

"We wait. I not ask much. I . . ." She paused, trying to come up with the right word. "I insist this."

"Oh, alright," John was clearly not pleased. "But no more than one week. The funeral one week hence. The coronation a week after that." Gundrea stepped back, somewhat mollified.

"Devereux," John resumed his haughty manner. "There's no need for a fancy coronation. We've spent too much of the Treasury's money on those of late. I won't sequester at the monastery. No long procession . . . just from here to the church. No fancy decorations that cost a fortune. Only the nobility and the royal family present . . . the proper way of a coronation. No elaborate feasts in the town. The people can see to their own celebration if they want one. It's not our duty to pay for that. No fancy banquets either."

"Yes, Your Grace," replied Devereux, still clearly nonplussed.

Again, Gundrea spoke up. "Must have banquet. Honor new king. Honor my father. Must have banquet."

"And what if I say no?" asked John.

"Queen is in charge of banquets," she said. "Will have banquet." This is a side of Gundrea none of us has ever seen. We had no idea she retained such intense loyalty to her father or that she was willing to stand up to her husband.

"Then it will be a small banquet," John acquiesced grudgingly. "I'll decide how much money can be spent and that will be that. You have my orders, Devereux. I expect them to be carried out." With that, he marched across the room and left us, Gundrea following, her head held high and the hint of a triumphant smile on her face. I can only imagine how he must have chastised her once they were back in their apartment.

It seemed the tone of my brother's reign was being set before our eyes. Though we all expected him to be more proud and demanding than any of his predecessors, the fact that he encountered resistance – from Gundrea, defiance even – in the face of his first attempts to exert his will means he could possibly become even more resentful of those around him.

Gwen and the Lady Petronilla, widow of King Harold, my father's elder brother, took charge of my mother, leaving me to speak with Lord Devereux. Rupert and Richard joined us as the others drifted away, leaving the family to our grief. Never before had I seen Lord Devereux so distraught. It seemed as if he'd aged visibly in the short time since my father's death was revealed.

"Alfred, it's true I've grown weary of funerals these past few years, but I don't know if I have the capacity to do this one. I never thought to be burying my friend . . . and certainly not so soon."

"Nor did any of us, sir," I tried to offer him some comfort.

"You probably don't know this – Rupert will remember – Edward was the first to make me feel welcome when my father brought me to court as a lad. We quickly developed a friendship that has lasted all these years and were both so pleased when you and Richard formed a similar bond."

"I remember it well," said Rupert. "You two were inseparable."

"I really don't know how to do this," Devereux shook his head sadly.

Richard placed his arm around his father's shoulders. "Let me do it for you, Father," he said. "You deserve to be able to grieve without having this extra burden."

"Are you sure, Richard?"

"Of course, Father. How could you doubt it?"

"You should know, Richard," said Rupert, "that I sent messengers to the Peaks, Lakes, and Kingdom Across the Southern Sea yesterday, as soon as I learned what had happened. I don't know if the kings will come, but there'll likely be dignitaries of some sort arriving, and they'll have no time to give us notice of their plans."

"That will mean lodgings and a banquet of sorts. John's not going to like it," said Richard.

"I've made no mention to anyone about the messengers, so let's just keep this our little secret. I did it for Alice. I'll speak to the steward so he's prepared to deal with whoever shows up and to organize a subdued banquet. It will do my nephew good to see how much Edward was respected by his fellow sovereigns. But it will do *no* good for him to find out in advance and try to put a stop to things."

"Thank you for that, Uncle," I said.

"Aye, Rupert," said Devereux, "well done as always."

"Don't forget, Richard," continued Rupert, "you have the bishop on your side in this. He's in the rather enviable position of not owing allegiance to John, so he can stand firm in not permitting anything to spoil the dignity of the funeral."

"Then there's the coronation," said Devereux. "The way he wants it done will be a disaster."

"We can work on that together," said Richard.

"We simply *must* find a way to make this a celebration for the people. The very idea of making them pay for it themselves." Devereux was indignant. "I've never *heard* such a ludicrous notion."

"I have an idea," said Richard, "but I need to speak to Phillip."

The door to my parents' bed chamber opened quietly, revealing Abbot André just inside. "Rupert . . . Alfred . . . it's time."

"Go," said Devereux. "Say your good-byes." My father's body will be taken to the monastery where it will be prepared for burial. The monks will hold vigil day and night from now until the funeral.

I put an arm around Lord Devereux's shoulder. "Come with us, sir. He would have wanted that."

Over the next few days, I spent many hours with my friend Samuel. As captain of the King's Own Guard, he blamed himself for failing to prevent my father's death. Samuel was my anchor in the two most difficult times of my life – when I first returned from captivity and again on a secret mission back into the Territories – and I'm doing my best to be the same for him now, letting him talk at length about the events of that day. He took me to the place where the fatal accident occurred. Slowly, he's coming to terms with what happened. It will take more time for him to fully accept that he truly *is* blameless. But I was pleased when he sought out Richard and me on the day before the funeral, asking to be allowed to lead the procession, as one final service to his fallen king. On the day, as he led the cortège, the way he rode the black stallion we use for such occasions told me that his pride in his role and in himself was returning.

Richard organized the perfect memorial for my father. At one point, when the King of Lakes arrived – the first of the neighboring kings to do so – John almost succeeded in turning the whole thing into a fiasco. He managed a hasty, unceremonious greeting and immediately summoned Rupert, Lord Devereux, and me to his public reception room.

"I want some answers," he demanded. "What's this all about? Who invited him? Why wasn't I told?"

Rupert was just about to attempt an answer when my mother walked in. "Oh," she said, somewhat taken aback. "I heard the King of Lakes has arrived. I thought you'd be receiving him here."

"I've said hello and ordered the steward to find them a place to stay. Now I'm trying to get to the bottom of this."

Once again, Rupert was about to speak when Mother intervened. In the days since Father's death, she'd recovered some of her usual composure and sensed what was afoot. "There's nothing to get to the bottom of, John. I ordered messages sent to your father's fellow sovereigns advising them of his passing. It's only fitting they should know, and I'm surprised you didn't think to do this yourself. Any decision they may have made to pay their respects to your father was theirs alone. I do hope you'll receive all our visitors properly." She's always been masterful at putting John on notice in the sweetest and most motherly of tones.

"Alright," said John, "what's done is done. Devereux, see that we have whatever receptions are in order."

"John, receiving a fellow king is not Lord Devereux's responsibility. You need to organize that yourself . . . you and Gundrea." She paused to make her point before adding, "I can help, if you wish."

"Oh, get out and leave me alone," he dismissed us.

Once in the corridor, Rupert went to my mother and kissed her on both cheeks. "Thank you for that, Alice. The mood he was in, he might have hanged one of us."

"You did it for Edward, Rupert, and I'm most grateful. Saving you from hanging is the least I could do. I trust you've taken care of lodgings and such?"

"The steward's been in on it from the beginning, my dear. We'll soon know if either of the others decides to make the journey."

In the end, all three kings came for the funeral, Goscelin, of the Kingdom Across the Southern Sea, arriving only hours before the service was to begin, having experienced a day's delay waiting for good weather for the sea crossing. By the day of the funeral, John had managed to convince himself that the kings had come for his benefit and so acted a proper host at the small banquet held that evening.

The greatest surprise of all, however, came as Mother and I were preparing to enter the church. Across the town square rode two men on horseback, clearly making directly for our small party. As they drew nearer, I recognized one of them as Lord Egon, one of the many feudal lords of the Unorganized Territories that border our kingdom to the southwest. Lord Egon and I have a history that dates back to the time when Ralf, son of Ranulf, held me as a captive in the Territories. It was at Egon's fortress that Ralf had the blacksmith put me in shackles and chains. Egon's displeasure was obvious, though he did nothing to interfere. When Harold's ill-conceived plan to intimidate the Territories with military exercises on our border and John's unauthorized raid resulted in the massing of armies on both sides of the border, it was to Egon that I went to make the case that my father had no desire for war. And it was Egon who was willing to trust that my father and I were men of honor and withdraw his own men, leading eventually to a return to the normal state of peace in that part of our world.

"Wait," I said to Mother as the two men dismounted.

Grasping my hand in greeting, Egon said, "Lord Alfred."

"Lord Egon. I'm deeply honored."

"We heard the news of the death of your father. I am saddened by your loss and wished to pay my respects."

"You're most welcome here, sir. Please . . . allow me to introduce my mother . . . Lady Alice, now dowager queen of our kingdom. Mother, this is Lord Egon."

Egon bowed deeply. "My lady, please accept my deepest sympathy."

"Alfred has spoken of you often, sir. Edward would have been honored by your coming. I know he held you in high regard, despite the fact that you never met. I hope you'll accept our hospitality tonight."

"With respect, my lady, we shall be on our way immediately after the burial. This is a time for your kingdom and your people to share their grief. There will be other times for diplomacy." With that, he stepped back and motioned for us to go on ahead. I didn't get to speak to him again that day. As we left the church, I saw him and his squire riding away, true to his word. How, I wondered, will the tenuous alliance he and I have formed fare under John's reign?

Our other guests departed the next morning, choosing not to stay for the coronation. I couldn't help but wonder if they had agreed this together as a way of putting John on notice. What they couldn't have known is that he would miss the point entirely.

•   •   •   •   •

Immediately after the midday meal, we gathered in the king's private reception room for the reading of the will. The bishop began by showing each of us in turn the intact seal, then opened it and showed us my father's signature and his own as witness. Finally, he began to read.

"The arrangements previously made by my brother, the late King Harold, for the Lady Petronilla and her daughter are reaffirmed. I ask my brother Rupert to take up the role of guardian for young Lady Richenda."

"Another girl to find a husband for," said Rupert quietly.

"Well, you've done quite well for your own three," said Mother with a smile. "I suspect he thought you had the necessary experience."

The bishop continued. "For my dear wife, Alice. She shall have apartments in the castle suitable to her status as dowager queen for the remainder of her life and an annual stipend sufficient to her needs as determined solely by she herself." It escaped no one's notice how carefully my father spelled things out, knowing it was up to him to ensure John couldn't reduce her status or means.

"To my brother, Rupert, I leave the country manor and the estate on which it is located, including all the income from its produce and rents, with the sole provision that Alice be permitted to reside there at any time and for any duration of her choosing."

"Whenever you like, Alice," said Rupert, and Catherine added, "Our home is yours, my dear."

"The royal library is bequeathed to my son Alfred, to be held in trust for the kingdom. No disposition is to be made of the room or any of its contents without Alfred's explicit permission. I charge him to protect and enhance this legacy for the benefit of our people." Once again, making sure John can't run roughshod over something he doesn't value.

There were small bequests to his squire, Donal; to Matthias, the steward; to Mervyn the Younger, our long-time stable master; to the monastery; and to the church.

"Finally," read the bishop, "the remainder of my personal fortune shall be divided equally between my sons, John and Alfred. For each of them, this inheritance is free of conditions and both are at liberty to manage and dispose of these assets as they see fit." Making certain I'm free to pass the legacy on to my own sons.

This was the biggest surprise of all, not only for me but clearly for John. No doubt he'd expected to receive the entire estate. And true to form, he couldn't restrain himself. "That's not possible," he said directly to the bishop. "Let me see the will."

The bishop allowed him to read the words but didn't relinquish control of the document.

"This can't be," John said again. He practically leaped from his chair and began pacing about the room.

"It can be and it is, my son," said the bishop calmly. "A king's will is inviolate. That's the law of the land."

"I'm the king now," John rounded on him. "I'll simply change the law."

The silence in the room was palpable. Would he really go so far? It was unthinkable.

Finally, the bishop spoke again. "I'd think long and hard before pursuing such a course, my son. The laws governing transition of rule and the king's will are ancient and have served the kingdom and your predecessors very well indeed. Is it your assertion that you're so much wiser than all your forebears that you would discard what has been valued for so long? And think ahead, to when your days are numbered and your son takes the throne? Would you really want him to be able to disregard *your* wishes so readily?"

John stopped his pacing. "Is that all, Bishop? The entire will?"

"Yes, that is the complete will and testament of our late king, which I will return to the church vaults for permanent safekeeping."

"Very well, then. I have some arrangements that are required. Mother, consult with the steward and find an apartment that's to your liking. I intend to move into the king's apartment in three days."

"That's very little time, John."

"Perhaps you could just swap with John and Gundrea," suggested Gwen, "and move back into your old rooms on the corridor with us."

"That won't be possible," said John. "My son and heir requires his own household. His mother will be in charge of his household and will remain there with him and his sisters."

It was Gundrea's turn to look stunned. Apparently, she'd had no idea that he intended to move into the king's apartment without her. "Is not right," she protested. "Queen lives with king."

"You'll be in charge of my son's household and his upbringing until he reaches the age when I begin his military training," John repeated.

"Tell him, Bishop," Gundrea pleaded desperately. "Is not right queen not live with king."

"I can't interfere with the arrangements a man makes for the rearing of his son, my dear, unless he's committing a sin or a crime." Then he added, attempting to mollify her a bit, "Even though I might agree with you such an arrangement seems highly unusual in this family." Gundrea slumped in her chair, her anguish visible.

Ignoring his wife, John continued, "So, Mother, you'll need to find other rooms that you deem suitable.

"Alfred, we need the nursery in that corridor for the exclusive use of my children. If you want to move your own apartment to a place nearer a suitable nursery, you have my permission to do so." So there's to be a major upheaval.

"Three days," and he turned on his heel and left the room. Gundrea followed slowly, in complete and utter dejection.

"Alfred," said the bishop, "I wonder if you might walk out with me?"

"Of course, Bishop."

I followed him out of the room, and we walked in silence toward the staircase. As we descended – when no one was in sight or within earshot – he reached into his robe and produced a folded document bearing what I immediately recognized as my father's seal. "I was to give you this, Alfred, in the event there were no special instructions. Your father was exceptionally fond of you, my son. I hope there's something in this to give your some comfort."

And thus I find myself alone in the library with my father's letter, trying to suppress my incredible sadness, for I can hear his voice in my mind as I read the words on the page.

My beloved son,

If you are reading this, then you know that I have taken no steps to alter the succession. Whether that will be my conscious decision or whether fate will intervene to take that decision from my hands is unknown as I write this. Perhaps that is for the best, for it frees me to say the words that are in my heart and in my mind, unencumbered by any foreknowledge of what may transpire.

This choice is the most daunting I have ever had to face. We both know what sort of king John will be. I have no wish to inflict that on our kingdom. But if I alter the succession, I fear the consequences may be even worse. John would not hesitate to oppose you . . . even, I fear, to the point of raising troops against you. And there can be no possible good outcome from civil war.

Of one thing I am certain. You are as well prepared as anyone could be to cope with the coming challenges and to find ways to make things better for our people, regardless of what John may do. Your four friends are your best allies. Use their counsel and assistance well. You have the trust and respect of all the lords, even including Meriden who, I've no doubt, will align with his peers if he perceives any threat to the future of the realm . . . and especially if he perceives a threat to his own hide.

Despite my sadness, I'm forced to smile. Father had a knack for seeing the light-hearted side of even serious matters. I'll miss that dreadfully.

I hope Rupert is still at your side. Though he never voiced it openly, I believe your grandfather thought Rupert was the most capable of all his sons, and over the years, I have come to agree. Your uncle will never steer you wrong.

Abbot André and Prior Warin consider themselves your friends and protectors. Allow them to be just that.

Do not forget Alice and Gwendolyn. They will see things you may not. They understand nuances of human behavior that may seem foreign to a man's mind. And your mother can manage John's behavior when no one else can. Let her judge how best to do that. John would never harm her, but excessive pressure from her might cause him to banish her from court and then you would lose her influence entirely.

As I write the word . . . influence . . . I am reminded how important it is for you to recognize that that is where your power will lie. You cannot oppose John directly . . . only through others.

I know John's reign will be regressive. My greatest fear is that it may be repressive. Our people have no memory of that, for two, perhaps three, generations have lived their entire lives in an enlightened, progressive society. If he is too harsh or if the people's lives become intolerable, they may rise up against him. Such an uprising might succeed if . . . and only if . . . the people and the nobles are united.

If it occurs, Alfred, that is where you would face the greatest danger. If there is an uprising, it must be clear beyond any doubt that it is against John. There must be absolutely no hint that it might be in your favor, for John has neither the clarity of thought nor the desire to perceive that any action in your favor could happen without your direct personal instigation. He would immediately brand you a traitor and would be quick to pursue what we both know would be the inevitable outcome.

And that is my most important advice to you, my son. Whatever happens, you must survive. I know not if your grandfather was right in foreseeing an important destiny for you or what that destiny might be. I know only that you cannot fulfill it if you are not alive. Retreat from public life if that seems best. Go into seclusion if necessary. Flee, if you must, for you would be welcomed and protected in any of our neighboring kingdoms, including, I think, even the Territories. But no matter what, stay alive. Even if your destiny is no more than to prepare Geoffrey and little Edward to be advisors to future kings, that is a worthwhile endeavor and they will need your wisdom and guidance to become such men.

You are a good man, Alfred, and I am exceedingly proud of you. My only regret in this life is that I could find no safe way to leave you the throne. But I leave my legacy and that of your grandfather in your hands . . . and perhaps that is even more important.

Edward

I fold the letter and place it inside my shirt. Perhaps . . . in time . . . I'll share it with Gwen. Perhaps also with Rupert – he deserves to know the esteem in which his father and brother held him. For now, I'll place it for safekeeping in the strongbox in my dressing room. And if that should ever prove not to be as safe as I now think, my father's words are forever etched in my heart and in my mind. I recall Grandfather's words, as he tried to teach a young boy the value of knowledge. "Men may take everything from you, Alfred," he said, "but the one thing they cannot take is what is in your mind. With knowledge, a man can rebuild a life . . . even a kingdom."

Gundrea's family is expected any day now. There's been no message, but there was little time for such formalities. In point of fact, no one is even certain if she knows if her father is still alive. If there's been any communication between them since she's been here, it's been entirely in secret.

In the meantime, the steward is trying valiantly to help us sort out the new living arrangements. "Perhaps, my lady," he offers, "you'd like the rooms now occupied by Lord Alfred . . . to be nearer your grandchildren in the heir's household. Lord Alfred's family could move to this corridor, where there's a large enough nursery" . . . 'this corridor' being the one where Petronilla's apartment is located and where we've gathered in her sitting room to try and work things out.

"It's a lovely thought, Matthias, but I rather doubt my advice will be either sought or welcome when it comes to the rearing of the king's children."

"Then perhaps you might all move into the old castle, my lady . . . and Lady Petronilla with you," he suggests. His reference is to the original part of the castle, at least two centuries older than the wing where we now reside. It was built by my ancestor on a rise at the point where the river becomes navigable by larger craft, and the town sprang up on the lower ground, outside its walls. The modern wing was built by my great-grandfather, and the lawns and gardens were added under my grandmother's guidance. "There are some very comfortable rooms there, and you could all be on one corridor," Matthias adds.

I have serious reservations about the wisdom of such an arrangement. Though he might not conceive of it immediately, I wouldn't put it past John to decide we were setting up some sort of separate court and creating a threat to him. Before I can voice my concern, Gwen chimes in with a much more practical consideration. "Another lovely idea, Matthias, but not so good for the children, I fear. They need plenty of light and fresh air. The windows in those rooms are very small . . . what few of them there are. It's quite acceptable for visitors, but not the atmosphere our children need to grow up happy and healthy. Besides, just think how much it would cost for all the candles we'd need to have enough light."

Matthias throws up his hands in defeat. "Then I suppose we have no choice but to rearrange the lodgings of the lords at court and make everyone's lives a misery."

A knock on the door interrupts his sigh. Petronilla's maid opens it to Rupert and Catherine. "We find them at last, my dear," says Rupert, squeezing his wife's hand.

"Do come in," says Petronilla. "Maybe you can think of something that's escaped us. This is all such a mess."

Rupert winks at Catherine. "What do you think, dear? Should we let them keep fretting or put them out of their misery?"

"Ignore him," says Catherine. "We have it all worked out. There's really no reason for us to maintain an elaborate apartment here. We spend most of our time at the port, and now, with the country manor—"

"And especially with my nephew in charge," Rupert interrupts her.

"I suspect our visits here will be even less frequent."

"But, my lord," the steward objects, "your father was always quite insistent that any prince of the realm required a residence in the castle suitable to his status."

"Aye, Matthias, but something tells me the new king won't be so inclined."

"That's incredibly generous," says Mother. "Are you certain?"

"Quite certain," says Catherine.

"Then here's what we'll do," says Mother. "Petronilla will remain here. Gwen, you and Alfred take Rupert's apartment, and I'll have John's old room down the hall."

"But, Mother Alice," Gwen says, "it seems to me you should have Rupert's apartment."

"Nonsense," says my mother. "There's only me and Nona. You and Alfred have a family to raise and need the extra space."

"We'll claim Alfred's room for when we visit," says Catherine.

"If we visit," adds Rupert.

"Ignore him," says Catherine. "I'm sure even John will have to have some sort of court ceremonies."

"Then it's settled," says Mother. "I suppose we'd best get on with it, Matthias.

"Of course, my lady. There's just one more thing."

"Yes?"

"The visitors we expect . . . the queen's family."

"What about them?"

"Well, it's the rooms I've chosen. I've been thinking . . . it's likely going to take quite some work to remove the stench once they've left. So I'm not giving them the very best."

"You'll get no objection here, Matthias," Mother replies. "If John or Gundrea has anything to say about it, send them to me."

"Thank you ever so much, my lady. Now, I'd best be off and get things underway."

When the door closes behind him, Mother lets out a sigh. "It will be good to have all this finished so life can get back to normal."

"Whatever normal is." Rupert's in quite a cantankerous mood today.

"Well, whatever it is," I say, "I think we need to make a bit of what Father would have called a tactical retreat."

The women all look at me with puzzled expressions.

"Ever since John became king, he's met with some sort of resistance to everything he's tried to do. If he starts feeling like he's being thwarted at every turn, he'll get hostile, and that won't do any of us any good. We need to step back and let him have his way for a bit . . . allow him to feel like he's fully in charge."

"Wise thinking, Alfred," nods Rupert. "Unless one of us sees him about to do something that's going to cause real damage, best we lay low for a while."

"There *is* one other thing we need to put our minds to," says Mother. "We need to find something for Donal."

"Isn't John providing for him?" asks Catherine.

"From what I've learned, he made a small effort – assigned Donal to be squire to his son. Donal was completely dismayed. 'M'lady, a baby be having no need of a squire,' he told me.

"I also heard that Gundrea intervened. Told John she would never share lodgings with a man who wasn't her husband. I think she thought that might get her into the king's apartment because there would now be a man in the heir's household. A serious miscalculation, it seems. John simply told Donal there was no place for him and that he needed to find himself a new master."

Rupert rolls his eyes. "I can't make out which of the two of them is the bigger fool."

Petronilla's been quiet through all this, but now speaks up. "I might have a solution." Everyone looks her way. "When Goscelin was here, he renewed his invitation for me to visit his court. I'd been planning to go, but with everything that's happened . . . If I go, it would be useful to have a man in the traveling party."

"Donal would be perfect," says Mother. "And while you're gone, Alfred and Rupert can work out something for him to do once you return."

"I'm a bit worried, though," says Petronilla. "What if John forbids me to travel? Does that come under the auspices of Alfred's tactical retreat?"

"Nonsense," says Mother. "You're free to travel where you wish and visit whom you wish."

"Yes, but this is John we're talking about," laments Petronilla.

"There's no need to confront him directly," says Rupert. "Plan a long visit with Catherine and me. Bring Richenda and her nurse and Donal for safety on the journey. Richenda can stay with us while you're abroad. John should be completely disinterested in your visiting the port.

"For now, I'll speak with Donal and tell him not to fret . . . that we're working things out for him. And I'll get Matthias to find him a place to stay where his presence won't be noticeable to John."

•　　•　　•　　•　　•

Tonight will be our last night in these rooms where we've spent our entire married life – the place where our children were born – the place where being in love has lasted and love has grown. We're both nostalgic, reminiscing about our first night together here and many special nights since. We'll miss this place. Our upheaval, however, is nothing compared to Mother's. Her generosity of spirit in the face of John's pettiness is nothing short of amazing.

•　　　•　　　•　　　•　　　•

Just as all the turmoil of moving has begun to settle down, Gundrea's family arrives. Brother Nicholas has come to once again help with translation. Gundrea has been pacing the corridors like a caged animal these past three days, looking out every window for any sign of travelers coming our way. When the runner arrived with news that they were approaching the town, she disappeared into her bed chamber.

Mother, Gwen, and I are all at the front entrance with Brother Nicholas to welcome our guests. Gundrea's absence is puzzling. John's is not. He announced he would only receive Gundrea's father formally in the king's public reception room, a move that's no doubt intended to make it undeniable to Lord Erik who now holds the position of power.

Just as the travelers enter the courtyard, Gundrea rushes out to join us. She's changed into one of her old black frocks.

Two men on horseback lead the traveling party. Judging by the difference in ages, they're likely father and son. Behind them, an odd-looking wagon like the one in which Gundrea had arrived . . . sort of a hut mounted on the bed of a wagon, with a door and folding steps at the rear. Behind that, two more horsemen, one of whom is Kjeld – one of the minders Erik had sent with Gundrea when John first brought her here.

The two men in front dismount and Gundrea runs toward them. She stops in front of the elder man and starts to curtsey, but he takes her elbow and raises her up before she can complete the obeisance. Nicholas translates his words. "You are a queen now, my child. You bend the knee to no one but God."

Gundrea takes her father's hand and leads him up the steps. The introductions begin, repeated in both languages. The younger man is called Gunnvor and is, indeed, the son of Erik whom John befriended in the tavern. While all this is happening, Kjeld and his mate have dismounted and opened the back of the wagon. The first to descend is Tove – Gundrea's other minder – and she's followed quickly by a younger woman who runs to Gundrea and embraces her at length. Finally breaking the embrace, Gundrea says, "My sister, Gunhild."

Hearing the pattern of the names, I now understand why John's heir is called John Gundar. I must remember to ask Brother Nicholas if there's any significance or just a family preference.

Mother gestures toward the door, inviting our guests inside where Matthias is waiting. He struggles to suppress an involuntary wrinkle of his nose for the visitors are, indeed, just as malodorous as we remembered from Gundrea's arrival. When they've been hustled off to settle in, Mother goes to the entrance and opens the door herself. "Let's get some fresh air in here. I don't know how we're going to cope with that for a week."

"Maybe we should have all our meals outdoors," I tease her.

"Don't laugh, Alfred. That thought crossed my mind just now. If the weather cooperates, I'm sure Matthias would be only too happy to arrange it."

The formal reception is just that . . . very formal. Watching John, I can't decide if the way he's holding his head and looking down his nose is intended to display regal haughtiness or if he simply can't stand the stench of his wife's family. Not for the first time, I wonder how he coped when he was in their home. Rebellion, it seems, drives other strange behavior. There's no doubt, though, that John's attention is drawn to Gunhild.

As they're leaving, John calls to Brother Nicholas, "A word, brother."

"Sir?"

"See if you can get them to take a bath. We can't do anything about the smell of their clothing, but perhaps a bath would help." Then, turning to Gundrea, "Explain to them that it's our way."

"Can *not* force to bathe. Is not normal in my kingdom. Only two times each year. Christmas and Easter."

"Then tell them a coronation is just as special an occasion."

"Cannot force. Will ask."

"*Beg*, if you must." And with that, he waves us all out of the room.

·　　·　　·　　·　　·

Coronation day has arrived. It somehow seems a somber occasion. The ladies don't have new gowns – Mother decreed they should honor John's wishes for a low-cost ceremony as part of our tactical retreat. Gundrea is clad in one of her black, high-necked gowns with her hair completely contained inside some sort of old-fashioned head piece.

Bootsteps that sound like a military parade precede John's appearance in the entrance hall of the castle where we've been ordered to wait. "That won't do," he barks when he lays eyes on Gundrea. "Go back upstairs and put on a proper gown. And take that thing off your hair. Your head must be free to have the crown placed on it."

Gundrea tries to protest. "Father not approve of other dress."

"I don't care what your father does or doesn't approve of. You're my wife and queen of my kingdom. You'll dress as our people expect you to . . . just as you've been doing until two days ago."

I smile to myself. For perhaps the first time in my life, I agree with John about something. I also realize that Gundrea's feelings for her father are not simply respect but are mixed with a very large dose of fear.

And so we wait for her to change. When she returns, she looks quite lovely in a green gown that matches the color of her eyes, with her long black hair hanging loose, ready to accept the crown. But she can't quite conceal how anxious she is about what her family will think. She takes John's arm, and we walk out to the waiting carriages.

The coronation is unusual, to say the least. The church looks almost empty, so few people are present. Once we're all in our places, the musicians begin to play processional music for the entrance of the king and queen. Ignoring the music entirely, John marches up the aisle as if on a military parade ground, leaving Gundrea to follow in his wake. He walks past the two prie-dieux placed before the altar and sits on the throne. Gundrea is at a loss for what to do.

Those of us near the front can hear the bishop address John quietly. "Not yet, my son. There are parts of the ceremony that precede your ascending the throne." He gestures toward the prie-dieux indicating that John should kneel there with his wife.

John waves his hand in dismissal. "I'm not interested in ceremony, Bishop. Just crown me, and let's be done with it."

The bishop is unmoved. "I'll crown you properly, according to our tradition and God's laws . . ." He pauses. ". . . or not at all." He gestures again toward the prie-dieux, where Gundrea has already taken her proper place.

At first, John doesn't move. The bishop merely waits. Finally, John rises from the throne and takes his place, and the usual prayers are recited before the bishop addresses the congregation. "Is there anyone here present who disputes Lord John's claim to the throne?"

John actually turns around to glare at the audience, threatening anyone who might even think of raising a dispute. The silent pause seems endless, as if the bishop is hoping for someone to come forward, despite his certain knowledge that John is the true heir. Finally, he can wait no longer. The look of triumph on John's face when the crown descends onto his head is something I'll never forget. Nor, I expect, will anyone else who's lived in dread of this day.

The crowd gathered in the town square as we depart is small, the king's acknowledgment of them perfunctory. Gundrea's banquet is restrained, but very proper, while in the town, the people have their own subdued celebration thanks to donations from my family and the Devereux and to Phillip's help in getting the Assembly delegate to organize it.

Predictably, John wastes no time. The first Council meeting is the very next day. Rupert's been ordered to attend as well. The tension in the room is palpable as we wait for the king to arrive. He marches down the corridor and stops in his tracks in the doorway. No one speaks or moves. Eventually, realizing what's expected, Devereux rises from his seat, and we all follow suit, a practice Grandfather dispensed with decades ago. John walks slowly to the head of the table and takes his seat. No one dares look at him. He makes us wait. And then, finally, "Take your seats." Not even 'take your seats, *gentlemen*'? This is going to be brutal.

"First item of business. Sir Gamel, rise," John addresses the knight commander. Gamel scrambles to get back up as the king continues. "Sir Gamel, you're hereby relieved of duty as knight commander."

Gamel somehow maintains his military bearing.

"Furthermore," John continues, "you're discharged from the knighthood with no commendation and no pension." There's a collective gasp around the table as everyone realizes this is retribution. John has always claimed his dishonorable discharge from the knighthood was unjust, and it appears Gamel is to be the victim of his revenge since the man who actually discharged him has retired and is no longer within reach.

"Turn your command over to your deputy and prepare to be gone by the end of the week. You're dismissed."

Gamel manages to keep his face a complete blank as he leaves the room, but he has a small triumph by not bowing as he passes the king.

John doesn't even notice. Gamel is no longer any of his concern. "I'll announce a new commander when I return from my progress," he tells us.

"Also, I've relieved Sir Samuel as captain of the King's Own Guard." Not a complete surprise, since each king chooses as captain someone to whom he's willing to trust his life. But then he continues, "He's replaced immediately by Sir Mauger." Another collective intake of breath around the table, this time with slightly more discretion. Lord Bauldry raises his hand somewhat tentatively.

"You wish to speak, Bauldry?"

"With all due respect, Sire . . ."

John pounces. "I believe, Bauldry, that the proper address for your king is 'Your Grace.'" Yet another change from the conventions established by my grandfather and affirmed by both Harold and my father.

"Begging your pardon, Your Grace," Bauldry resumes, "and with all due respect, it's my recollection that the man named Mauger hasn't been a knight for quite some time." Mauger was one of the four men who accompanied John on the ill-fated raid and was also expelled from the knighthood. "I can't speak for my fellow councillors, but I would certainly rest easier knowing that your safety was in the hands of someone whose military skills are at their peak."

"I've signed an order restoring Sir Mauger to the knighthood with full honor. He has always demonstrated a willingness to follow my orders. I trust him to be in charge of the safety of my family and that should be enough for everyone in this room, Bauldry. Anyone else have anything to say on the subject?" No one does.

"Good. Now about the progress. I intend to leave in three days. This won't be a leisurely ramble . . . more like an extended patrol. It's important for the people to see their new king, and I intend that they see I mean business.

"Thorssen, your place first. I'll spend one night in Great Woolston on the way there, so you should have ample time to prepare. As for the rest of the route, my squire will advise each of you of the plan, what day I expect to arrive at your estate, and whether the stay will be one night or two. Be back here and prepared to meet again two days after the completion of the progress. That is all." As John pushes his chair back in preparation for rising, everyone around the table clambers to their feet.

When we can no longer hear his footsteps in the corridor, hushed conversation begins. I catch Rupert's eye and incline my head toward the door. He nods, indicating he'll stay here with the lords. There's something else I need to attend to.

I rush to our apartment to find Osbert. "I need your help, Osbert."

"Anything, m'lord."

"I want to have drinks in the tavern late this afternoon with Richard, Phillip, and Samuel. Samuel's been replaced as captain of the King's Own Guard."

"Aye, m'lord. Sir Samuel be needing the company of friends. Mayhap he knew it would happen, but he be in such a state since yer father died."

"Indeed, Osbert, but there's more. John's relieved the knight commander and discharged him with no pension."

"That not be right, m'lord. But methinks yer brother never forget 'twas Sir Gamel sent him home in disgrace."

"You've gone straight to the heart of the matter as usual, Osbert. So find Gamel and tell him I'd be most grateful if he'd join us at the tavern. If he hesitates, just tell him it's really important to me. I think that should be sufficient.

"Then if you could arrange for our wives to join us after we've been there about an hour, we'll take our supper in the tavern. Come to think of it, I've no idea if Sir Gamel is married. Do you know?"

"Aye, he be, m'lord. But his wife mayhap be needing somebody to watch their two children."

"I'm sure the nursery can handle two more children for a few hours."

Gwen had wandered in while I was speaking. "Handle which two more children?"

I tell her quickly what's happened and what I have in mind.

"Of course. I'll speak to Nurse. Osbert, you tell Sir Gamel's wife to bring the children here, and we'll go together to the tavern after we get them settled in."

"Anything else, m'lord?"

"Just one thing, Osbert. I'm going to try to find Samuel and spend some time with him, just the two of us. Do you think you might arrange with the innkeeper for us to have that corner table set aside for us? It's big enough for everyone and won't be quite so noisy if there's a crowd."

"Ye leave it to me, m'lord. Just take care of Sir Samuel." And with that, he's off to do what he does so well.

"I don't think you'll need to go searching for Samuel," says Gwen. "He was looking for you earlier. I told him you'd likely come here after the Council meeting. Now let me go speak with Nurse."

She opens the door to find Samuel standing there, his fist raised, ready to knock. She gives him a quick kiss on the cheek and says, "He's all yours, Samuel."

Samuel crosses to the couch and sits down while I close the door. "You've heard?"

"I've heard."

"I know I shouldn't be surprised, but I can admit to you that it really feels like a blow to the gut."

"That's only because of what came before, my friend."

"I keep reminding myself. But tell me, is it true what I've heard about what he did to Gamel?"

"Discharged him with no commendation and no pension."

"That's unconscionable! Gamel's served honorably, never disciplined, never even reprimanded. What was he thinking?"

"As usual, only about himself. It's petty and vindictive and completely unfounded. All I can think to say is that he had the sense to stop short of a dishonorable discharge. That would've angered the lords, among other things."

"It might have driven the knights to mutiny," says Samuel. "Even *this* is a slap in the face of their commitment to the knight's code of honor. Is there nothing that can be done?"

"Nothing to keep him in the knighthood. John made that much clear. But I've asked Gamel to join us in the tavern later. There *are* some things we can do to help him adjust. Now tell me, what are *you* going to do?"

"I haven't had time to give it much thought. On the one hand, it might depend on who becomes commander. On the other, Alfred, I may just want to go home. One of my father's tenants recently passed away without any family to take over, so the largest and prettiest cottage on the estate and some land to manage are available right now. It might suit me, for a change, to be a gentleman farmer."

"Have you spoken with Tamasine?"

"Not yet, but we need to talk about it soon. I know my father will allow me plenty of time to decide before leasing to a new tenant. But I must admit, it seems rather appealing at the moment."

"Have you thought about taking over from Sir Ronan as head of training?"

"No, that hadn't occurred to me. We all assumed it would be Gamel."

"You'd be perfect for it, Samuel."

"What makes you think John would even consider it?"

"Nothing, quite frankly. I can't fathom his mind. But it's something I might spend whatever influence I have with him to make happen if you wanted it."

"I don't know, Alfred."

"Just think about it. I can't tell you why I have this feeling, but something tells me your knightly skills are going to be terribly important in the not-too-distant future. It's just as vague as when my grandfather used to tell me he was sure I have some important destiny. But it's strong enough for me to ask you to think really hard about staying at the top of your form. Strong enough for me to put pressure on John if that became necessary."

"That's pretty daunting, Alfred. I don't know what to say."

"Say nothing for now. Just please tell me you'll at least consider it."

"Of course. Anything that important to you is worth more than a passing thought."

"Let's go meet the others in the tavern."

We arrive to find Richard and Phillip are already there and have ordered the first round of ale. Just as we finish toasting Samuel, Gamel comes through the door. I rise from my seat and call, "Sir Gamel! Over here."

He joins us. "You were there, Lord Alfred. You know it's no longer 'Sir.'"

"Indulge me, Sir Gamel. You've earned the honor, despite the king's action. No one at this table thinks otherwise."

"None of the councillors thinks otherwise, either," says Phillip.

"Thank you for that, gentlemen," says Gamel. "I still haven't fully taken it all in yet."

"That will take more than a few hours," says Samuel. "Take my advice, though. Don't try to deal with it alone. I know most of your friends are among the knights. But you can talk with any of us here."

"Thank you for that too. I've told my wife already, and I know she's terribly worried about what we'll do for money . . . how the family will survive without my knight's pension. Frankly, I don't know either. Her family are tenant farmers who get by, but we know they can't afford four more mouths to feed, so I have to find some sort of work."

"Maybe that's something we can help with," I say. "Talk to Lord Rupert. It's not out of the question he might be in need of help with security around the port." What I actually have in mind is that my uncle and my friend Laurence may have an entirely different need for Gamel's services in their intelligence-gathering network.

"If that doesn't work out," chimes in Phillip, "I know the sheriff of Great Woolston is looking to retire within the year."

"I'm afraid, your lordship, that those positions normally go to honorably retired knights," replies Gamel.

"I don't seem to recall the king mentioning anything about dishonor. Do you, Alfred?"

"Definitely not."

"So technically, there's no impediment," says Phillip. "And I'd be willing to put in a good word with the mayor on your behalf."

"I'm overwhelmed, sirs," says Gamel. "I . . . I don't know what to say."

"Say you'll have another round with us before our wives arrive," says Richard. "I think Alfred is buying," he laughs as he signals to the innkeeper.

The trial of Ralf's sons takes place today. It will likely be simple and straightforward, as the lads have been only too happy to tell anyone who would listen how they obeyed their father's instructions to cut the cinch on my father's saddle so that it would give way under the stress of riding, throwing him violently from his horse. It's Ralf who should be on trial, but he seems to have gone to ground – no one's even asked about the boys, much less attempted to rescue them, and Rupert's best efforts haven't turned up any signs of him.

John has shown no interest in justice for our father's death and refused to delay his progress for the trial. But the people need to see that justice for such a crime is fair but swift and inexorable. So it falls to Rupert and me to represent the family.

The hearing room in the town hall is crowded – every seat on every bench taken and people standing shoulder to shoulder at the back and around the sides of the room. Those who couldn't get inside are milling about in the square as we arrive. At the front of the room, there's a table and chair where the magistrate will preside and a bench on each side, one for the accused and the other for witnesses. The hum of conversation goes quiet when the magistrate takes his place and orders, "Bring in the accused." The two young men are brought in under guard, their hands tied behind them. We've learned that their names are Drogo and Ran. I wonder, not for the first time, if the latter is Ranulf's namesake.

The witnesses recount what we already know. Samuel describes the fateful jump over the hedgerow and recovering the saddle later to discover the sabotage. Elvin tells how the boys came to him looking for work. "Did you have any knowledge at the time of who they were, Master Elvin?" asks the magistrate.

"Nay, sir. They say they be from the east . . . from a village they say be near Devereux Castle. But I never heard of the village so I forget the name." This explains why Ralf and all of his sons were once spotted in that area. He wanted the boys to be able to give a reliable account of place names and the surrounding landscape.

"And was their work satisfactory, Master Elvin?"

"They be fair workers, sir. They be lazy like many young lads, but the work they did were good enough."

Somehow, Rupert has managed to keep Alf out of all this to protect one of his best agents, instead testifying himself that he ordered everyone rounded up when he arrived at the castle and learned what had happened. Since the boys have never denied their actions and John's not here to insist on getting to the bottom of everything, that proves sufficient to needs.

When the magistrate addresses himself to the boys, naïveté and devotion to their father cause them to seal their own fate. The magistrate carefully leads them through everything they did, then addresses the older one. "Drogo, you lads are old enough to understand the difference between right and wrong. Is it right or wrong to take the life of another man?"

He doesn't answer directly. "Men be killing each other in war, sir."

"But we aren't at war. Do you know what the Bible says about killing one's fellow man?"

"Me mother tell us God say not to kill. But me da say a soldier obeys the orders of his commander and mayhap he be ordered to kill."

"Are you a soldier, Drogo?"

"Not a proper one, sir, like the knights with their fancy banners. But when me and me brothers ride out with me da, we be on patrol, just like the knights."

"Did your father say what would happen if you didn't follow orders?"

"When we be lads, sir, when Da tell us what to do, if we dinna' do it and do it quick, he beat us. He say, now we be men, if we dinna' obey, then we have to fight him so he can show us proper-like how he be stronger and the one who say what we do."

"Do you think you'd lose a fight with your father, Drogo?"

"Aye, sir. He be strong and fit. And if we show any sign of not losing, our brothers would join in to help him."

Then the magistrate turns to the younger one. "Ran, do you agree with what your brother's just told me?"

"Aye, sir."

"And did your father tell you what might happen to you if you obeyed his order and the king should die?"

"That be what were supposed to happen, sir," answers Ran. "Me father say it be a great honor to us to be the ones who finally see things set right."

"Did he say that you might be punished?"

"Nay, sir. He say come find him and our brothers, and we celebrate."

The magistrate shakes his head and looks around the room at the spectators. "Is there anyone else who knows something I should consider before passing judgment?"

There's complete and utter silence in the room. No shuffle of a foot, no rustling of clothing, no squirming of bodies, not even a nervous cough, though the magistrate waits a very long time for any response.

"Very well. Before I pass judgment, I have instructions for everyone here. I'm certain there's a crowd in the square eager to know what's happened. The sheriff's men are about, to keep calm and order, but to make their job easier, I'm asking that you not speak of what's happened in this room until after I announce the judgment.

"It's also important that the king's justice be properly administered – that the crowd doesn't take matters into their own hands. So the accused will remain here under guard while I proclaim the verdict. Once it's safe to do so, their guards will return them to their cells in the castle.

"Are my instructions clear?" He scans the room intensely, making sure everyone knows he means business.

"Very well. Drogo and Ran, please stand to receive the king's justice.

"Drogo, you are accused of regicide – of intentionally causing the death of our late King Edward – a crime that is tantamount to treason. I find you guilty as charged. Furthermore, as you have openly and without coercion admitted and described your intent and your actions, you have forfeited your right of appeal to the Crown. Drogo, I sentence you to be hanged from the neck until dead." He looks directly at Ran and repeats the same judgment. The boys look stunned and cower as the guards move closer to take charge of them. I suspect it's never occurred to them until this very moment that their actions would actually cost them their lives.

"These sentences are to be carried out simultaneously," the magistrate continues, "three days hence at midday in the market square. They will remain hanging in the square for three days as a reminder of the consequences of regicide. Anyone attempting to claim the bodies must be brought before me. If no one claims them, they'll be dumped in the old pauper's pit on the far side of the river.

"The accused have made it clear they acted on the orders of their father, Ralf, son of Ranulf. I therefore declare Ralf a fugitive from the king's justice. Anyone knowing his whereabouts and not reporting it to the proper authorities or anyone giving food, shelter, or comfort to Ralf is therefore guilty of harboring a criminal and subject to the penalties prescribed in our laws. These proceedings are now concluded."

As everyone leaves the room, I hang back. "Go along if you wish," I tell Rupert. "I'd like to have a word with the magistrate when he returns."

"I had the same thought."

The cheering we hear outside tells us the crowd is satisfied with the verdict and the sentence. There are probably also some who are just looking forward to the spectacle of a hanging. I've never understood that side of human nature.

It's not long before the sheriff appears at the door and beckons to the guards. "The crowd's dispersing quietly," he says. "Let's get those two back to the castle."

The magistrate returns as they're leaving, head down as he walks into the room. He seems startled to see us. "My lords, forgive me. I didn't expect to find anyone here."

"We wanted a private word, Magistrate," says Rupert, "to thank you for the way you conducted the proceedings."

"It was worthy of my father," I add.

The magistrate mops his brow with a kerchief. "May I?" he gestures to a bench, asking our permission to sit.

"Of course," says Rupert.

"I've thought of nothing else since I heard of King Edward's death and that those two had been detained. I knew it would fall to me to pass judgment, so I've had many sleepless nights these past three weeks, reading and re-reading the laws and asking myself over and over again, 'what would he have done?'

"I studied with him, you see, in preparation for taking this post. I so admired him and wanted to do right by him."

"You've done just that," I say, clapping him gently on the shoulder.

"I considered trying to use them to get to Ralf . . . offering to reduce their sentence to life imprisonment if they could get their father to come forward. In the end, I decided the people wouldn't understand. They'd expect whoever actually committed the crime to be punished. So I did the only other thing I could think of."

"I think that's exactly what Edward would've done," says Rupert. "Now, maybe you can finally get a well-earned night's sleep."

We arrive back at the castle just as Gundrea's family is leaving. No one will be sorry to see them go – not even Gundrea, I think. Before he left on progress, John was paying far more attention to Gunhild than to his wife. Letty says talk in the servants' hall is that Gunhild was seen coming and going from the king's apartment in the hours when the rest of us were sleeping. It's hard to believe Gundrea wouldn't have heard the gossip. I only hope Lord Erik never finds out.

The priest who came with her family stayed behind, and she's moved him into the vacant dressing room in her apartment. It seems he says mass for the queen and her children every day in the castle chapel – twice on Sundays, Letty tells us.

·　　·　　·　　·　　·

The morning of the hanging dawns darkly, with storm clouds on the eastern horizon. The westerly wind means we'll escape any bad weather, but the heavy morning sky does nothing for my mood. With Rupert back at the port, I have the grim duty of witnessing the gruesome event on behalf of the family. Samuel asked to come with me. "I think maybe if I see justice carried out, I can finally put that whole business well and truly behind me," he said.

We ride rather than walk – to stay out of the press of the crowd and to have a better view. If Ralf decides to attempt a last-minute rescue of his sons, he'll try to blend in with the crowd and will be easier to spot from horseback. The sheriff, it seems, has the same idea. Joining us at the edge of the square opposite the platform where the gibbet's been raised, he says, "I've got men in all four quarters, but I can direct them better from up here." Samuel and I find a reasonable vantage point while the sheriff continues to make his way slowly around the perimeter.

At the appointed hour, they bring the boys out and make them climb the stairs onto the platform, a priest following them, reading from the Bible. Ran is crying, tears running down his face that he can't wipe away because his hands are bound. Drogo's eyes dart around the crowd, and he seems to be keeping up a running conversation with his brother. We learn later from those nearer the platform that he kept saying, "Dinna' cry, Ran. Da'll be here. I know he will. Look for him like I be doing."

As the church bell begins to toll midday, the priest closes his Bible and goes to each lad in turn, saying a prayer and making the sign of the cross over each of them. Then the guards put them up on stools and pull the nooses over their heads, adjusting the knots around their small necks. Drogo takes Ran's hand, and the priest leaves the platform. When the last bell sounds, Ran screams, "Daaaaaaaaaaaaaaaaaaaaaaaaaaaa!" – an ear-splitting, heart-rending cry that slowly fades to a whimper. And the guards kick the stools out from under them.

There's not a sound from the crowd. There's no one here to mourn them. People just slowly turn their backs and wander away, back to their day's routine. Perhaps, like Samuel, they came only to see that justice was truly done for the king they'd loved.

It's quieter than usual around the castle with all the lords off attending to the king's progress, but Phillip has hurried back to prepare for the meeting of the commercial Assembly. "Are you sure it's wise to go ahead with it while he's away?" I ask.

"Better, I think, to stick to business as usual," he replies, "since the meeting's been scheduled for months. Just think of the turmoil a delay would create – we could be back to all that grousing and complaining in an instant."

"Or you could have John grousing and complaining instead," I tease him.

"The meeting should be done and everyone gone by the time he gets back. And anyway – he didn't tell me to cancel it, so I'm just doing my job."

The Assembly was constituted by my father as an antidote to a growing sense of unrest among the commercial interests and has been more successful than even he had imagined. They've had their debates – some of them quite heated – but in the process, they're beginning to recognize just how complicated all the moving parts of the kingdom's governance can be. One of the most contested issues was the building and operation of a woolen mill to provide cheaper cloth for people of limited means, and now, with the mill in full production, they all boast about its success and their part in making it happen. The delegates are chosen by the merchants and traders in the towns they represent, but the makeup of the Assembly hasn't changed much from the first meeting . . . and there are no new faces when they gather this time. Ouistreham from Neukirk Market, Hewse from the port, Jolland representing the interests of the castle town, a trader named Gand from

Great Woolston, and – much to my delight – Amelia Greslet, the most influential merchant in Abbéville Market.

Amelia holds a fascination over me that I am completely at a loss to explain. I'm still very much in love with my wife. And yet, I'm drawn to Amelia like the proverbial moth that occasionally incinerates itself in my bedside candle. Both my father and Gwen have told me at one time or another that being attracted to a beautiful woman is just how men are made. The trick, it seems, is avoiding the fate of the moth.

With little else to do, Richard and I sit in on the Assembly meetings. The first day is spent almost entirely on discussing the operation of the mill. Surprisingly, it's Hewse and Gand – once the loudest voices in opposition – who urge an increase in production this year. For once, Phillip has little to do but watch as they sort things out for themselves. The next morning, the subject is taxes. "It's *always* taxes," says Phillip, rolling his eyes as we chat over the midday meal. "Maybe Richard should put them to work sorting out how to balance his accounts every year."

"Good God, no!" Richard doesn't hesitate. "It's complicated enough without five more people meddling." He pauses for a gulp of ale. "You just need to find something different for them to argue about."

"Any ideas?" asks Phillip.

The afternoon discussion has settled into a familiar pattern when suddenly the door bursts open and John marches in, stopping just inside the room. Everyone scrambles to their feet and into a hurried bow. "This Assembly is dismissed," John announces. "We have no need of advice from a collection of shopkeepers. I'll run the kingdom as I see fit. You go back to running your shops. Be gone by midday tomorrow."

Turning on his heel, he adds, "Thorssen, present yourself to me as soon as you've dismissed this lot." And then he storms out. No one moves a muscle until the sound of his boots in the corridor fades away.

And then they start talking all over each other. "Did he really just call us shopkeepers?" "What's the meaning of this?" "I thought the Council authorized this Assembly." "Does he really mean it?" "Thorssen, what did you know about this?"

Finally, Phillip restores order. "Madam . . . Gentlemen . . . I'm as surprised as you. I had no idea."

"My lords?" Amelia poses it as a question to Richard and me.

"No idea at all," says Richard as I shake my head.

"I heard," says Ouistreham, "that the king didn't want the Assembly when it was first proposed."

"He did express some reservations during the Council debate," says Richard. "But the Council voted overwhelmingly to proceed, and we've been very well satisfied."

"So," says Gand, "I suppose this is it. We pack our bags and go home. How disappointing!"

"Let's not give up so easily," says Phillip. "The king may not want to continue the Assembly in its current form, but as Lord Richard said, the lords *do* find your insight valuable. So here's what I propose.

"We obey the king's order. But I invite all of you to visit Thorssen Castle soon. Expect a written invitation for a visit of several days as soon as I can sort out the details. Expect some of the lords to be there as well. My apologies, Madam Greslet, that the distance will be so great for you, but I hope you'll find it worth the journey."

Amelia's eyes light up in recognition of Phillip's cunning solution to the problem. "I'll look forward to the invitation, your lordship. I've never been to Thorssen Castle, but I understand the views of the sea are quite spectacular."

"Excellent!" says Phillip. "Now, I suspect you all have preparations to make for your departure. I, it seems, must wait on the king."

As we leave the room, Amelia hangs back to walk with me. "I take it from the expression on your face that you didn't see this coming."

"You take it correctly. That doesn't mean, though, that I'm unaccustomed to my brother taking me entirely by surprise."

We walk in silence as the others rush ahead, still angry about what just happened and in no mood to linger. Near the end of the corridor and with no one in sight, she reaches out and touches my arm. "I'd hoped we might have an opportunity for another ride in the woods. I'd really like to see that little paddock beside the stream again."

I place my hand over hers. "Perhaps there'll be another time." I bring her hand to my mouth and kiss it in farewell, but find myself lingering rather longer than is really necessary. Why, I ask myself once again, am I so intrigued by this woman? And once again, I brush it off as a harmless flirtation. But is it as harmless as I choose to pretend?

•   •   •   •

So John has returned. I wander back to our apartment, which is empty, so I go to the nursery, where the girls are singing and the boys are playing with the dogs. Watching their simple fun lightens my mood.

As Gwen and I settle down to a private supper in our sitting room, Osbert pokes his head through the door. "Begging yer pardon, m'lord, but Lord Thorssen say he really be needing to talk t'ye."

"Invite him in, Osbert," says Gwen cheerily. "I'm sure we have enough food if he's hungry."

Phillip falls into the nearest chair, looking totally exhausted. I go to the cabinet in the corner and pour him a brandy, which he downs in one gulp. "I have *never*," he pauses while I refill his glass, "*never* been so insulted in my life. My father would have been appalled.

"He orders me to wait on him, and then he makes me sit in the public reception room for three hours. *Three hours*! Absolutely no one else comes or goes during that time. Finally I'm invited into the private reception where he berates me nonstop for a full quarter hour for conducting the Assembly meeting without his permission.

"I foolishly tried to explain that the meeting was planned long before he became king. That only set him off on another rant. You would never have known he was speaking to a lord of the realm. Does he even know, Alfred, what the traditional relationship is between the Crown and the lords?"

"He was taught, Phillip, just as I was. Right now, he can't see beyond the fact that he finally has power. You know how much he's always resented the efforts of my grandfather and my father to restrain his behavior. The restraints are off now, so I fear we may be in for quite a few surprises."

"I just hope we get through this 'drunk with power' phase quickly." Phillip is starting to relax a bit under the influence of the brandy.

"I have to tell you, my friend, your solution for the Assembly was nothing short of brilliant. Did you make that up on the spot?"

"Not quite," he replies a bit sheepishly. "I remembered how adamantly John had opposed the Assembly proposal and decided I'd best be prepared if he was foolish enough to try to disband the whole thing. So Richard and I came up with this estate visit idea. We have to keep the commercial interests engaged in some fashion. If we don't, the pot that was simmering before will simply boil over." He pauses for a sip of brandy. "Richard's willing to invite them to Devereux Castle from time to time as well and says his father approves."

"I rather suspect some of the other lords will follow suit once they see firsthand what you're doing. You *are* planning to invite them to your little party, aren't you?"

"Naturally."

"Is there any way the Treasury can support this? It isn't usual that the lords should have to personally bear the cost of conducting the kingdom's business."

"Richard suggested something of the sort. But he's cautious until he has a better idea how much attention John will give to Treasury operations."

"I wouldn't dare to hazard a guess what he might do."

Phillip finishes his brandy. When I offer to refill his glass, he raises his hand in restraint. "Thank you, but I'd best be going. Addiena will be wondering where I am, and I've clearly interrupted your supper. It did me a world of good to talk to you, Alfred."

"Maybe I've found my new role. André said it would become clear in time."

Phillip cocks his head and looks at me quizzically.

"Sounding board to everyone John manages to offend." We both laugh.

"That, my friend, could turn out to keep you well and truly occupied."

On his way out, Phillip turns at the door. "By the way, I trust you know about the meeting of the lords he's called for the day after tomorrow?"

"First I've heard of it."

"Well, it's supposed to be everyone. Ernle is having to rush to get back, since he was the last stop on the progress. There's no way Peveril will even be notified in time, much less be able to complete the journey." Lord Peveril is our ambassador to the Kingdom Across the Southern Sea. "I was told you and Rupert are expected to be there as well."

"I suppose my invitation has been delayed," I grin.

Phillip rolls his eyes, and then he's gone.

My summons to the meeting of the lords is delivered to Osbert by John's squire at midday the following day. I sincerely hope someone's been more diligent about informing Rupert. Barely, it turns out, for he arrives at sundown, clearly having pressed his horse to cover the distance more quickly than usual.

As we assemble in the Council chamber, the usual friendly conversation is subdued. The bishop is conspicuously absent. All are here except Peveril. Richard's presence is presumably because he's on the Council.

John arrives with his usual air of arrogance. He's taken to wearing a coronet at all times, an affectation eschewed by his predecessors for all but the most formal occasions. Leaving everyone standing with heads bowed for just a little longer than is really necessary, he finally says, "Take your seats and listen while I tell you how I intend to run this kingdom.

"First, I've chosen a new knight commander – Sir Louve. He may only have risen to troop captain, but Sir Mauger tells me Louve will be diligent in executing my orders and ensuring that our knights are prepared for any eventuality."

There are furtive glances around the table. No one knows anything about this Sir Louve. If what John said is true, then it would seem obedience is his primary attribute.

"Next," he plows ahead, not pausing for any questions or discussion, though I rather doubt anyone would venture a comment just yet. "The Treasury. I'm assuming personal control immediately. Richard Devereux, your services are no longer required." Lord Devereux places his hand on Richard's arm – a signal, I think, to say nothing.

"And while we're on that topic . . . I intend to run this kingdom properly. If I require advice from the nobility, I'll seek it from the lords of the realm. The role of the heirs is to apprentice with their fathers – nothing more. Richard Devereux, your presence is no longer required."

Richard ventures a glance in my direction. His eyes reveal his seething frustration. I shake my head almost imperceptibly to indicate we'll talk later. To his credit, Richard rises from his seat and bows, saying, "Yes, Your Grace" and then, gesturing to the door, "With your permission, Your Grace?"

"Yes, yes," John replies brusquely. "Get on with it." He waits until the door closes behind Richard before proceeding.

"Thorssen knows this already, but I want to make it official. The commercial Assembly is disbanded. You all know I opposed its creation in the first place, and I'm taking steps to rectify that ill-conceived decision. This afternoon I'll sign a proclamation formally disbanding it and rescinding any laws . . . anything . . . associated with it."

Bauldry has apparently had enough of silent acquiescence and raises his hand to speak.

"You have something to say, Bauldry?"

"With your permission, Your Grace."

"Very well, let's hear it."

"It's my impression that the Council has been well pleased with the insight we're receiving from the Assembly. Why would we want to undo something that's working so well?"

"*You* may have been pleased, Bauldry, but I remain unwavering in my belief that there's no value and only risk in ceding power to the lower classes. The Assembly is disbanded, and that's that." Bauldry shakes his head in disbelief.

"Next," John goes on. "Our embassy in the Kingdom Across the Southern Sea. Peveril will be recalled and the embassy discontinued. I see no need for us to spend money maintaining a presence in a foreign land. That money can be put to other uses."

Montfort raises a hand hesitantly.

"What is it, Montfort?"

"With respect, Your Grace, I believe if you speak with our traders, you'll find that the ambassador has been very successful in helping to arrange favorable terms with the great weaving houses and the winemakers in the Kingdom Across the Southern Sea."

"In that case, Montfort, it sounds as if Peveril's job is done and he can come home." Montfort can do little but look at the ceiling in dismay.

"I am today creating three new lords - Benoist, Morphew, and Puchot." This time, he pauses and looks around the table for reactions.

Meriden looks puzzled. "Puchot, Your Grace? That's an unusual name. In fact, the only man I've ever heard of bearing that name is a tenant on my estate."

"In which case, Lord Meriden, you should already have an acquaintance with the new Lord Puchot."

Meriden can't contain himself. "A tenant farmer named lord of the realm? How can that be, Your Grace? What has this man done to distinguish himself?"

"He hasn't done anything, Meriden. It's what was done to him that must be set right. Puchot and the others were dishonorably dismissed from the knighthood for doing no more than following their captain's orders." Suddenly it's clear to everyone who these men are - the other three knights John took on his reconnaissance raid into the Territories.

"If memory serves, Your Grace," Bauldry ventures, "that raid was in express violation of the orders of the knight commander. My recollection is that orders of the commander supersede those of a captain."

"We're not here to discuss military command structure, Bauldry. These men were treated dishonorably, their lot in life greatly reduced through no fault of their own, and that must be rectified. I intend to reward their loyalty by including them among my advisors and to that end, they're to be made lords." He stops and looks around the table again.

Devereux tries a different approach. "Your Grace, if I may?" he asks before speaking.

"At least someone here still has some manners," replies John. "Go ahead, Devereux."

"While no one here denies the king's right to create a lordship for the bearer's lifetime, I'm curious how you intend to provide land and a source of income for them."

"As Meriden has pointed out, Puchot is a tenant farmer on his estate. The others are tenants on other estates. I intend to grant them the land they now hold as a tenancy. They have no need of income beyond supporting their families, and they're already doing that with the proceeds of their farming. Those proceeds will increase because they'll no longer owe rent to their landlord."

Meriden explodes. *"You can't do that!"*

"I am the king. I can. And I already have. And *you* need to be mindful of how you speak to your king, Meriden."

Lord Ernle has been quiet until now but raises his hand to speak.

"You have something constructive to add, Ernle?" says John.

"I was wondering, Your Grace, if perhaps you might be forgetting some of the history of this kingdom."

"I'm not sure what the history of the kingdom has to do with this matter, but I'm sure you'll tell me how you think it's relevant."

"If you recall, Your Grace, when this kingdom was consolidated from the ancient fiefs, each of the fief holders was granted hereditary rights to their own lands for their descendants in perpetuity, in return for nothing more than being honor-bound by a pledge of loyalty to the king – that very pledge you accepted from each of us when you ascended the throne."

I came to know and respect Lord Ernle when he took me into his home and under his wing after my return from captivity. My father often referred to him as a crafty fox. Crafty, indeed, to so subtly point out that John has already guaranteed the integrity of the hereditary estates by accepting the lords' pledges.

"And your point, Ernle?" Did he really miss it altogether or just choose to ignore it? It'll be interesting to see how Ernle finesses this.

"There are no doubt far better lands that could be granted to the new lords. Lands that would be much more in keeping with their new status. Grants that would permit you to maintain the honor of the Crown." The nods around the table are subtle but unmistakable.

"I'll keep your words in mind, Ernle. Perhaps there are indeed better properties for the new lords." No one misses the significance of that first comment. Ernle may have preserved the integrity of the hereditary estates, but likely at the cost of never again being invited to sit on the Council or advise this king.

"Now, for the makeup of the new Council. Bauldry and the three new lords. There's no need for anyone else from the royal house. No need for the bishop. Sir Louve will be invited only if military matters are to be discussed. Meetings will be at my discretion with ample time for travel, so there's no longer a reason for any of you to maintain a presence at court."

"With respect, Your Grace." Bauldry. "The lords have a traditional right to request a Council meeting at any time. How can we do so if we're not at court?"

"The king has a traditional right to decline such a request." John is correct, but it's a right no king has exercised in a century or more. "I have *no* wish to incur the expense of maintaining lords at court."

"Once again with respect, Your Grace." Bauldry again. "We pay our own expenses. We buy our own food, our own wine, pay our own servants, maintain our own wardrobes—"

John interrupts him. "And you use my fuel to cook your food and warm your rooms in winter, my kitchen staff to prepare your meals, my stable for your horses and my barns for your carriages, my grooms and stable boys and meadows to feed your animals, my water, my guards to ensure your safety, my laundresses . . . Shall I go on?"

Bauldry wisely says no more.

"Are we clear?" asks John. There's silence around the table, which he takes for assent. "Then we're finished here." He rises as the rest of us scramble to our feet. It seems as if no one exhales until the echo of his footsteps in the corridor is finally silent.

Devereux goes to Ernle and claps him on the shoulder. "We owe you a debt, my friend."

"No doubt it will cost me dearly in some other way, but it had to be done," says Ernle.

"Gentlemen," says Devereux, "we're going to have to find new ways to look out for the welfare of this realm and its people. But we have to be careful . . . and I think we'd best not discuss it here."

"Interestingly," says Rupert, "the fact that he doesn't want us at court may very well make things easier. Thorssen, what's this I hear about your planning some sort of country party?"

"Indeed I am, though my steward doesn't know it yet," replies Phillip. "Addiena tells me my life will be much simpler if I speak with him before actually issuing invitations," he adds with a chuckle. It's just enough to lighten the mood in the room.

"Rupert," Devereux resumes, "I think it falls to you to bring Peveril into the picture as soon as he returns. He'll be dismayed by such an abrupt recall."

"I'll meet his ship when it docks. We don't need to let him run afoul of the king right away."

"Bauldry, you're going to have your work cut out for you in this new Council."

"If it ever meets at all," says Bauldry.

"Indeed. Now, I must go reassure my son that he's suffered no more than any of us at the hands of our new king."

"Tell Richard he should join Phillip, Samuel, and me at the tavern later," I tell him as he makes his way to the door.

"Aye," Phillip chimes in. "Tell him Alfred is buying."

Over the past week, the lords have all departed. Richard and his family returned to Devereux Castle with his father. Three days ago, Samuel came to me with the news that he and his family are leaving also. "Sir Ronan and I had it all worked out, Alfred. He's ready to retire and was overjoyed that I'd consider taking the post . . . so much so that he wanted to give his personal recommendation to the king.

"I'd already decided to go ahead and accept father's cottage and land against the day when I really do need it. The plan was to lease it to Ronan so long as I remain in the knighthood. Then, when I'm ready to retire, he could stay on to help me with the running of the place."

"So what went wrong?" I asked.

"Your brother, of course. He rejected it out of hand. Berated Ronan for having the temerity to think he would have *any* say in the choice of his successor. Said he would look to Sir Louve and him alone to recommend the next head of training. Then he stopped pacing, pointed a finger directly at me, and said, 'And you can be absolutely certain, Ernle, that it will *not* be you.'

"His exact words! Not even the courtesy to call me Sir Samuel." He threw up his hands in dismay. "I'm sorry, Alfred. I know this was important to you."

"Not the post, Samuel. Just your skills. I suppose I should have thought it through more carefully before putting you in that position. I might have realized he wouldn't want any of the people surrounding him to have any connection to me."

"It's not your fault, Alfred, that your brother's—"

I quickly put my finger to my lips. I could imagine what he was about to say. "The walls have ears, my friend. Let's go riding."

A brisk gallop across the meadow seemed to help Samuel dissipate some of his frustration, and we made our way into the woods, to the dilapidated hut we had called our lodge when playing there as boys. Dismounting and setting our horses to graze, we went inside. "This place doesn't seem to have changed much since the first time we found it," he remarked. "Can it really be that we've changed so much since those days?"

"I'm not sure it's we who've changed, Samuel. Oh, we're older and know more about the ways of the world. But deep inside, I think we're still who we always were. Even John, which is why he's so dangerous as king."

We talked at length – reminiscing about our youth – sharing our uncertainties about what's to come. Finally, I asked him, "So what are you going to do?"

"Louve assigned me to command the western garrison. I have to either take it or retire."

"And?"

"Frankly, I'm so disgusted with the way things are going that retirement seems like a really good option. But I can't get your 'vague feeling' out of my mind. So I'm going to stick with it. Being that far away from here should mean I don't have to witness the insanity on a daily basis. Tamasine and the children can live in the cottage. There's a sort of keeper's lodge we can fix up nicely for Ronan. He's agreed to oversee the farm and provide protection for the family. I'll be close enough I can easily go there when I'm off duty."

"You don't have to do this for me, Samuel."

"I know. But like I said, your vague feeling is lodged in my own mind now, and I can't shake it. All in all, this may be a better solution anyway. And with what John's done to the lords, having his grandchildren nearby should be good for my father as well. Besides," he claps me on the shoulder, "I'm not sure I'm entirely ready to be a gentleman farmer just yet."

Samuel's family left yesterday and he departed at dawn this morning in command of the replacement troop for the garrison. Petronilla left at midday for her visit to Rupert and Catherine ... and of course, onward to Goscelin's court.

The castle is so quiet now that it's almost eerie. The town, too, seems subdued. With the lords and their families and servants gone, there are fewer people in the shops. And the ripple effects are just beginning. John ordered the steward to reduce the staff of the kitchens and the laundry by half. Mervyn the Younger was forced to retire. "I need only one stable master, Mervyn – you or Elvin," John is reported to have told him. "You decide." Half the stable-boys and a third of the grooms were also dismissed.

With nothing to occupy my time, I turn my attention to the horses. I've chosen a two-year-old son of Star Dancer to train as a gift to Lord Egon. He'd once expressed admiration for Star Dancer, and we spoke briefly of discussing horses at some future time. Working with these magnificent animals has always given me both pleasure and comfort, but somehow, this time, even they can't fully ease my feeling of helplessness in the face of everything that's happening around us.

•   •   •   •   •

Petronilla has returned and joins us for a private supper in Mother's chamber on her first night back. "I had the most delightful time," she exudes. "Goscelin's court is such a remarkable place. His collection of art is beyond anything I've ever imagined. Artists come there just to copy the works as a way to perfect their skills. There's a music school too, and a concert on the lawn every Sunday afternoon when the weather is fine."

"Tell us about Goscelin himself," Gwen implores.

"He's everything his letters led me to believe. Impeccable manners. Real kindness. He gave a ball in my honor and would dance with no one else."

The door bursts open, and there stands John. "So the prodigal returns," he says.

We all look at him aghast. "Whatever do you mean, Son?" asks my mother.

John continues to address himself to Petronilla. "I hear you've been across the southern sea. Set sail three weeks ago, according to my information." So he has his own spies. Laurence and Rupert will need to know this.

"And?" asks Petronilla.

"And I want to know what you were doing there."

"Accepting a friend's invitation to visit," she replies evenly.

"Don't be coy with me."

"John," says Mother, "what's your interest in Petronilla's trip?"

"I demand to know what you were doing there," still ignoring Mother and speaking directly to Petronilla.

Mother's had enough. "That is no way to speak to your aunt, John."

"I'm the king and I'll speak to anyone however I wish," he retorts.

"John, do you remember nothing of what I taught you of court manners? Petronilla is not only your aunt, she's a dowager queen. She's entitled to your respect.

"And by the way," she adds, "I'm growing quite annoyed with your new habit of barging into a room without knocking. It's unseemly."

"It's my castle, and I'll enter any room I choose."

"And what if we'd been having a fitting with the dressmaker and were all standing here in our shifts while she made adjustments to our gowns? There's no need to be boorish, John. It's unbecoming."

Then she quickly changes the subject. "Now that you're here, why don't you join us for supper? Let's send for Gundrea and make it the whole family."

"She won't come. And anyway, I didn't come for supper."

While he's talking, Mother rings a bell, and Nona pops in from the dressing room. "Nona, please go ask the queen to join us for supper. Tell her the king is here, and we'd be delighted to have her company as well."

"Yes, m'lady." Nona drops a little curtsey and hurries off.

"She won't come, I tell you."

"Why are you so sure, Son?"

"Because she hasn't come to any of my suppers."

"Have you asked her?"

"She knows when I dine."

"That's not what I asked, John. Having denied her right to share your apartment, what makes you think she'd just put in an appearance to dine with you unless you invite her?"

"Why are we talking about this?"

"Patience, Son. Let's see if your wife comes. In the meantime, do sit down. Alfred, pour your brother a glass of wine."

Mother has a remarkable talent for completely changing the subject on John in such a way that he can't figure out how to bring it back. In short order, there's a knock on the door and Nona enters. "Queen Gundrea, m'lady."

Gundrea is dressed in one of her black, high-collared frocks, and she seems a bit hesitant, unsure why she's been invited here. "Sit," John says. "It seems they want us to have supper here."

The remainder of the meal is rather stilted, but we manage to keep the conversation on children and the weather and far away from Petronilla's trip. I offer John a brandy, which he refuses, eager now to get away from all this family togetherness. Gundrea leaves with him, though I doubt she'll be going anywhere other than her own apartment.

When they're gone, Petronilla visibly relaxes. "Thank you for that, Alice."

"Of course, my dear. Though I fear it may only be temporary. Now tell us, what do you think Goscelin will do next?"

"I can only wait and see."

"Would you accept him if he proposes marriage?"

Petronilla smiles. "I think I just might. But I'm glad to have ample time to talk with you about it before having to make a decision."

Phillip's country party is an enormous success, but it's obvious the whole affair is costing him a king's ransom – or maybe the right phrase is "a kingdom's ransom." Future gatherings will need to be more low-key, but Phillip insisted this first one needed some of the trappings of past Assembly meetings.

The first day is a formal Assembly meeting, but unlike previous ones, all the lords decide to sit in to listen. "Everything's changing," says Jolland. "First, there's the folks that were dismissed from the castle staff. Most of them have nowhere to go, so they're sleeping in alleyways and scrounging for odd jobs and bits of food. But there's no one to take them on. The shopkeepers and trades are trying to keep their helpers on, but I don't know how long they can afford to if the court doesn't come back."

"The traders in the port are already starting to speculate about orders dropping off," says Hewse. "It's not bad yet, but their mood is dour. They're sure it's only going to get worse."

"Things are more or less normal in Neukirk Market for now," says Ouistreham, "but I'm worried about the harvest. Not that it will be bad, but that it will be good. So much of the harvest usually goes to the castle and the port, but if they're not buying, I dread to think what might happen."

"How are the people without work getting by?" asks Phillip.

"Badly," replies Jolland. "The church is doing what they can but it's not much. The monastery has given temporary shelter to a few families, but their resources are limited too. Mostly, people are just living day-to-day, hand-to-mouth, wherever they can. No one I know has ever seen anything quite like this."

The next day seems intended to lift everyone's spirits, and the weather seems happy to do its part. The dowager Lady Thorssen is totally in her element, presiding over an outdoor feast much like those she used to organize when her husband was alive. Holding court on a blanket spread on the lawn, she commands Lord Devereux, Phillip, and me to join her for gammon, fresh paindemaine, and small ale.

Hoofbeats are the last thing anyone expects to hear, but the sound is unmistakable. And as they get louder, a mounted troop riding under the king's banner gallops up the lane, coming to a stop at the edge of the lawn. John – wearing his coronet – jumps down from his horse and marches toward Phillip as we all scramble to our feet. Everyone, that is, except the dowager Lady Thorssen, who has always done things her own way and remains seated, continuing to enjoy her food.

"Thorssen," John barks.

"Yes, Your Grace."

"Quite a gathering you have here. Why was I not invited?"

"There are those among the party, Your Grace, with whom you've made it clear you have no wish to consort. I sought to spare you the awkwardness, Your Grace."

"Oh?"

"Indeed, Your Grace. Those you refer to as shopkeepers . . . and the heirs of the lords are also here . . . though my own son isn't quite of an age yet to take much interest."

"Hmph. Sounds like you might be trying to conduct business of the kingdom behind my back."

"Not at all, Your Grace. As you can see, we're having an outdoor meal. Tomorrow, there'll be a hunt. And if we have any luck on the hunt, we'll have a feast the following day with local musicians for entertainment."

The dowager Lady Thorssen chimes in. "Do sit with me, Your Grace, and have some of this fine food and small ale. Or if you prefer, I can ask my son to send for some regular ale for you and your men."

"I think not, Lady Thorssen. We're on patrol and patrols don't divert themselves with country parties." With that, he turns on his heel, marches back to his horse, mounts up, and leads the troop away.

Patrol indeed. Checking up on us, more like.

When they're out of earshot, Lord Devereux claps Phillip on the shoulder. "Nicely done, Thorssen. You're a credit to your title and your father's legacy."

"He has his moments," says his mother, with grudging admiration.

Devereux laughs. "Why do I suspect he doesn't get all his talents from his father, Lady Cecily?"

"You are *quite* correct, Lord Devereux. Now, you gentlemen do rejoin me to finish this meal. I don't fancy having you all standing there looking down at me."

We leave at the end of the gathering with more questions than answers . . . more consternation than constructive ideas about the problems John's creating. Perhaps I've been too optimistic about our ability to make a difference. Or perhaps, as Gwen points out, it's too soon for people to accept that this isn't just a temporary setback but a real sea change. But I don't think the hereditary lords are under any illusions about the present or what the future is likely to hold.

With so much time on my hands, I've finished the young stallion's training quickly. He's smart and well-mannered, which made it that much easier, and he seems to be as reliable as Star Dancer and Sirius. I named him Polaris, for the star that mariners use to navigate on the open seas. Training him has helped me navigate the changes around me. I hope he can also help steer a successful course through the nascent dialogue Egon and I have started.

Tonight, during out bedtime chat, I broach the subject once again with Gwen. "You've had remarkably little to say about this journey. I can't work out if that's because you're anxious about my going to the Territories again or if there's some other reason."

"I'm not fearful of your visiting Egon. He seems to be a man of honor, and I'm sure no harm will come to you in his domain. Now if you were thinking of going anywhere else in that part of the world . . ." She suddenly sits up straight and looks directly at me. "Tell me you're not thinking of going somewhere else, Alfred." Her tone leaves no doubt as to her opinion of *that* idea.

"I don't know. I'd thought maybe . . ." I pause for effect, watching her brow furrow and her posture stiffen. "Oh, I don't know . . . maybe stop in at Ernle's . . . maybe see how Samuel's getting on."

She swats my arm. "That's not funny, Alfred." But the smile that replaces the furrow says otherwise. She settles back down on her pillows.

"In any event, you must have some opinion about what I'm doing . . . why I'm going there."

"I understand it. Egon took considerable risk in coming to pay his respects to your father, not knowing if he'd be welcomed here."

"No more risk than I took in seeking his help to end the border hostilities."

"Perhaps. But a risk nonetheless. So his coming was clearly a gesture of friendship. I certainly don't disagree with your wanting to reciprocate."

"But there's something else on your mind."

"I'm just wondering if this is the right time. Ordinarily, I'd say yes. Forging a friendship with Egon could lead to . . . oh, I don't know . . . reduced tension, better understanding . . . maybe even an alliance someday. Perhaps this could be that mysterious special destiny of yours.

"But John is *so* unpredictable. What if things go terribly wrong? It's not just that the path you've started down would be disrupted, but what if Egon began to question your motives? The outcome could be far worse than if you'd done nothing at all."

"I've thought about that too. But something visceral . . . something I can't really explain . . . tells me it's worth the risk."

"Then go with my wholehearted support. And make sure you tell Tamasine how much I miss her company."

•   •   •   •   •

"Why ye not be riding Star Dancer?" Osbert asks as we leave the stables shortly after dawn.

"I want to see how Sirius will handle a long journey. And if he doesn't do so well, at least you won't laugh at me like my mates would." And then I tell him how they almost got Star Dancer to dump me on my arse in the dirt the first time I rode him.

He chuckles. "I be thinking ye be missing yer mates these days, sir."

"More than you know, Osbert."

The night before we enter the Territories, we stop in the village on our side of the border. It's the first time I've actually been in the village, but the people know my story and feel like they played some part in my homecoming, so they're generous in their welcome. The innkeeper insists on giving us our supper and lodgings for free, but I leave a few coins for him under the bar before we depart.

It's midafternoon when we reach the track that leads up to Egon's fortress and the town below it. As we turn off the main road, I'm pleased that this time I feel no sense of hesitation or dread. Sentries appear on the palisades of the fortress, but that's no surprise. When we pass the smithy, the blacksmith waves a greeting of recognition, which I return. We go slowly through the gates. The sentries stand watchful but make no move to detain us. Osbert seems a bit apprehensive, but follows my lead.

Once inside the outer courtyard, we dismount and begin to lead our horses toward the gate into the inner bailey. The retainer who first greeted me when I came here with Samuel comes through the gate and approaches us. "You come back?"

"Yes. Come see your lord."

"You wait here," he says and starts back toward the inner bailey. Halfway there, he turns to be sure we're complying.

Egon comes through the gate, his arms spread expansively in welcome. "Lord Alfred! What a pleasant surprise!" He embraces me as one would a good friend not seen in a long time, then snaps his fingers, bringing two guards running, and says something to them I don't understand. "Please. Allow my men to stable your horses, and come inside and drink with me."

"Of course they may stable the horses, but they're not all mine." I give Sirius's reins to the sentry but keep Polaris's lead in my hand. "Lord Egon, I recall you admired the stallion I rode when I was last here."

"Indeed I did."

"I also recall we said that one day we should speak more of horses, so I've chosen a son of that stallion and trained him as a gift to you." I hand Egon the lead. "I call him Polaris, but you may, of course, call him anything you like."

Egon walks around the young stallion, admiring him. As he reaches out to stroke the horse's nose, I retrieve an apple from my pouch and toss it to him. Osbert suddenly finds his voice. "M'lord, Lord Alfred here be well known in our kingdom fer giving apples to his horses."

Egon laughs out loud. "Is he, indeed?"

"Aye, m'lord."

"My squire, Osbert, Lord Egon. His mother came from somewhere on your side of the border many years ago as a young girl."

"Well, I am pleased that you have returned to your mother's homeland, Osbert." Then he turns back to the horse and offers him the apple. "A magnificent animal, Alfred. He is ready to ride?" I note he's abandoned the formalities.

"I've been riding him these past three weeks."

"Then we should go riding tomorrow so I can try out my new mount. Polaris. I know this name . . . the guide star. He will be our guide for the future."

"I was hoping you might agree with me on that."

We spend the following day and night with Egon. He seems quite pleased with Polaris. "You have trained him well. His manners are excellent as are his gaits. He will be a fine addition to my stable."

I'm equally pleased that Polaris adapted so easily to a different rider. But there's one thing that has troubled me from the time I decided on this path: I have no way of knowing if Egon is one of those men who treat their horses with brutality. So I turn the conversation to how I treat my own animals. "I wish you could have met old Master Mervyn – the man who helped me train Star Dancer and taught me everything I know about horses and horsemanship. I'll never forget one thing he said: 'You'll get along ever so much better if you help him learn what you want than if you just try to force him to do things.' He's the one who got me started with the apples."

Egon is quick on the uptake. "Among my entourage, Alfred, no one is allowed to abuse a horse. A man never knows when he will have to trust his life to the abilities and instincts of his mount. So we must earn their respect against such a day."

We've quickly dropped the formalities and settled into comfortable conversation. Egon introduces me to his son, who, as it turns out, is the man I mistook for his squire when they came to Father's funeral. "As yet, Goron has little of your language, but I am teaching him. It is my hope that will be important for our future."

"It troubles me that I have no more than a few words of your language, but I have no one to teach me."

"Perhaps your squire could teach you," he suggests.

"Alas, he has none of it either. His mother wanted him to fully assimilate into our society, and she mistakenly believed that knowing her language would be an impediment to that."

"Perhaps she was not so mistaken at the time."

"Perhaps."

"Some of our people emigrate to your kingdom from time to time. Maybe you could find a teacher among them."

Our conversation then turns to the most important reason for my visit. I wanted to be the one to tell him what a different sort of king John is from his predecessors. Egon is deeply thoughtful as I describe the new state of affairs to him. "How will your lords and your people react?"

"It's too early to know – either what John might do or what reaction it will cause. In fact, it won't entirely surprise me if he simply tires of being in charge after a time and abandons things to take their own course. We've seen before that he can lose interest in something just as quickly as he takes to it. Our lords will keep a careful eye on him."

"Why are you telling me this?"

"We've both seen how badly things can go wrong through misunderstanding." A reference to the massing of troops on both sides of the border during Harold's reign. "If I can give you whatever understanding I have, then maybe we can avoid something like that happening again."

"Do your lords know you are here?"

"No one knows I'm here except my wife. At the right time, I'll discuss it with one or two of them that I trust the most. For now, there's no need."

"Then we must continue our dialogue. I also would not wish to repeat the previous confrontation. You must be careful, Alfred. Do not let your brother come to believe that you oppose him. That would not serve either of our purposes and might be dangerous for you."

A smile comes to my face. "Another wise man gave me the same advice . . . and I fully intend to heed it."

To lighten the mood I turn the conversation back to horses, telling him of the beautiful mares of Gwen's dowry – the silver-white horses with the long, dense grey manes and tails from the Kingdom Across the Southern Sea. "We've crossbred them with Star Dancer's lineage, and the offspring are very impressive. We acquired a stallion of the breed two years ago and are now trying our hand at purebreds. The first foals seem to have all the traits of their parents."

"I have never seen horses like you describe."

"Then I'll bring one on my next visit." I would much prefer to invite him to come and see our breeding operations for himself, but that would be unwise at the moment.

On our way home, the first stop is Ernle Manor. Over Lord Ernle's excellent brandy, we talk late into the night. I hold nothing back from this man who's like a second father to me, telling him how utterly helpless I feel watching what's happening and being unable to exert any influence over events. "It seems the only useful thing I can do, sir, is stay at the castle to observe what's happening firsthand, since I'm the only one who hasn't been sent packing."

"What worries me, Alfred, is that there may be a more insidious reason you haven't also been sent away."

"Oh?"

"He wants you where he can keep an eye on you . . . know everything you're up to. He's obsessed that you're still a threat. That's yet another reason why you have to leave things in our hands."

"I'm keenly aware that I can't oppose him . . . or even do anything he might misconstrue as opposition. In fact, it's the inaction that's so foreign to me and the source of all my frustration. Isolated there, I struggle even with how to ensure the lords know they have my support."

"We know, Alfred. It seems to me, though, that you have friends in many of the noble families. I doubt even John could object to your visiting your friends, especially if your family accompanies you often enough to dispel suspicion. I presume the reason for your visit here is to see Samuel."

"Not entirely, sir." I had thought long and hard as we rode here from Egon's what to say about my sudden appearance on the Ernle estate. There will be talk in the village of having seen us go into the Territories with three horses and come out with only two, so I mustn't give Ernle any reason to suspect deception on my part. "Lord Egon – the nearest Territorial lord to our border – came to Father's funeral. He remained discreetly in the background and departed immediately after the service. It was a gesture of respect for Father's role in withdrawing our troops at that time when conflict looked imminent. So I took him a horse as an expression of gratitude."

"I'm quite impressed, Alfred. It's the small gestures like that that are the first steps toward great alliances."

"Gwen – and now you – are the only ones who know, and I'd prefer to keep it that way for now. The villagers will have seen us coming and going, but that talk will die down soon enough with the routine of daily life."

"You're more and more like your grandfather every day . . . though I don't know why I should be surprised by that." He raises his glass. "To small gestures."

"I *did* come to see you and Samuel as well. I was planning to stop by the garrison tomorrow, as we leave, to chat with him for whatever time he can spare."

"You can do better than that. He's off duty for two days, beginning at sundown today, so he'll be at the cottage. We'll ride over in the morning and surprise him."

"How's he doing, sir? I'll ask him myself, of course, but I'd like to know your assessment as well."

"I think you'll be pleased. Time is having its healing effect, as is having a command once again. And I've noticed that having his own home is far more agreeable to him than I would've predicted. Tamasine and the children are thriving, and Sir Ronan has a surprising knack for managing the farm."

I drain the last drops of brandy from my glass, and he moves to refill it. "I think not, sir. One more glass of this magnificent stuff and I'll fall asleep sitting here. Best I should find my way to bed while I still can."

He laughs. "I found this stuff in the Kingdom Across the Southern Sea when I attended Harold's wedding to Berengaria. Rupert's been importing it for me ever since. I'm surprised you've never had it before."

"Perhaps my uncle's been keeping the secret for himself." And with that, we go our separate ways for the night.

●　　●　　●　　●　　●

As we ride up the lane toward the cottage, someone parts the curtains on one of the front windows to peer out. Before I can dismount, Samuel bounds out the front door. "Oh my God, Alfred! You should have told us you were coming." Tamasine stands in the doorway, watching our reunion.

Lord Ernle remains astride his horse. "I'll leave you to it, then, and get back home. Tamasine, bring the children to the manor next week to play with the puppies. They're from Luna's line, Alfred. Tell Gwen they're thriving." And with that, he turns his horse's head back toward the manor house.

Over the next two days, I discover Lord Ernle was entirely correct in his assessment of Samuel's spirits. He's happier than I've seen him since before my father's accident. "Having a command again was exactly what I needed, Alfred," he tells me. "Come with me to the garrison on your way home. I want to show you some of the changes we've made." Which suits me just fine. I want to be seen at the garrison in case John has eyes and ears there. "Bring Gwen and the children next time you come," Tamasine exhorts as we prepare to ride off on Sunday evening. "It's lovely here, but I do miss them terribly."

I execute a mock courtly bow from my saddle seat, "That I most certainly will do, my lady. I know she misses your company as well."

Our final stop before we make for home is the monastery. It's been too long since I've seen Prior Warin. The place is much the same as I remember it, change not being a great attribute of monastic life, but they do have a small new orchard near the back gate. "We're experimenting with a new type of apple from some seedlings brought by one of the immigrants," says Warin. "The trees aren't big enough to produce much fruit yet, but they're healthy and growing, so we're hopeful."

I tell him the whole story about the overtures of friendship between Egon and me, going all the way back to when we first laid eyes on each other. Because of the work he does here on the border, it's important that he know. He's intrigued, but also wary. "What you're doing is admirable, Alfred, and long needed in this part of the world. I'll pray for your continued success. But I'd also caution you to concern yourself with the son. He could be as different from his father as John is from yours."

"I've thought about that. And that's one reason I want to learn their language . . . so the son sees I'm making as great an effort as what his father is asking of him. Do any of your brothers speak their tongue?"

"Most of us have little more than the pidgin that's spoken in the village, but there's one among us who seems to have a knack for languages. Since you can't spend time here without arousing John's suspicion, I have another idea. I'll assign Brother Eustace to perfect his knowledge, and then he could go into André's service. Time you spend there will be unremarkable to anyone, even your brother. I'm sure André would gladly send me someone in return."

"That's more than generous, my friend. I don't know how I could repay you."

"Repay me by continuing on the path you've started."

"That I can promise."

On the last day of our journey home, Osbert is strangely quiet so I ask him what's on his mind.

"I be thinking, m'lord. I be thinking mayhap the king be asking where we've been."

"If he does, Osbert, I'll tell him I've been to visit friends, and that is the truth of the matter. If he wants details, then I'll tell him we spent time with Lord Ernle and with Samuel and his family and with Prior Warin. The knights at the garrison know we came from Ernle Manor with Sir Samuel."

"I be thinking, too, m'lord, that someone mayhap be telling him we left leading the horse ye've been training and we be coming back without it."

"In which case, I'll tell him we gave the horse to Prior Warin for use at the monastery. The good prior will be only too happy to confirm our story if the king should be so silly as to ask him. And Osbert?"

"Yes, m'lord?"

"Thank you for thinking of these things. I'm really a lucky man that you choose to stay in my service."

"I be the lucky one, m'lord, and I be knowing it since the day yer father ask me if I be willing to be yer squire." And for the rest of the journey, Osbert is his usual voluble self, confident now that he knows exactly how to protect my interests.

Private suppers in our apartment have become routine. With no one at court, there've been no formal court dinners, and the king never invites anyone to dine with him. I'm not sure the dining hall has been used at all since the coronation. Remembering how much he despised the formality of court dinners when we were young, I'm tempted to wonder if John banished the lords from court just to avoid the hated dinners. If only it were that simple.

Mother and Petronilla join us most nights. This evening, Petronilla seems distracted, pushing her food around her plate without really eating and fidgeting in silence while the rest of us chat as we dine. Finally, Gwen asks, "What is it, dear? You look as if you're about to burst."

Petronilla's face lights up. "I am." She puts down her knife and reaches into her pocket for a folded piece of paper that she hands to Gwen. "I've read it over and over and still I can hardly believe it." Gwen unfolds the page and smiles as she glances at the bottom. "Read it aloud, Gwen," says Petronilla. "Maybe if I hear it, it will seem more real."

Gwen glances around at each of us in turn and then begins.

My dearest and most adored Petronilla,
In the weeks since you left, I have lapsed into a most unfamiliar state of distraction and inattentiveness to the duties of my position. When I should be studying court documents, I find myself listening for your voice in the corridor. When I am exercising my horse, I wish I were instead taking a turn around the gardens in your company. When the court convenes for dinner, I look to my left and am dismayed to discover that you are not there. Not since the weeks following the death of my beloved Jacquetta have I felt this kind of longing for someone who is absent.

I can only hope that my love for you is returned in some measure and that you, too, might wish that we could live out our days together. I therefore beseech you, my dearest Petronilla, to relieve my suffering and do me the great honor of becoming my wife and my queen. I want for nothing more than to embrace you into my life and to welcome Richenda as my daughter and raise her as if she were my own.

I know that your position requires you seek your king's permission to marry, but I cannot imagine he would withhold it. So I beg you to hasten your reply and tell me that my days of longing for your presence will soon be at an end.

In loving anticipation,

Goscelin

"Oh, how wonderful!" Gwen exclaims. "But oh, how much I'll miss you. And Juliana . . . she'll be heartbroken to see Richenda leave . . . they've become such fast friends. But you can't let that hold you back."

"It's all so much to take in," says Petronilla. "How have I been so lucky? To be loved by two good men and now to twice be a queen. It's more than I could ever have dreamed."

"It's no more than you deserve, my dear," says Mother.

"I'm just trying not to get my hopes up. I still have to get John's permission. What if he forbids it?"

"He wouldn't dare." Mother's face is as stern as her voice.

•   •   •   •   •

"I absolutely forbid it!" John sits up straighter on his throne and slaps his palm on the arm for emphasis. He'd made Petronilla wait an entire week before granting her an audience, and now he's just dashed her hopes.

She insisted we accompany her. "I don't want to face him alone," she said over last night's supper. "He's so unpredictable." It seems her instincts were better than ours.

"With respect, Your Grace," she struggles to keep the disappointment out of her voice, "may I ask why?"

"You may ask. But I'm not obliged to answer. You have my decision and that should be sufficient."

No one says a word. Aside from the fact that we're all rather taken aback – not only would this marriage make Petronilla happy, but it would also be greatly advantageous to the kingdom – we all know how much John likes to talk about his views of the world. We need only be patient.

And as if on cue, he leans forward on his throne and speaks directly to Petronilla. "You want to know why I deny your request? Because I don't want to be under any obligation to grant Goscelin any favors when he inevitably comes asking."

"That's not how it works, Your Grace." I feel compelled to come to Petronilla's defense. "Dynastic marriages are about forging alliances, about common interests, about avoiding conflict."

"That's exactly what I mean," John retorts. "Common interests. First thing you know, he'll be coming to me asking for help against some enemy or other. I have absolutely no interest in fighting anyone else's battles, especially someone who let our king get slaughtered without lifting a finger to prevent it."

Petronilla winces briefly at the reference to Harold's gruesome death, despite the fact that she knows John is grossly distorting the truth. But she quickly composes herself and tries a different approach. "Perhaps you're forgetting, Your Grace, that as queen regent, I accepted your own marriage even though you hadn't secured my approval in advance."

"And perhaps *you're* forgetting," John's tone drips disdain, "that I already had Harold's permission to marry."

The room is silent once again. I've no idea what other approach to try. This time, it's Mother who breaks the silence. "I think there may be something else you haven't considered, John."

He glares at her. "And what might that be?"

"Have you considered the cost of maintaining two dowager queens? Two sets of suitable lodgings, two stipends, two people to feed . . . And Petronilla is still quite young. She could easily live as long as you do. The sooner she marries, the sooner you're relieved of that extra burden on the Treasury. And if she marries Goscelin, she'll be a queen once more and never again dependent on you financially."

John rubs his chin and contemplates the floor at his feet. I can imagine him trying to do the sums in his head. Mother has cunningly found the one thing he can't resist.

Finally, he waves his hand at Petronilla dismissively. "Very well. You have my permission. Now leave – all of you. I have more important things to do."

We're halfway down the corridor before anyone dares to speak, and even then, Petronilla keeps her voice low. "I don't know how I can ever thank you, Alice. That would never have occurred to me."

"And it's just as well it didn't," says Mother. "He knows he can't threaten my position, so I wasn't putting myself at risk. But if anyone else had mentioned it, it would have given him an excuse to deny your marriage and cut you off financially at the same time."

"Then I thank you twice over. Now I need to go write to Goscelin and give him my answer."

"Actually, my dear, what you need to do is pack your things and leave as quickly as you can. Don't give my son the slightest opportunity to change his mind. If Gwen and I help you – Letty and Nona too – you can be on your way the day after tomorrow. Osbert and Donal can arrange the coach and wagon. And from the tone of Goscelin's letter, I suspect he'll be all too happy to get your answer in person."

"It's not how I wanted to go." Petronilla is almost in tears.

"I know, dear," says Mother. "But let's not risk anything standing in your way."

I leave the women to their plans and go find Osbert to tell him what's afoot. Another reminder of better times being torn from us. But at least Petronilla and Richenda will be out of John's clutches.

The weeks proceed apace and turn into months. I've begun a correspondence with King Goscelin related to our shared interest in finding important volumes for our libraries. I ride every day when the weather is fair, exercising both Star Dancer and Sirius. I correspond by letter with Richard, Phillip, and Samuel, but we dare not discuss in writing anything other than pleasantries and news of daily life and family events. There's little else for me to do, and a certain malaise is starting to settle in.

From time to time, John has summoned me to wait on him for one reason or another. The first summons came two weeks before the annual herding competition. After making me wait for an hour while he dealt with others – thus making it obvious to everyone that he accords me no special status – he invited me into his private reception room.

With no preamble, no inquiry after my health or the well-being of my family, no pleasantries whatsoever, he launched into what was on his mind. "This herding competition. I want it clear there's to be no money from the Treasury spent on the organization of the event or any prizes. Entertainment for herdsmen does nothing to advance the interests of the Crown." I notice he doesn't speak of the interests of the kingdom but only those of the king.

"That's quite a break from tradition, John," I ventured as he walked across the room toward his throne. He's had a throne placed in this room also and removed all the other seating so that those who must deal with him here are forced to stand.

Hearing my words, he abruptly turned on his heel and glared at me. "What did you just call me?"

"I called you John, as I always have. I'm your brother, after all, and we're alone here."

"And *I* am your king, and you will address me properly."

I hesitated long enough for him to wonder what my reaction would be. Knowing, however, that this wasn't worth an argument, I finally said, "Very well . . . Your Grace. But the point remains valid that this is a significant departure from tradition. After all, these herdsmen support the Royal Kennel, and the King's Prize is well and truly coveted. In my opinion, that can only strengthen the people's loyalty to their king."

While I spoke, he resumed walking to his throne and deposited himself there in his usual slouch. "I care little for your opinion, Lord Alfred, and the people owe me their loyalty with or without any prizes. Perhaps I didn't make myself clear. There are to be *no Treasury funds* spent on this event.

"And now that you mention it, not one coin from the Treasury to subsidize that kennel of yours. If you want to keep your stupid dogs, then pay for them from your own purse. Now get out of here. I've other business to attend to."

Gwen's reaction was a breath of fresh air. After all, she's the Patroness of the Royal Kennel, and the herding competition was her invention. "Well, your brother's a right bastard, isn't he?" she said with a lilt in her voice that brought a smile to my face. "But I've no intention of letting his pettiness spoil the herdsmen's pleasure. This is the first competition since your father's death, so we'll simply rename the top prize as the King Edward Prize and fund it ourselves. We'll make a grand gesture of honoring your father and no one need be the wiser." Always inventive is Gwen. For the hundredth time, I remind myself what a lucky man I am to have her in my life.

"What about the kennel?" I asked. "It would be a shame to see all of Brother Adam's efforts go to waste."

"And they won't. The Royal Kennel will continue as usual. Adam is almost entirely self-sufficient and needs very little money. I'll simply support him from my own funds."

I cocked my head to one side and looked at her quizzically.

"You know the two gold coins my father gave me for luck when we married? The ones in the little purse that Letty guarded so carefully?" I nodded.

"Well, I took Petronilla's advice and invested them with her banker. He's already made me more than twice again their original value, so I can well afford to support the kennel."

"Well, well. I am indeed astonished."

"I hope you're not displeased," she sounded slightly apprehensive.

"Not at all. It was your money to do with as you pleased. And I'm actually quite delighted."

Her smile returned. "You know, Petronilla's really rather astute when it comes to money. She's become quite wealthy, so I thought it would do no harm to see what her banker could do for me."

"No harm at all. Money that John doesn't know anything about could well become important in the future. In fact, I might want to put a bit into your little scheme as well for just that reason. And I think it would be best if you do the investing . . . as if it were your money. I certainly wouldn't want him to get wise to what I was up to."

"That'll make it even more fun," she laughed.

My second summons came quickly and was even sillier . . . and again I was made to wait. This time, he came out to me rather than inviting me in. "What's this I hear about you not wanting to change your banner, Lord Alfred? After all, you're now second in line of succession. I should think you'd want that recognized by all and sundry."

"Everyone already knows, Your Grace," I replied, "and I see no need to incur the expense when it's most likely you'll have other sons who'll displace me."

He was in no way mollified. "I have no other sons now, so you should do things properly. Besides, I despise that sleeping lion. Change your banner at once." And with that, he turned on his heel and marched back to his private chambers.

To avoid incurring his wrath on such a petty matter, I changed my banner to incorporate the single lion rampant of the second in line. But I didn't lose the lion dormant, the symbol awarded to me by my grandfather. John may despise it, but it's my personal symbol, and I have every right to use it.

Weeks passed before I was again summoned. It happened just before the Harvest Moon, which marks the time when children return to school. Gwen had been concerned about the lack of other children in the castle school, thinking it undesirable for our children to be taught alone. Her attempt to convince Gundrea to allow the king's children to attend was futile, so she had arranged with the mayor of the town that the castle school would be open to the town's children, much as in the old days when my grandfather first began his efforts for universal literacy.

"I'm putting a stop to this right now," John said, a scowl on his face.

"To what, Your Grace?"

"Your wife's scheme to have children from the town schooled here. To begin with, it isn't right for noble children to mix with the lower classes. And beyond that, I won't have a bunch of children running around the castle getting underfoot and disrupting important business."

"If you recall, Your Grace, it's how school was done when we were lads. Besides, the schoolroom is nowhere near where you conduct your business."

"Must you dispute everything I tell you, Lord Alfred? Tell your wife to find a different solution."

"She's tried, Your Grace. Her first idea was to have your children and ours schooled together. Unfortunately, the queen rejected the plan."

"That's her prerogative. She has charge of my son's household and his upbringing."

"With respect, have you spent any time with your children lately?"

"What business is that of yours?"

"In truth, none. I simply wondered if you knew how much time they're spending with the queen's priest."

"Again, what business is that of yours?"

"Only to the degree that it might affect the future of the kingdom. The priest, you see, has none of our language, so your son is growing up speaking the language of the Eastern Kingdom more than our own."

"For the third and final time, Lord Alfred, what business is that of *yours*?"

"I merely wondered, Your Grace, when your son begins training in the skills of a knight and the art of kingship, how will you be able to influence him if he doesn't speak our language with ease and fluency?

How will he manage conducting royal business if he can't read our language with the same ease?"

At last, I had his attention. He shouted for his squire, who came rushing in from the public reception room. "Fetch the queen here immediately." Bowing hastily, the poor man scurried off.

Not a word passed between us until the two of them returned. From the odor that wafted into the room in Gundrea's wake, it was immediately clear she had abandoned the practice of regular bathing. The squire was hard-pressed to avoid wrinkling his nose, but John had no such scruples.

"Good lord, woman, when have you had a bath or clean clothes? You'd best go back to those ways if you ever want to be in my presence again."

Gundrea wisely said nothing.

"Now what's this I hear about how you're educating my son? I'm told he only speaks with the priest and only speaks your language."

Gundrea glared at me before replying. "Priest knows what son should learn. Is best he learn from priest."

"I don't care who he learns from so long as he learns it in our language. Does he speak our language at all?"

"Some words. If you want him know this language, best if king and queen live together and children with them. Then John Gundar learn from father. Learn best that way." Gundrea hasn't given up on finding an angle to get herself into the king's apartment.

"Learn best," John began, unconsciously imitating his wife, and then growled at his own lapse. "He'll learn best by speaking it all the time and learning to read it. I don't care if he speaks both languages. I do care that he speaks mine best. Make sure that happens from this moment, understood?"

Gundrea said nothing.

Impatient, John waved her away. "Go on, then. And for God's sake, take a bath."

As she started to leave, he turned to me. "You, too, Alfred. We're finished here."

Gwen was more exasperated this time. Her plan to have the town children here would have been beneficial to them and to our own in so many ways. It didn't take long, however, for her to move from exasperation to a new plan. "If John doesn't want children underfoot, then so be it. We'll simply move the castle school into town."

"Should we be concerned about the children's safety, going back and forth every day?"

"I wouldn't want to send a signal to the people that we're fearful. What if Osbert accompanied them?" As usual, she solved the problem neatly.

The most recent summons was more disturbing. No waiting this time – John's squire took me immediately into his master's presence.

As usual, there was no preamble, no exchange of pleasantries. "This will take but a moment. I simply need to tell you that I'm commandeering all those broodmares and young horses of yours. You're to have no more to do with their breeding or training. The young ones are to be trained as war horses."

"War horses, Your Grace? Are you planning to go to war?"

"Knight's horses, then. It's the same thing . . . and you know what I mean. We're in need of more horses for the growing number of knights."

"I'm sorry, Sire," I replied, venturing the somewhat less formal address, "but you can't do that."

He glared at me and then rolled his eyes and shook his head. "Alfred, Alfred, Alfred," he said in what I presume he took for a fatherly tone of voice. "When will you finally get it into your head that *I* am the king, and I can do *whatever* I decide to? I know you still resent that Father didn't pass me over in favor of you, but it's time to put that aside. I've decided to commandeer your horses and that is that."

"It has nothing to do with resentment – of which I have none, by the way – but with the fact that the horses aren't mine for you to commandeer. The original mares were part of Gwendolyn's dowry. Our marriage contract specifies that those mares and any offspring of any breeding program she chooses to undertake belong to Gwendolyn alone in her own right."

"Very well, then, I'm commandeering Gwendolyn's horses, and you will so inform her."

"Setting aside for a moment that I would then be guilty of breaking my marriage contract, there's no doubt the bishop would get involved, which could cause you no end of difficulties. And more than likely, Gwen's father would appeal to his cousin, the King of Lakes, to intervene. Do you really think it's worth creating an international incident over a few horses?"

Never able to hide his thoughts or emotions, John started pacing in frustration at being once again thwarted by the brother he resents and by his inability to muster a cogent defense of his little scheme. "Very well, then. But that space will be needed for the new horses we'll have to find. See that all your horses – and Gwendolyn's – are gone from here by the end of the week."

"I presume, Your Grace, that we're entitled to keep our personal mounts in the stables?"

"Yes, yes," he replied impatiently, "but just one mount per person. Now get out and attend to getting them moved."

"I'll ask Elvin to help me move them as soon as may be, Your Grace."

"You'll do nothing of the sort. Elvin is busy with the needs of the king's stable. He is *not* your personal errand boy. Figure out how to do it on your own." And he waved his hand toward the door in dismissal.

"A week?!" Gwen exclaimed. "Is he crazy? The mares are in foal and really shouldn't be moved at all."

"I know, but it looks like we have little choice."

"Where can we take them? They need proper supervision, especially when it comes time for foaling. It needs to be nearby so we can go there even in winter. André can't take them. He doesn't have room for that many animals. And I won't split them up."

This time, it was Gwen who continued to seethe over John's unreasonable demands, and I was the one with the plan. "What do you think about moving them to the country manor? The stables there are nearly as spacious as here, and there's even more good pasture."

"Oh, Alfred, do you think Rupert would mind?"

"I'll send him a message, of course, but I'm confident he'll have no objections. He's made it quite plain to me that he still views the manor as a family home and that he's merely its caretaker of the moment."

"It's not as close as I'd like, but I do think it's good for the horses." She moved closer on the couch where we were seated and hugged me tightly. "And thank you, Alfred," she said.

"For what?"

"For protecting my interests so well."

"And why shouldn't I? After all, anything that's important to someone I love as much as you is just as important to me." Her glowing smile was the only thanks I needed, but she gave me another hug followed by a very long, very un-chaste kiss.

With the help of Osbert, Mervyn the Younger, and two of his grandsons, we managed to move the horses with no mishaps and apparently no ill effects for the broodmares. Mervyn stayed long enough to be sure all the animals settled in well, and we've employed one of his grandsons to help the local stable master with the extra responsibility.

The Christmas season is more subdued than I can ever remember. We decorate a yule tree in our own apartment and celebrate the arrival of Saint Nicholas with gifts for the children, but the rest of the castle is drab. No yule log in the main hall. Not a single sprig of holly or garland of evergreen in sight. The comforting aromas of fruit pies baking in the kitchens, the fragrance of pine boughs, the scent of spices as the mulled wine is made . . . all are missing. Even the Christmas Eve and Christmas Day services in the church are more somber than usual. I notice there, for the first time, that some of the women have taken to dressing more in the style of the queen, though whether this is a nod to fashion or to their state of mind is difficult to discern. Gwen is certain it's both. The uncertainty the townsfolk feel about their future has undoubtedly put a damper on what should be a happy time.

A few days after Christmas, we travel to the country manor to celebrate the New Year with Rupert and Catherine. Leaving the town, we pass the collection of shacks that have sprung up along the creek, cobbled together by the unfortunate people who have neither work nor homes. They're tiny – made of whatever scrap wood or stone could be found. Some are no more than lean-tos built next to a slightly more substantial neighbor. Six . . . eight . . . ten people huddle together in a single room, the crowding perhaps helping to create enough warmth to ward off the winter chill. But if illness breaks out in these miserable conditions, the crowding could become deadly in the blink of an eye.

Just off the road are the remains of a hut that burned. Desperate for warmth, someone had built a fire too close to the shack and when the wind shifted, the whole thing went up in flames. Most of those inside, I'm told, perished in the fire. The two who were lucky enough to escape now have nothing but the clothes on their backs, having lost whatever blankets or cloaks they had to the flames.

The only positive thing about this shameful situation is that the people at least have fresh water from the stream before it flows into the river. At this point, the river hasn't flowed far enough downstream to dissipate the effluent it picks up from the castle and the town.

Before we left the castle, I'd asked Letty and Osbert to gather up all the leftover food they could find, and the cook even gave them several new loaves of bread. We stop while Osbert rides over to deliver the sacks of food. When two women start quarreling over who gets what, I call out, "Don't squabble over the food, ladies. It's not much, but if you share it around, there should be some for everyone."

A man I barely recognize as once having been one of Elvin's grooms – he looks so different now, with unkempt hair and a scraggly beard – walks up and strokes Star Dancer's nose. "God bless ye, Lord Alfred. Ye be a fine man fer sure."

I'm glad the children don't have to see this sad sight, but Gwen apparently has other ideas, opening the curtains on the coach and pointing things out to Juliana and Geoffrey. "That's why Letty was collecting food this morning," she says. "So we could help these people who need it."

"Why do they have to live here?" Geoffrey asks.

"Well, some of them used to live at the castle, but now that they're no longer working there, they don't have any other home."

"Can't they work somewhere else?"

"I'm sure they want to. They just haven't found new work."

"Why can't they work at the castle any longer, Mama?" Juliana asks.

"Sadly, Juliana, the king doesn't want them to."

"But why not? Doesn't he know it's wrong to make people suffer?"

"I don't know, dear. But that's why your father and I think it's important to do what we can to help."

Juliana reaches into her pocket and takes out a small parcel. "Here, Papa." She hands the parcel out the window. "It's a sweet cake Cook gave me to eat on the journey. Give it to that man who was nice to Star Dancer."

This isn't the first time Juliana has asked questions about the changes in her world. How do I teach my children that they have a duty to respect their uncle the king despite the fact that he regularly fails to embody the virtues *they* are asked to demonstrate?

Despite the difficulty of winter travel, Richard has brought his family, too, so Avelina can celebrate with her parents. We put on a show of lightheartedness for the sake of the children, even planning a New Year's feast with musicians for entertainment and dancing. But none of us is truly in a celebratory mood.

The evenings find Richard, Rupert, and me in long conversations over brandy in the drawing room where a blazing fire keeps the winter chill at bay. On the first evening, Richard remarks on the presence of all the horses. "Can't remember when I've ever seen the stables so full. And Sirius here as well. I thought you were using him regularly as an alternate mount," he says.

My tale of John's orders to vacate the stables leads them to shake their heads in dismay. "We've decided to use Sirius for all of this year's breeding, since we won't have access to other stallions in the castle stable."

"Lucky Sirius," jokes Richard, getting a laugh from all of us.

"And once Gwen got over her fury at John's ridiculous demands, she's decided how to get the better of him. If he wants any of her horses, she'll be more than happy to sell them to him."

"So tell us what else my idiot nephew has been up to," says Rupert. Richard, who was taking a sip from his glass, nearly chokes on the brandy and looks at Rupert wide-eyed.

"Don't look so shocked, Richard," laughs my uncle. "I've been calling him that for years and see no reason to change now."

They manage a chuckle at some of John's sillier stunts, but share my overall concern. "I especially don't like the expansion of the knighthood," says Richard. "What are that many knights going to do?"

"And that reference to war horses," I add. "He may have passed over it as just a slip of the tongue, but my fear is that it actually reflects what's going on in his mind."

"I suspect your fears are justified, Alfred," says Rupert. "After all, belligerence in one form or another is about the only thing he does well."

"There aren't many people who'd describe belligerence as a skill," chuckles Richard.

"There aren't many people quite as good at it as my brother," I reply, to which Rupert raises his glass, "To belligerence!"

The following evening, Richard has equally dire news. "There was an abundant harvest," he tells us, "so the farmers couldn't demand as high a price for their produce. Even with low prices, much of the harvest went unpurchased. The traders are worried they won't be able to sell as much or get as good a price because of the uncertainty here, and they don't think they can make up the difference in their profits by trading abroad. They're not stockpiling as much in their warehouses as they've done in the past.

"So the farmers sold less than usual at a lower price than usual despite having the best harvest in many years. They're disillusioned almost to the point of despondency. My father, brothers, and I bought as much of the surplus as we could, but I'm not sure we really had much impact. There's still a lot of produce rotting in the farmers' storerooms.

"What happened with the harvest put the shopkeepers on edge, so they're starting to dismiss their helpers."

"What's happening to those people, Richard?" I ask.

"They're huddling in the alleyways or trying to find shelter in stables or in the church – wherever they can find a bit of warmth. But I fear some of them won't make it through the winter. The church tries to feed them what it can, but it's not enough.

"And it's not just Neukirk," Richard goes on. "I had a letter from Phillip just before Christmas. He's heard from Madam Greslet, who's terribly worried about what's going to happen when shearing season comes around. The sheep must be shorn, but she's fearful that buyers will be few, even if prices are lower. Phillip says the mayor of Great Woolston has similar concerns. Doesn't John have any notion that all this is a direct result of his actions?"

"Sadly, I rather doubt it," replies Rupert. "He's never been able to make the connection between actions and consequences – and most especially when it's his *own* actions that are involved."

"Indeed," I add. "If he's even aware of what's happening, his view is that it's the people's own fault, that they should look out for their own well-being, and if they'd done that better, they wouldn't be in this situation. I can't even follow that line of thinking."

"There's something else," Richard resumes. "Avelina noticed it in Neukirk on market days. The first time she saw a small group of people gathered around a priest at one end of the market, she thought nothing of it. Two weeks later, she saw the same priest with a larger group of people and asked me if I knew anything about him – which, of course, I didn't.

"So next market day, I went with her, and we stood at the edge of the crowd to listen. Bit of a fire-and-brimstone message he has, but no one seems to know where he's come from. He's an unkempt, rather dirty-looking fellow but enough of an orator to hold the crowd's attention. I talked to the deacon at the church, and he has no idea who the man is, where he came from, or where he stays. Neukirk's resident priest continues to offer much the same guidance in his homilies as he always has, but the deacon says he's noticed that fewer people are coming to church services, preferring to listen to this itinerant."

"You know," says Rupert, "I've seen just such a fellow in the port recently, haranguing people with a similar message. I didn't think much about it because he was spending his time around the brothels and the taverns where the sailors go drinking and whoring when they're in port. It's not entirely unusual for the clergy to try to save drunkards and prostitutes, but now that I hear your story, I wonder if something else is afoot."

"Maybe I should ask the bishop if he knows anything about them." I muse.

"What I can't quite work out," says Richard, "is why this appeals to people. Is it just that they have little to do and listening to these priests occupies their time? They've always had the church in their lives."

"It's simpler than that, Richard," says Rupert. "They're frightened. They don't know why things have gone so wrong so quickly, so they're looking for an explanation . . . for someone to tell them what caused their problems and how to fix them."

On the final evening before we're all to depart for home, Rupert seems morose. This is so out of character for him that I'm compelled to ask why.

"I'm simply realizing how much I'm going to miss your company," he replies.

"I enjoy these gatherings, too, but at least you have your work to occupy you."

"I wish that were so, Alfred, but Catherine and I will be staying here."

"What on earth are you talking about?" I ask.

"I haven't said anything before now – didn't want to spoil the holiday. But tomorrow I have to confront it head-on. The day before Christmas, John showed up unannounced. It seems my services are no longer required. He's decided to put the tax collectors in charge of collecting tariffs and to let the local dockmen organize the arrival and departure of ships and the loading and unloading. It's going to be utter chaos – the same sorts of gangs running the port as before Father put me in charge."

Richard frowns and shakes his head in dismay. "Is there no end to this insanity?"

I try to offer my uncle some consolation. "At least you have a nice house and the society you've formed over the years."

"Alas, no longer, Alfred. He's appropriated that as well. We're to be out by the end of the month. The servants will have begun packing our things by now."

"He can't do that!" I'm beginning to feel like that's all I ever say about John. "That's your home, and you've a right to continue living there even if you're no longer the commissioner."

"That's not how he sees it. His view is that it's the king's house, and whoever lives there does so at the king's pleasure."

"Didn't Grandfather give the house to you?"

"Yes, but it was never codified in a will or a contract, so I have little ground to stand on. Actually, I think this is John's revenge for the fact that your father left this manor explicitly to me. He's been annoyed about that ever since the will was read."

"He doesn't really need the house – he never spends any time in the port."

"Oh, he has all that neatly worked out as well. He intends to install Gundrea and the children there. Says his son's household requires finer, more spacious surroundings than what they now have. He gets rid of me and Gundrea in one simple stroke."

"I'm truly sorry, Uncle. This can't be easy. At the same time, though, consider helping us with our horse breeding. I'm sure Gwen will be delighted to have you in charge down here."

"Thank you for that, Alfred, and of course I'll look after your interests. After all, there's little else for me to do. I won't be able to manage my networks from here, and our information is going to grow stale rather quickly, I fear."

Rupert suddenly goes completely silent, realizing he's spoken as if I were the only other person present. All three of us stare into our brandy glasses, avoiding eye contact.

Finally, Richard breaks the awkward silence. "Don't concern yourself, Lord Rupert. The lords have known of the central spy network for many, many years. It's a secret passed from the lord to his heir – most often as a separate portion of the will designated for the heir's eyes alone. Occasionally, the information is passed on during the lord's lifetime. Father holds little back from me, so when young William was breeched and he believed the succession was secure, he gave me the knowledge.

"We don't speak of it openly, but it saves us the trouble of having to run our own extensive . . . and I might add, expensive . . . networks. Not that we don't have our own sources of information, of course," he adds with a chuckle.

Rupert laughs out loud, visibly relaxing. "You know, Richard, I've always suspected as much but never dared to ask. It's one of the difficulties of this business – asking questions without revealing something the other person might not know."

"No doubt," says Richard, "John has his own spies. And I think we can all be fairly certain who's in charge of *them*." This draws a laugh from all of us.

"You know, Uncle," I muse, "this may not be such a setback after all. We may be able to use it to our advantage."

"How so?" asks Rupert.

"Well, now you're free to attend the gatherings of the lords. I've been worried about the risk if I'm invited to those and the king isn't."

"It's worth thinking about, Alfred. But *you* would lose the advantage of hearing things firsthand, and the lords would likely regret not having your ear and your insight."

"Your insight is at least as good as mine, Uncle . . . probably better. It shouldn't be hard for us to discuss what you learn. John won't think anything at all of my bringing the family and Mother here for visits. Think of it as the inverse of spying – gathering information out in the open."

"Interestingly," says Richard, "Father and I have been talking about exactly the same concern. Our idea was to invite the king each time and hope he refuses, but this gives us more options."

Rupert raises his hands in mock surrender. "Alright . . . alright . . . you've convinced me," he laughs. "Seriously, though, Richard, I think your father's right about inviting the king. But at least this way you can do it occasionally, when convenient, rather than take the risk of having him decide to show up when it's least desirable."

Then turning to me, he adds, "Are you certain, Alfred?"

"Absolutely, Uncle. Difficult as it may be, I need to avoid being the focus of John's attention."

We're all silent for a long time, staring into the fire and sipping our brandy. At long last, Richard raises his glass. "To a better world. Let's hope we can make it so."

As we depart the next morning, it appears Rupert's mood has lifted entirely – it's good for a man to have a purpose in life. Alas, this only serves to remind me that I've surrendered yet another piece of mine.

The weather is fair so the journey is pleasant, if chilly. As we go through the town, I notice a crowd gathered at the end of the square near the church. Sending the rest of our party on to the castle with Osbert, I go to investigate.

There's a man standing on an overturned crate holding forth to a small group of people. His long hair and beard are unkempt, and his monk's robe looks well worn. He doesn't appear to be particularly clean, but as I'm staying back from the crowd, I don't notice if he smells. His voice, however, is that of an orator . . . almost stentorian in strength.

"You ask," he says, pointing to people near the front of the crowd. "You ask," he repeats, "why God has allowed these bad things to happen. We are good people, you tell yourselves. We serve God. We serve our king. We've done nothing to deserve this." He pauses for dramatic effect.

"But are you really so good? Is this kingdom really so free from sin? I say look around you. You've striven for years to better yourselves. Is that not the sin of greed? Is that not the sin of covetousness? Why should you long for more than what God has allotted you? To do so is a *sin*!" He emphasizes the last word by raising the volume of his voice.

"Look at your women. They wear baubles and frills. They go about in the marketplace. They toil in shops. They argue and dispute with their husbands and fathers. Some even have their own money or property. Is this the way of the Lord? I say it is *not*," he shouts.

"And is it the way of the Lord for men to waste their time with reading and with books that are not holy? Once again, I say it is *not*. God put priests on this earth to read the holy scriptures and the writings of the saints. God put priests here to understand the holy books and to tell the people what they need to know. Writing that is neither scripture nor words of the saints is sinful! It is blasphemous! It is *heresy*!

"You've given comfort to people who do not worship God. You've allowed these people to come from foreign lands. You give them work. You take them into your society. You must *shun* all who do not worship the one true God. You must banish them from your presence, for they are like the Devil among you."

He pauses to let his words sink in. A frisson of murmur goes through the crowd. When he resumes, his tone is quieter . . . more like a parent explaining something to a child.

"You ask, my friends, why God has allowed these things to happen. Your friends sleeping in freezing shacks. People with no work and no food for themselves or their children. Darkness upon the realm. You bemoan your lot in life and place the blame on God." Another pause, briefer this time. "And yet, in your heart, you know the answer. God is punishing you for your sin.

"When God saw the world was wallowing in sin, he sent the flood to cleanse the earth, and the sinful perished. When Lot's wife looked back longingly at wicked Sodom, God punished her by turning her to a pillar of salt. God has sent these new trials to awaken you. To make you aware of your sin. You may think you suffer now. But what you suffer now is as *nothing* compared to what God is capable of.

"Turn away from your sin!" he shouts. "Return to the ways of God. Renounce greed and covetousness and decoration and reaching beyond your station in life. Turn your backs on non-believers . . . *banish* them from your midst. Accept your lot. Humble yourself before God. Return to the natural order of things.

"*This* is the path to God's mercy."

He seems ready to go on railing against sin and preaching the path to forgiveness, but I've heard enough and ride away. I'm reminded of Rupert's comment about the people's fear and of the simplicity of Juliana's questions that so often start with "why." It would do little good for the people to know that their king has created this sad situation. These railing priests would simply assert that the king was acting as an agent of God. Though I'm wearing my winter cloak and the sun still hasn't fully set, I find myself shivering as I ride on to the castle.

The steward meets me at the door in a state of agitation that seems to be a peculiar combination of fury and dismay – something I've never seen before in this man who's always in complete control of every situation. "Thank God you've returned, my lord." He comes close to wringing his hands. "We're at our wits' ends with all the king's new orders."

"I'd like to get out of these traveling clothes, Matthias. Walk with me and tell me what has you so upset."

"It started the day after you left, my lord. First, he had us remove all the nice furnishings from the guest apartments in the old castle. Then he ordered bunks placed in all the rooms . . . six, sometimes eight bunks to a room. You see, he's run out of space for all the new knights and trainees, so he's putting all the trainees in the old castle. Even with the space that's there, those lads are going to be packed in shoulder-to-shoulder with barely room to breathe."

"I suppose he's not planning on having any guests any time soon." I'm not trying to make light of what's happening, but can't think of anything else to say.

"That's not the worst of it, my lord. We've done his bidding and all the rooms are ready to be occupied. But then he decided he wants all the knights and trainees to take their meals in the dining hall in the old castle. That means extra work for the kitchen staff, but we'll sort out a way to manage."

By now we've reached our apartment, and I go directly into my dressing room through Osbert's door to the corridor. The steward hesitates. "Do come in, Matthias. I gather there's more."

There's a bath ready, and Osbert begins helping me off with my traveling cloak and boots as Matthias continues. "Aye, my lord. Now he wants me to start preparing the knights' food in the old castle kitchen. That makes no sense, my lord. That kitchen hasn't been used since before your grandfather's time. I don't even know if the hearths and chimneys are safe to use. There's no water piped in there . . . we'd have to carry it from the new kitchen or from somewhere else. The cooks need their modern kitchen to properly prepare so much food. But the king won't be swayed, sir, no matter what I say . . . no matter how humbly I plead."

Standing now to begin removing my shirt and trousers, I say, "I agree it doesn't make any sense at all, Matthias, but I rather doubt anything I might say could convince him to change his mind. In fact, it might just make him more determined to do things his own way."

Matthias looks totally crestfallen. "I had so hoped, my lord . . ."

"Don't give up hope, Matthias. You just need a different ally. The one person who might be able to talk some sense into the king on this point is Lady Alice. I suspect she's had time to refresh herself by now. See what she advises."

The steward's face brightens. "I'll do that straightaway, sir." And he's off in search of the dowager queen.

Gwen asked Letty to arrange supper in our apartment this evening, as we're all tired from the journey, and Mother joins us. When Letty arrives with our meal, Matthias is with her, carrying a large tray of some sort of fowl.

"What have we here, Matthias?" asks Gwen.

"A feast, my lady. I was saving this grouse for the king's dinner tomorrow, but I think Lady Alice deserves it more."

"Oh? And what great deed have you done, Mother Alice, that we should have such a treat?"

Mother smiles sweetly and says only, "I'm sure Matthias would like to tell you."

And so he does, starting with all the changes and his dilemma over the use of the old kitchen. "The minute I told Lady Alice, she says, 'Come with me.' So we go straight to the king's apartments, and she asks me to wait in the public reception room. She orders the king's squire to admit her immediately, which he does, but she leaves the door ajar so I can hear what's happening.

"'What's this I hear about your wanting to use the kitchen in the old castle?' she asks the king. And he says, 'Why not? It's there and closer to the knights' dining hall.' So Lady Alice says, 'John, do you know how long it's been since that kitchen was used?' And the king says, 'Not really, but why should that matter?'

"And then Lady Alice answers him, 'It matters a great deal, John. That kitchen is ancient. It's not fit for cooking anything more than gruel and porridge. It might not even be safe for that, and I don't think you really want to risk having the kitchen staff injured or the room catch fire, do you?' So the king says, 'I want the men to have hot food. And that kitchen is nearest. If they have to carry food from the new kitchen, it will get cold.'

"Then Lady Alice says, 'Well, do you want your men to have piping hot gruel or warm meats, fowl, pottage, and bread? You get one or the other. The plan you propose simply won't work.' And then she goes on, changing the subject on him and getting him all flummoxed. 'If you'd let Gundrea fulfill her responsibilities as queen, you wouldn't get yourself into this kind of pickle. She understands about kitchens and banquets and what it takes to feed a large number of people. She could have advised you properly and saved all this commotion.'

"So the king answers, 'Gundrea has her own responsibilities with my son's household.' And Lady Alice says, 'A queen knows how to handle many facets of court life, John. She's perfectly capable of rearing your children and overseeing the preparation and serving of food at the same time.'

"So now the king is getting irritated. 'Has she put you up to this?' he asks. 'She's always trying everything she can think of to worm her way into these apartments, and I'm having none of it. She has her household, and there she will stay.'

"Lady Alice is all calm. She says, 'Gundrea has no idea about any of this unless you've told her. I'm merely pointing out that you have someone in your immediate family who can get these things right without throwing everyone into an uproar. Now I'm going to go find Matthias and tell him he should use only the new kitchen. Give me your assurance now that you won't countermand my order.'

"So now the king says, 'Just tell him the men better not be getting cold food.'

"And with that, my lady marches out of the private reception room and beckons for me to follow her. Once we're in the corridor with the doors closed behind us, she says, 'I trust you heard all that, Matthias, and know what to do.' And I say, 'I did, my lady, and I'm ever so grateful.'"

Through all this, Letty has been serving our food and Matthias pouring the wine, Mother looking serene and a little amused. "And now," says the steward, "it's time for you to enjoy your meal."

"Not quite, Matthias," I say. "There's one person who hasn't been served yet." He looks around, exceedingly puzzled. "You, Matthias. As you see, Letty and Osbert often share our meal when we dine in private. Tonight I invite you to do so as well."

Matthias beams. "I would be honored, my lord."

As everyone prepares to tuck into their food, I raise my glass and propose a toast, "To small victories." Glasses are raised all around and the steward adds, "And to Lady Alice."

By mid-January, winter has both the land and my state of mind firmly in its clutches. I have nothing useful to do. Oh, I exercise Star Dancer and Gwen's mare when the weather permits. And I've just finished a completely unnecessary inventory of the library – nothing has changed since the one I did right after Father's death except that every book is now in its proper place on the shelves – no little wooden sticks bearing a borrower's name anywhere in sight. Wandering around the corridors does nothing but remind me how empty and lifeless the place is. Sleepless nights have become more frequent.

I find myself spending more time than usual with the children. Today, Juliana and Geoffrey are practicing their writing while Little Edward plays with the dogs. "Why don't we pay a visit to the monastery?" Gwen asks. "I'd like to find out what Adam needs for the kennel, and you always feel more cheerful after a talk with André."

"Why not? I could use a change of scenery."

Juliana stops what she's doing, walks over, and takes my hand. Looking very serious, she says, "Please, Papa, may I go too?"

"Shouldn't you be in school?"

"Please, Papa? I'll do an extra lesson if you let me come with you. Brother Adam is teaching me how to train Willow and Primrose, and it's been ever so long since he was here. They always do better after Brother Adam shows me what to do. Please, Papa?" It seems she has something of a natural talent for working with the dogs. So far, she has them herding ducks so well that the ones that live at the nearby stream quickly take to the water or the air when they see her coming.

Gwen chimes in. "She really is doing very well with her lessons, Alfred. And it's not like this would be a holiday. After all, she'll be learning another skill."

For a moment, I say nothing, giving her what I hope is a stern, fatherly look. She stands quietly, not whining or pleading. So I let my expression change to a broad smile. "How could I possibly refuse two such beautiful ladies? We'll leave in time to have the midday meal at the monastery. Can you be ready?"

"Oh, yes, Papa. I'll be ready." She starts to return to her work table but then remembers something and comes back to take my hand again. "Thank you, Papa." I kiss her cheek and she practically dances all the way back to the table.

The day dawns fair and unseasonably warm so we decide to forego the coach. Juliana is thrilled, as she's been denied pony rides since late summer. With all the knights and trainees and horses milling about – all the trainees with weapons they don't yet know how to control – all the blacksmiths' fires making horseshoes and even more weapons – it's just not safe. I still can't fathom John's intentions. Is he just enjoying playing commander? If so, he'll tire of it soon and move on to something else. Or is he trying to create a show of strength to intimidate the people? He's said more than once that they need to be kept in line. But what if it's something more sinister? Could he really be planning to go to war?

By the time we arrive at the monastery, just the fact of being away from all that has lifted my mood somewhat. After a meal of simple but remarkably tasty monastery food, Gwen and Juliana are off to the kennel, leaving André and me to talk.

André is beginning to show his age. He seems in good health . . . complains of nothing. But then his monk's training would have taught him to accept his lot without complaint. In his presence, I always feel safe. I don't know if it's simply his calm demeanor or if it's visceral memory of the day he and his monks were my salvation after my escape from captivity. In truth, it matters not which.

He seems almost as morose as I am about the growing hardships. "We try not to turn people away," he says, "but we haven't the resources to take care of all the needs of so many. I've had to set a policy of limiting how much help we give any one person or family. It breaks my heart, but it seems more moral than exhausting our resources by giving too much to those who come first."

"Stay your course, André. From what I've heard about the wool merchants' concerns for the shearing season, I fear things are going to get worse before they get better." He shakes his head sadly.

I ask about the itinerant priests. He's heard about them, but has no more idea where they've come from or where they find a bed each night than anyone else. "The bishop was just as puzzled," I tell him, "though he promised to write to his fellow bishops and even to Rome, if need be, to learn more."

"I wonder," muses André, "if they are even legitimate priests. Tell me about this fellow you listened to."

As I recount the details of the message I'd heard, his expression grows grim. "This, too, breaks my heart."

"I'm sorry, André. I didn't come here to add to your worries."

He looks directly at me with a kind smile. "Indeed you did not. But I see there's much that's troubling you, and I suspect these things are only part of your burden. Hold nothing back, Alfred. I'm here to help in whatever way I can."

So I proceed to tell him about Rupert's new status, about how much the castle has become like an armed fortress, about my inability to divine John's intent, about the lack of purpose I feel. "It's no longer bound up in grief for the loss of my father. And in point of fact, it's worse than when I could lay some of the blame for my gloomy state on that event."

There's wine left over from our meal. André is pensive as he refills our glasses.

"I wonder," he begins, "what our neighboring kings think about what's happening here. Surely word is reaching them."

"I, too, wonder. But as we no longer have any ambassadors and Rupert has been banished to the countryside, our ability to gather information is severely hampered." I pause. "I trust you, too, know of Rupert's role."

"Aye, Alfred, I do, though none here but the abbot is privileged to know that information."

I chuckle. "I'm quickly learning this is the best kept secret-that's-not-a-secret in the entire kingdom . . . despite Grandfather's exhortations to limit the knowledge."

"Think of it as a carefully controlled secret," he grins and then looks serious once again. "I think that for such secrets, that is the best one can hope." He drinks from his glass before resuming.

"I suspect, however, that there are other ways to get information. If I recall, your wife's father is a nobleman of some rank in the Kingdom of Lakes . . . perhaps even some relation to their king? And is not Lord Thorssen married to a princess of the Kingdom of Peaks?"

The answers seem so obvious now that he's spoken them. I'm sure I must look a bit sheepish. "Of course you're right, André. And I'm exceedingly embarrassed that I didn't think of that myself."

"Don't chastise yourself, Alfred. Not only are you isolated in an armed fortress, as you call it – without like-minded men to stimulate your thinking – but you're also burdened with the knowledge of how circumspect you must be to avoid running afoul of the king. It seems John has done one thing exceptionally well."

"And what might that be?"

"He's effectively imprisoned you, all the while proclaiming to the world that you're a free man, second only to his own son on the ladder to power." He pauses to let this thought sink in.

"And I've let it happen."

"You couldn't have avoided it, Alfred. Not without risking getting yourself thrown into a real prison . . . or worse. But we both know your strength of mind. You'll see this through. Of that I'm certain."

"I wish I could be as sure."

"There's something I've been meaning to ask you to consider," André goes on.

"What might that be?"

"Future generations will need to understand what happened during this period. Historians will want to study it; future sovereigns will need to learn from it. I imagine the king is creating a record of his reign. But I imagine equally that it's a record excessively biased to the king's peculiar point of view. Someone needs to write a true history that describes in detail everything that occurs – a chronicle of all the kingdom, not just of the man who sits on the throne. Have you ever considered such an undertaking?"

"I have not, André, though it seems a worthy endeavor."

"Worthy indeed, Alfred, and of greater importance than you might realize at this moment. I ask only that you give it serious consideration. Perhaps this is the important destiny your grandfather foresaw for you."

I've grown accustomed to people attributing any number of events to my grandfather's deeply held view that there's some special purpose for my life . . . a purpose he couldn't discern but was convinced would manifest itself in due course. I generally dismiss such comments, for I don't consider myself special. I'm sure my life will play out as intended, and I'm not sure I believe in foresight. For the first time, however, spoken by André, those words seem to resonate with some sense of truth. Perhaps indeed . . .

"Trust the lords, Alfred. When the time is right and they believe the odds of success are high, they will act. I'm sure of it."

"As am I," I reply.

"It wouldn't hurt, either, for you to trust The Lord," his smile is fatherly. "Though I must say I agree with those who assert that He is not averse to human assistance in these things."

It's time to find Gwen and Juliana and start our return journey if we're to arrive home by sundown. Walking with me toward the kennel, André suddenly remembers something. "I almost forgot, Alfred. There's a new monk recently arrived here from the western monastery. He seems to have a remarkable command of the language of the Territories. I can't vouch for that myself, but I'm told the new immigrants find his skill more than passable. You must come back soon and spend some time with Brother Eustace."

So Warin has indeed followed through. "That's excellent news!" I say. "Tell Brother Eustace I'll be back next week and he'll have my full attention."

"Warin wrote to me of your promising friendship with Lord Egon. I'm most eager to see how it progresses."

"I only hope it doesn't get ripped apart by some whim of John's before we're able to build on the foundation we've laid."

As we ride home, I reflect on my renewed sense of purpose and how quickly it has broken through the gloom. By spelling out so clearly that I am indeed a prisoner, André has freed my mind to think differently. I feel almost lighthearted, and it seems Star Dancer senses the change – he's friskier than I've seen him in quite some time.

Allowing Juliana and Osbert to go on ahead, I turn to Gwen. "What would you think of a visit to your parents once spring arrives?"

Her eyes light up. "That would be lovely, Alfred!" She pauses for a long moment, apparently thinking something through. "I wonder, though . . . what would you think if we went a bit earlier . . . for Juliana's birthday. She's almost a young lady now, and I'm sure my father would like to throw a special celebration for her. I can even imagine he might invite all the relatives, including some we see only for ceremonial occasions. They've not seen Geoffrey since he was breeched, so even more reason for festivities."

How quick she is to grasp my motivation . . . and to find a device to achieve those ends that will look to all the world like ordinary family activity!

"Even better," I reply.

"I'll write to my parents in the morning." She, too, seems energized. "And don't worry, my love, I won't forget my letter will probably be read by John's spies."

Juliana and Osbert have stopped to wait for us. "Hurry, Papa, or we'll get home before you do and I'll eat up *all* the supper." We urge our mounts forward and the four of us ride the last mile together.

In the morning, I, too, have a letter to write, so I make my way to the library immediately after my morning ride.

Phillip,

I hope this letter finds you and your family in good health. I'm writing to tell you we're planning a visit to Gwen's parents very soon to celebrate Juliana's birthday, and Gwen is certain all her relatives will attend. We're both looking forward to seeing her family again as it's been more than a year since we were there.

I don't know when you might be planning to take Addiena and the children for a similar visit to her family. In truth, it's none of my business. But as I've been thinking about our own travel and the necessity of finding lodgings during the journey, it occurs to me to extend an invitation to you. Whenever you do undertake such a trip, Gwen and I would be very pleased to have you as our guests for a brief rest from the rigors of travel so you could go on from here refreshed and renewed.

Know that we would enjoy the pleasure of your company any time.
Alfred

I re-read it twice before folding the paper, assuring myself that I've found the right balance between innocuous correspondence and planting a seed in Phillip's mind. Satisfied, I summon Osbert and ask him to be sure it goes with the next messenger to Great Woolston.

"D'ye not want to seal it, m'lord?"

"I think not, Osbert. If my seal is visible, we can be sure it will be opened and read by the king's spies. Like this, it's much less likely to be noticed."

"Ye be a cunning one, m'lord," he grins. "Mayhap I send a little note to Alwin too – just this same way – so's there be two in the pouch."

"A most excellent idea, Osbert!"

"If there be naught else, m'lord, then I be off to take care of things."

"Nothing else, Osbert. I have things to do here for the rest of the day."

And thus I find myself sitting at my writing table, the blank paper before me, thinking how to construct a proper chronicle. It should be formal . . . and factual . . . and, to whatever degree any writer is capable, it must readily distinguish the narration of events from the opinion of the narrator.

Hesitating, I examine the three quills lying beside the ink pot. Am I really capable of such a weighty undertaking? Two of the quills need sharpening, so I take out my knife and reshape their points. Wouldn't André or perhaps even one of his brethren be better suited to the task? More neutral observers? His words echo in my mind: "We see only the outcomes, Alfred, and have no view of the causes." I look around the room and then back to the table top. The blank paper stares back at me.

Stop procrastinating, Alfred. You'll never have the answer until you try. And so I take quill in hand, dip it in the ink pot, and begin to write.

A history of the reign of John the 15ᵗʰ sovereign of our kingdom and the 1ˢᵗ to bear this name

being a true account of the reign of John the eldest son of Edward the 14ᵗʰ sovereign of this realm His wife Gundrea is the daughter of Erik a nobleman of the Eastern Kingdom At the time of his accession in the 213ᵗʰ year since the founding of the kingdom the king and queen have 3 children of which the youngest John Gundar is the 1ˢᵗ son and heir to the throne

The reader should know that this author is not entirely disinterested, being the second and only other son of King Edward It is nevertheless my intent to recount truthfully the events of this reign and to make clear to the reader insofar as I have the ability whenever I stray from the relaying of history to conveying an opinion thereon

The First Year

Foregoing many of the traditions of the kingdom John was crowned just two weeks after the passing of his father in a coronation ceremony notable for its austerity Within the first three months the new king took many actions that appeared to set the tone for how he intended to reign When he then took personal control of the Treasury the stage was set for rule solely by the personal power of the monarch a style of governing not seen in this kingdom in more than half a century

I find it easy to write dispassionately about the facts of the dubious military appointments, the creation of the three lifetime lords, the dissolution of the court, and the economic decline that is following on the heels of all this uncertainty. When it comes to how the legacies of my father and grandfather are being destroyed, the task is more difficult.

He then began to systematically dismantle the progressive policies of the 12ᵗʰ 13ᵗʰ and 14ᵗʰ kings Since the reign of the 12ᵗʰ king the Council established the rates of taxation King John now does so by personal decree During the reign of King Edward the payment of taxes was made less onerous People paid their taxes in the large town nearest where they lived and the mayors of those towns kept records of the taxes collected It was not uncommon nor was it illegal for mayors to allow people to pay in small sums when they had money so long as the entire sum was paid by the proper time Royal Tax Collectors called on the mayors to collect the tallies and only rarely did they have to pay a direct visit to a merchant land owner or farmer to demand payment The system worked as hoped The Treasury was always well funded and the people were less fearful and more compliant in their payments King John abolished this system in the following proclamation

The previous laws and practices regarding taxes owed to and claimed for the Royal Treasury having ceded the power of the sovereign to others of lesser rank are hereby revoked From this day forward taxes shall be collected only by the Royal Tax Collectors Be it known that anyone owing taxes is required to produce the full sum owed on the demand of a Royal Tax Collector at whatever time and place the Collector makes such demand Anyone who cannot or will not pay their taxes on demand will be subject to search of their premises for the money to fulfill their obligation and to seizure of assets equal to the value of the amount owed including crops livestock goods for sale furnishings land and even the home or place of business in question or imprisonment for failure to pay Anyone judged guilty of willfully refusing to fulfill their obligation to pay tax will be imprisoned for a period of no less than one full year

Enforcement of this proclamation cast a pall over the land Tax collectors escorted by troops of armed knights rode everywhere from farm to farm village to village town to town manor to manor demanding payments The presence of the knights was primarily to guard the money that was accumulated and ensure it arrived safely back at the castle but also served to intimidate the people to stifle any reluctance to pay and to conduct searches and seizures when necessary The constant presence of armed men demanding money did nothing but augment the peoples fear In another edict the king rescinded a proclamation of the 12th king concerning school attendance Parents he declared knew best what their children needed to know and the Crown had no interest in what children learned There was not initially a decline in the numbers of children attending schools in the towns because it was part of the fabric of life and people were doing their best to continue their lives as normally as possible There are signs in the countryside however of a notable decline in the number children being educated

It is also not difficult to write the facts about the appearance of the itinerant priests or of the astonishing growth of our fighting forces. But I can't restrain myself from adding an opinion at the end of that narration.

It is a dangerous and worrisome state for a kingdom that has been at peace within itself and with its neighbors for most of a century It is equally worrisome that the king seems oblivious to the effects of his actions

•   •   •   •   •

At the end of three days, after scratching through and rewriting numerous passages, I declare myself satisfied that I've made a plausible start. I copy the almost indecipherable pages as a clean manuscript and burn the others, making certain nothing remains but ash – nothing even remotely resembling paper – nothing that could be discovered by a scullery maid cleaning the grate or laying a new fire – in short, nothing that anyone would consider reporting to the king. I tuck the manuscript inside my shirt so I can walk unencumbered through the corridors without drawing anyone's attention. For now, whenever the document can't be in my possession, it will remain locked in my strongbox. Tomorrow, if the weather's fair, I'll ride to the monastery to show it to André and get his guidance on improving it. And I should also have my first language lesson with Eustace.

As luck would have it, we wake in the morning to a snow storm howling outside the windows. By early afternoon, the storm has spent itself, but there's snow on every surface and drifts up to a man's knee by the walls, where the wind could blow it no further. Because the temperature is in no hurry to climb above that point where water turns to ice, it takes the sallow sun two more days to melt the snow and begin to dry the roads to a passable state.

When finally there's a morning without a coating of ice on the water troughs, I saddle Star Dancer and head north to the monastery. I'm surprised by the number of mud holes in the road. A single horse can circumvent them easily enough, but a wagon would find some places impassable. If John has allowed this road to fall into such disrepair, what, I wonder, are the conditions of the other main roads in the kingdom?

Impatient as I am to get on with my new projects, I arrive at the monastery earlier than usual, while the service of Terce is still in progress. Looking for something to occupy myself, I wander over to the kennel where I find a brand new litter of puppies. Little more than a week old, by the looks of them, their eyes not yet open, they're climbing all over each other and their mother seeking a free teat for a morning snack. The mother eyes me warily at first, but I approach slowly, and she quickly decides I'm no threat. Eight of them. Brother Adam is going to be quite busy raising this lot.

I stroll around the monastery grounds for a bit then make my way back to the chapel, where the service has just ended. André seems genuinely pleased to see me. He turns to the monk nearest, "Find Brother Eustace and ask him to come to my study."

Before the monk can leave, I interrupt, "Actually, André, there's something I'd like to discuss with you first."

"Of course. Half an hour?"

I nod. The monk acknowledges his new instructions and goes on his way.

"I'd have come sooner," I tell André, "but for the snow storm."

"Take heart," he replies, "that the snow-melt will be good for preparing the ground for planting."

In his study, seated before the fire, I take out my manuscript. "I'd like your opinion on this. I found it took quite some work to get started, but having done that, I think I want to continue." He takes my pages and reads in silence.

"You've made a good start, indeed, Alfred." I suddenly feel my shoulders relax, though I hadn't been fully aware how anxious I was for his approval.

"I admire the trouble you've taken to differentiate between the recitation of events and your opinions. If I might suggest, however, your opinion may be more valuable than you think. Future students of this period will be as interested in the 'why' as in the 'what.' And you have a unique perspective as a firsthand observer who also has a deep understanding of your brother's character."

"Insofar as anyone can actually understand him, I suppose."

"Oh, I think you've captured his character and motivation quite masterfully already. Now just continue to apply that insight to your account.

"In fact," he adds, after a moment's thought, "I won't be surprised if you find yourself revisiting these pages at some later time. With the benefit of hindsight, you may choose to elaborate further on how one thing led to or influenced another." He returns the manuscript to me.

"Actually," I tell him, "I've been thinking about this. It might be wiser for me to leave the completed portions with you for safekeeping. Even though I have a strongbox, there's no way of predicting if John might suddenly take it into his head to search my belongings or seize the box. I think both the manuscript and my own hide would be safer with the document in your possession." I hand it back to him.

"You may be assured it will be safe from prying eyes here, Alfred. We're happy to do what we can," he chuckles, "to protect the hide of a man such as yourself."

There's a knock on the door, to which André responds, "Come." A young monk, short of stature and a little on the chubby side, with blond hair and intense blue eyes, enters the room, closing the door behind him and waiting there for further instructions.

"And now," says André, rising from his seat, "I believe it's time for your first language lesson." I rise as well, as André motions for the young monk to come forward.

"Lord Alfred, this is Brother Eustace, of whom we spoke." The monk bows his head slightly, though whether in deference to me or to his superior is impossible to discern. "You may have the use of this room for your lessons. I'll see that you're not disturbed."

And so we begin. "You'll find," says Eustace, "that their language has some similarities with that of the Kingdom of Peaks, if you know any of that tongue. It is, however, a more ancient language, I've come to believe. Let's start with a few words and phrases so you get a feel for the sounds and how to pronounce words."

At the end of our first session, my head is spinning with both the exhilaration of this adventure I'm embarking on and the recognition that it's been a long time since I was learning Latin as a lad. I'll simply have to apply myself and become a good student once again.

I arrive back home just as a patrol is returning. While we're attending to our mounts, I take the opportunity to ask the captain about the roads. "The winter seems to have been particularly hard on the road to the monastery. Is that the case where you've been as well?"

"'Tisn't just the winter, my lord," he replies, "though that hasn't helped. There's been no repair to any of the roads for almost a year now. We make our reports – same as always – but nothing seems to get done. I can't remember when my troop's been ordered to help repair a road or a bridge. Used to happen regular – like clockwork – but seems all we do now is ride with the tax collectors or go on training exercises."

Then, as if suddenly remembering to whom he's speaking, he adds, "No disrespect to your brother the king, of course, sir."

"Of course not, Captain," I reply. "I asked you a question and you gave me an honest answer. Please don't ever do any less whenever we have a chance to talk."

When I ask John about the roads, his response is predictable. "What business is it of yours?"

I bite my tongue, so tempting is it to ask him if that's the only thing he knows how to say to me. "Well, as a free man of your kingdom who uses the roads for travel from time to time, I'd like to know they're safe and passable. I suspect that's not an uncommon concern."

He shrugs his shoulders. "Be that as it may, there's not enough money to hire road builders right now, so it will just have to wait. The knights have to be fed and trained and prepared; and the Treasury isn't limitless, you know."

"Isn't it customary for troops to be detailed to conduct some repairs? Surely you wouldn't have to hire road builders for everything."

"My knights are a military force, Alfred, *not* road builders," he replies vehemently.

"If I remember my history correctly, the Roman Legionaries were master road builders. We still use some of their roads today. That hardly seems a bad example to follow."

"It's an irrelevant example, and I've nothing more to say on the subject. If you're so concerned about road building, spend some of your own money to get it done."

He is pig-headed, as usual, so I take my leave. But as I open the door to exit the room, I turn to him with one final comment. "You might change your priorities when the supply wagons can't get through to the garrison or to your training exercises."

He glares at me. "Get out," is all he says, so I know my remark has had the desired effect of reminding him of something he hadn't properly thought through.

After weeks of anticipation, we're at last on our way to visit Gwen's parents. Everyone is going, including my mother, Nurse . . . even the dogs.

"With no one at court, there's no one to look after them while we're away," Gwen had bemoaned.

"Couldn't Matthias assign someone to do that?" I asked.

"I'm sure he'd do so willingly," she replied, "but I don't fancy coming home to learn that John got wind of it and had the dogs done away with. There's no way we could explain that to the children." And so the dogs are part of the traveling party.

Two coaches carry the women, the children, and the dogs; a wagon is laden with all our baggage. Osbert and I ride alongside, often at the front to check the condition of the road. So far, the weather has been fair and the roads dry, though we've observed quite a few places where the ruts were somewhat deeper than usual from heavy wagons going through in the mud. At one point, our drivers had to guide the coaches over a particularly nasty spot, putting the wheels on the center of the road and on the verge to avoid getting stuck.

Once we're over the border into the Kingdom of Lakes, the roads are smooth and in excellent repair, despite the harsher-than-usual winter. Even such a small thing as this has the effect of restoring my belief that the normal rhythm of life still exists somewhere. I'm briefly tempted to wonder, "What if we just decided to stay here?"

We arrive at midafternoon of a day that is starting to feel as if spring might be in the air. Lord Godwin and Lady Margaret are overjoyed to see us, fawning over everyone, including the dogs. Lady Margaret takes charge. "Your rooms are all prepared. Gwen, you and Alfred will have the big front corner room on the first floor. The nursery is all freshened up – we haven't had children there since your youngest sister visited a year ago. Alice, you'll have the room next to ours. It has a lovely view over the garden toward the lake. Now, I've ordered hot baths for everyone, and you should have lots of time to refresh and rest before supper." And with that, she begins herding everyone indoors, like a mother hen . . . or perhaps, it occurs to me as I watch with amusement, the dogs following behind, making sure everyone is moving forward . . . just like one of our little four-legged herders. Osbert takes charge of the baggage, with help from some of the servants.

Godwin claps me on the shoulder and shakes my hand heartily. "I'm so glad you've come, Alfred. All is in train as Gwen requested. Juliana will have as fine a birthday celebration as any young lady ever had. The king was only too happy to accept my invitation. It seems he, too, has been trying to work out how the two of you could meet."

We walk up the front steps and into the house. "I trust you remember how to find your room?" he asks and without waiting for a reply, continues, "Top of the stairs, turn left. I suspect there'll be plenty of bustling about. You'll find it."

"No doubt Osbert will find me if I get lost," I chuckle.

"We'll talk more over brandy this evening, after you're refreshed from travel. Now off with you."

Though there's still a bit of winter chill in the air, the days are getting noticeably longer. For four days running, we wake to bright sun in a clear blue sky, and my morning rides with Godwin are a real pleasure. It's also refreshing to see the children able to run and play outdoors with no comings-and-goings-of-knights to restrict their freedom.

The house fills with guests, including Gwendolyn's sisters and other assorted relatives. Late in the afternoon of the day before Juliana's birthday, the king's party arrives. Observing the manner in which the members of this extended family greet one another reminds me of the comfortable informality that once existed within my own. That fleeting thought about the possibility of staying here crosses my mind, unbidden, once again.

The king joins us for our ride the next morning on what is yet another picture-perfect day. Back in the stable, we turn our horses over to the grooms and head toward the house. "I wonder, Godwin," says the king, "if I might commandeer your study for a few hours. There's much that Alfred and I need to discuss."

"For as long as you like," Godwin replies. "I'll see that you're not disturbed."

"Well," says the king, "a bit of food around midday might go down easily."

"Without question. Ale or wine?" Godwin asks.

"What say you, Alfred? Ale? I suspect we'll be sampling the best wine in Godwin's cellar at tonight's banquet, and I'd hate for him to run out."

"Ale it is," I reply.

The morning sun on the windows and the early morning fire, now reduced to glowing embers, have made Godwin's study cozy and comfortable. We choose chairs near the fireplace, and the king immediately puts me at ease, much in the manner of my father or grandfather, treating me almost as an equal. "I must compliment you, Alfred, on finding a ruse by which we could meet. I myself hadn't been able to work out anything plausible."

"I can't take full credit, sir. The notion of the visit was my idea, but it was Gwen who recognized right away that a party for Juliana would be the most innocent of all reasons for us to be in the same place."

He laughs. "Oh, our Gwendolyn is indeed the bright one. You're a lucky man to have her."

"A fact of which I'm reminded every day."

"You know, we were all rather concerned when she became of marriageable age."

"How so? I'd have thought every noble in your kingdom would've been pressing the suit of one or another of their sons."

"And so they were. But Godwin and I both knew we had to find someone special for her. A man whose intellect matched her own . . . and more importantly, a man who would let her intellect and progressive ideas thrive. When Edward told me he and Alice were looking for suitable candidates for your bride, I knew we'd found the answer. I trust you two are happy together?"

"Without question, sir."

"Excellent!" he pronounces himself satisfied, then adds, "And enough of this 'sir' stuff in private. You're as near to a peer from your realm as I suspect I'll have the opportunity to converse with. Your brother, it seems, can't be bothered even to acknowledge my invitation for him to come for a state visit. I'm fairly certain that means he's rather unlikely to reciprocate."

I chuckle. "As you've discovered, John isn't known for his diplomatic skill . . . or even his manners."

"Our kingdoms have been friends and allies for so many years, Alfred. I'm deeply troubled by what I hear about what's happening there."

"We've none of us known anything like this in our lifetimes."

"Enlighten me," he leans back in his chair, inviting me to talk.

I've given a great deal of thought to how much I should reveal. Remembering how much my father trusted this man, I've come to the conclusion that it's best to tell him everything. Only in that way can he be well prepared to protect his kingdom and to support our lords if and when they decide to take action. And so I begin my story.

He's intensely attentive, occasionally inserting a question or remark, and incredulous when I describe the banishment of the lords from court and the Council-in-name-only that John has created. When I get to the part about Rupert's dismissal and our fears for conditions at the port, he sits forward in his chair. "If what I've heard is true, your fears are already being realized. We knew your uncle was no longer in charge at the port, but not why. Your tax collectors are accosting our traders with armed knights as escorts and demanding inspection of their goods and immediate payment of tariffs, which they seem to make up on the spot. That intimidation is bad enough, but it gets worse."

"How so?"

"It seems the dockmen have organized into gangs, each of which controls a section of the dock. The ship captains have to pay the gangs for a spot to tie up, else they're relegated to anchoring mid-river and having to ferry their goods to and from shore in small craft. As I understand it, the traders also have to pay the gangs to get access to the ships for loading or unloading. And whoever pays the most gets moved to the front of the line. A trader might be second in line at the start of the day only to find himself relegated to the back by noon, as the bribery seems to be continuous.

"That's a prescription for violence to erupt. I've become quite concerned for the safety of our traders, but have no idea how to counter the risk. If I send armed knights with each trading expedition, that would automatically be seen as a provocation."

"Not just by the gangs," I interject, "but by the king as well."

"Believe me, that thought has also crossed my mind. I could arm the traders, but they aren't trained in the arts of fighting and so would probably come out on the losing end of any altercation."

We're both silent for a moment. There's an idea taking shape in my mind. "It's taking me a while, but I'm starting to learn how to think about things in a totally unconventional way," I tell him. "This meeting, for example. In the past, I would never have presumed to meet with a foreign ruler behind my own king's back. So what I'm about to suggest may seem more than a little odd at first."

"Let's hear it."

"What if your armed knights went along on the expedition disguised as traders? It would require trusted men with the skill to be watchful for danger but know how to conceal their arms and their abilities unless the traders were actually threatened. That would provide protection without unnecessarily provoking either the gangs or the king."

"It's actually quite brilliant, Alfred."

"It's not without risk. If things were to get out of control, there would just be that many more armed men in the fracas. If John's knights step in to break things up, your men could find themselves arrested, and I've no idea how that would play out. If it became known that some of the traders were knights in disguise, I can't predict how the king might react."

"Your assessment is valid. But the question I have to ask myself is how do I best protect our trading interests in general, our trading routes, and our traders themselves? We're mostly a landlocked kingdom, and your port is our best access to the sea. Oh, we have a harbor in the far northwest, as you know, but it isn't set up for the great trading ships. And using it adds a week, maybe ten days to the sea voyage even when the winds are fair. Not to mention the longer overland journey. In winter and early spring, the storms in the Western Sea make that route risky at best . . . as a practical matter, unwise even to consider. So I must find ways to keep our trade flowing through your port or we'll begin experiencing the economic collapse you're already suffering.

"The disguised knights would also give me a solution to another problem that's only just begun."

"Oh?"

"Aye, in the last month I've received two reports of trading expeditions being stopped just across the border by armed knights. In both cases, all their goods were searched thoroughly while the drivers and traders were held at sword-point. No one knows what they were looking for, as they eventually rode off without any explanation."

"That's really disturbing. Especially as I've no idea whether they were acting on their own initiative or on some sort of new orders." I pause for a moment to reflect. "One thing does occur to me, though. I wonder if they might have been looking for immigrants being smuggled in among the trade goods."

"That doesn't make any sense. We've always had free passage across our borders – in both directions."

So I tell him about the itinerant priests and their messages, including the message about intolerance of immigrants. "I'm given to understand that their numbers have increased such that they're everywhere in our realm these days. Many of the people who have no work seem to be latching onto the notion that the reason they're in dire straits is because the immigrants are taking the jobs."

"That sounds ominous."

"If the outcry has reached John's ears, I can imagine his solution to silence it would be to eliminate the immigrants."

"Beyond that, the whole thing with these wandering priests is unnerving. Has your bishop no power to stop them?"

"They seem to believe he has no authority over them. They simply ignore any suggestions from the regular clergy to be on their way. Oh, they may wander off to the next village for a few days, but they come back eventually."

The king shakes his head in dismay. "I most fervently hope we don't see them here."

The servants have unobtrusively laid out food and a jug of ale on Godwin's desk, so we pause in our conversation to fill our plates and mugs. "Nice," says the king after tasting the ale. "If Godwin's wine is as good as his ale, we'll have a very fine banquet indeed."

Settling in again before the fireplace, I tell him about John's rapid expansion of the knighthood and the training of archers. "There's no one around the castle these days but a few servants and dozens upon dozens of knights and trainees."

"What does he intend to do with this army?" asks the king.

"I wish I knew. One possibility is that he simply enjoys playing at soldier and has no vision for what to do as king other than to create a big army. There's no doubt he excelled at fighting skills when we were in training together. And there's even less doubt that he has no vision. My fervent hope is that he'll simply get bored with it after a few more months and turn his attention to something else."

"Why do I think you don't believe that's likely to happen?"

I smile. "Because he's far more bored with anything that requires thoughtfulness or the application of whatever intellect he may have. And because having and leading a strong army is the single most obvious and visible thing he can think of to demonstrate his personal power."

"If you had to hazard a guess?"

"I think it most likely he'd target the Territories first. That was the site of his greatest humiliation, and he's blindly determined to prove he wasn't in the wrong and to 'set right,' as he would describe it, 'all the injustices that followed.'"

"And if not the Territories?"

"I simply don't know. If he thought strategically – even if he were just a good tactician – any of us could anticipate his possible moves and work out the right counters. But he seems only to act in one of two ways – reacting to whatever he sees standing in his way at the moment or redressing his personal grudges for some real or imagined offense.

"That's why I'm holding nothing back from you. You have to be well informed if you're to protect your realm and its way of life. One thing I can assure you. Whatever actions you may have to take will have the full support of our hereditary lords. Even if they can't directly support you, they'll take no action to interfere."

"Have you spoken to the King of Peaks?" he asks.

"I have only the flimsiest of pretexts for such a visit. But my friend Phillip – Lord Thorssen – is married to a princess of the Peaks. I've encouraged him to take his wife and family for a visit."

"You're becoming quite the sly one, Alfred," he laughs.

"Well, as I said, it's taken me some time to figure out how to think this way, but I'm trying."

"Perhaps I'll visit the Peaks king as well. We haven't had a state visit in," he pauses, thinking, "almost three years now. Surely it's time."

I refill our mugs with the last of the ale and raise mine. "To state visits!" He laughs as we drink the toast, clearly understanding my enthusiasm for these two kingdoms to have a coordinated approach to whatever might happen in ours.

"May I ask you something of a more personal nature, Alfred?" He's quite serious now.

"Of course."

"With what you've told me about the atmosphere at the castle, I'm surprised you continue to live there. Wouldn't your family be more comfortable – perhaps even safer – somewhere else?"

"You pose a fair question, sir." I can't help myself . . . the 'sir' just seems natural. "With all the lords banished from court, I've felt it was my duty to remain so someone could observe firsthand what was happening. The lords need to know. You need to know. The interests of the people need to be protected. And John needs to know that others are watching.

"But lately – especially over these last few days as I've watched Gwen and the children thrive in a place that's like what our home used to be – I'm beginning to question my decision."

"Duty takes many forms, Alfred," says the king gently. "I can't fault your logic for remaining in the castle. But consider this. Perhaps your duty is more to the future than to the present. There's so little you can do to affect what's happening in the present – without putting yourself at grave risk, that is. Perhaps it's far more important to keep your family safe and to prepare your sons to be a strong influence for good on the next king . . . even, perhaps, to be around to exert such influence yourself."

For a long moment I don't respond. I must have looked saddened in some way, because he continues, "I hope I haven't overstepped. That was *not* my intent."

"Oh, no, sir. Not at all. It's just that, listening to you speak just now, I could hear in my mind the voices of my father and my grandfather. I was thinking perhaps they, too, would have given me similar advice."

He smiles kindly. "You've given me much to contemplate, Alfred."

"Likewise, sir."

"And now, I think maybe we'd best go see how the preparations for this evening's festivities are progressing."

Back in our room, I find those preparations well underway. "Alfred . . . at last!" exclaims Gwen. "We were just about to despair of your returning in time to dress for the banquet."

I give my daughter a peck on the cheek. "You don't really think I'd miss any part of this celebration, do you?"

Gwen smiles. "No, but your daughter was starting to get worried." Gwen is dressed in the new gown she had made for the occasion . . . the blue of our family coat of arms that is so striking on her. She's looking through her jewel box, choosing just the right adornments to match her gown.

Letty helps Juliana into her new frock, just as if she were a proper lady . . . which, in fact, she is, if still a very young one. Once all the fastenings are done up, Letty seats her at the dressing table and arranges her hair. Somewhere, they've found some late snowdrops and Letty works two or three of them into Juliana's dark curls. The effect, with her silvery-white dress, is stunning, making her look every bit the princess.

Gwen reaches back into her jewel box and takes out a delicate gold chain from which dangles a single, small, pear-shaped amethyst. Fastening it around Juliana's neck, she says, "This was my very first piece of jewelry, and now it's time for it to be yours."

"Oh, Mama, it's so beautiful!" Juliana beams with pleasure. "Is it really, truly mine?" She fondles the pendant carefully.

"We'll store it in my jewel box for safekeeping, but yes, it's yours and yours alone to wear for special occasions."

Juliana springs up from her seat and hugs her mother. "Oh, thank you, Mama. Thank you, thank you, thank you."

"And now," Gwen disengages her embrace, "let's see what your father thinks."

Juliana turns to face me. Can it be possible that the baby I first held on the day I returned from captivity is this amazing young girl standing before me? I cross my arms over my chest and put one hand to my chin, appraising her thoroughly for effect. "You, my dear, are a vision of loveliness . . . as beautiful, I daresay, as your mother."

Her face lights up with pleasure. "Really, Papa? As pretty as Mama?"

"As pretty as Mama." I hold out my arms and she comes to me for a hug.

Gwen has taken a seat in front of the fireplace and now calls Juliana to her. "Now, this is your first grown-up banquet. Remember, you're the guest of honor tonight, so you won't sit with us but in the place of honor between Grandpa Godwin and the king."

"I remember, Mama."

"And do you remember your manners?"

"Yes, ma'am. I eat properly with my fork and knife. Take small bites of food. Don't talk with food in my mouth. And don't speak unless someone speaks to me first. And when I'm not eating, I keep my hands in my lap."

"That's right. And when you're introduced to the king?"

"I curtsey, but I don't say anything unless he speaks to me. And when I answer, I call him 'Your Grace.'" She pauses. "And after that I call him 'Sire.'"

"Perfect again," says Gwen. "And what if you get confused or don't know what to do?"

"I watch you and do the same thing as you."

"And if you need my help?"

"I pull on my ear and you'll come." Gwen gives her a kiss on the forehead.

"I'm sure you'll be the perfect lady," I tell her, "and that there'll be no need for any ear-pulling tonight."

"Now, Alfred," scolds Gwen, "you'd best hurry. Osbert's waiting for you. But we need to be downstairs in half an hour, so no dallying."

I grin and, for Juliana's benefit, say, "Yes, ma'am," and go into the dressing room where Osbert is indeed waiting with all my clothes laid out.

The banquet is a great success. Juliana is the perfect young lady, and I'm pleased to see both Godwin and the king engage her in conversation frequently. After the meal, the entertainment begins, and Juliana dances with her father, her grandfather, and the king before Gwen decides it's time to bundle her off to bed. My heart is filled with pride.

The next morning, the king's party departs. Gwen's sisters remain for a week, all of them catching up on whatever it is sisters talk about and do when they're together. We'll stay yet one more week after that before beginning our return journey.

One morning, during the last week of our stay, as I return from the stable after a solitary morning ride, I find my mother taking a turn in the garden alone. "Walk with me, Alfred," she says. "I'd be glad of the company." Settling into step beside her, I notice she looks more rested and relaxed – younger, even – than I've seen her in months.

"It's been a pleasant few weeks here," she begins. "Not at all like the tension that pervades the castle. I'm afraid I'm actually dreading going home."

"I have to admit I've quite enjoyed it myself."

"I can see that, Alfred. I've watched the care fall from your shoulders. You've become your old self again during our time here."

"Is it really that obvious, Mother?"

"To those who care for you, yes," she replies. We walk on in silence. Finally, she continues, "Have you thought about moving with your family to the country manor? It would be a better place for the children, and you'd no longer have to be reminded everyday of all the things that are going wrong and that you're powerless to address."

"I've actually thought about little else over the last few days," I reply. "Would you agree to come with us?"

She stops in her tracks and turns to me, smiling. "You have to ask?" We resume our walk. "Of course I would," she continues. "In fact, Catherine and Rupert urged me to move quite some months ago, and I'd have been happy to do so. But I felt I had to stay at the castle to protect your interests."

"I'm a grown man, Mother," I chide. "I think I can look out for myself."

"Oh, I've no doubt about that. But I also know I'm the only one who can restrain John. And I've been living with the worry that I'm the only one who could intervene if he decided to do harm to you or your family. In the country, we'd be out of his sight . . . and you wouldn't be a daily reminder to him that the only reason he's king is because no one could come up with a way to prevent it."

I tell her how André described my situation as being John's prisoner. "That's when I first began thinking that maybe I'd allowed my sense of duty and of what I believed to be the proper role for a son of the royal house to cloud my judgment. This visit – seeing how you and Gwen and the children are thriving in the kind of world we all *should* be living in – has caused me to rethink everything. I've been wrapped up in thinking about what I couldn't achieve when I should've been thinking about what I *could* do."

"I'm pleased, Alfred. Gwendolyn will be too. And I know your father would agree. Remember his advice: 'Retreat from public life if that seems best.'"

I stop in my tracks and turn to her. "Yes," she says, "he showed me the letter he intended to leave for you."

"I've often wondered. I expected no less."

We resume our stroll. "You needn't concern yourself about the lords, either. I've written to Lord Devereux, and he agrees it would be better for you to be away from John's clutches."

"I'm surprised you've been willing to commit such thoughts to writing. I've become quite circumspect about anything I write, knowing John's spies most likely read all my correspondence."

She laughs out loud. "Your brother knows that if I get even a hint he's spying on me, I'll bring the wrath of three kingdoms down on his head, and he'll be deposed within the month."

"And why would he think that?"

"Because I told him as much."

I smile and shake my head slowly. "Mother, you are a marvel. But what makes you believe he took you seriously?"

"Two things. First, the way he reacted. He turned and looked out the window for a few moments then turned back and said, 'Oh, very well. Now get out and leave me alone' – his usual response when he's forced to admit defeat."

It's my turn to laugh out loud. Her imitation of John – both his demeanor and his tone – is so perfect I could almost imagine him standing in her place.

"But the second is the greater proof," she continues. "None of my letters – sent or received – has ever been tampered with. No seal broken. No clumsy patching from trying to put broken wax back together. No distortion of the seal image. No letters delayed or out of sequence."

We finish another circuit of the garden. "Mother, I think you've just given me a new lease on life. Devereux was my biggest remaining concern. This is the sort of thing I would've liked to speak with him about, and you've solved that problem tidily."

"Then we'll move?" she asks as we approach the terrace.

"I'll speak with Gwen tonight . . . but I rather doubt she'll have any objections," I assure her.

"You won't regret this, Alfred," she replies.

Gwen is equally pleased. We're having our familiar bedtime talk when I broach the subject. "I've been so in hopes you'd come around to that decision," she says.

"Why haven't you said anything?" I ask incredulously.

She takes my hand. "You needed to find your way there yourself, my love. My asking to leave would have just seemed like whining . . . like asking you not to pursue what you felt was your duty. And if you'd heeded my advice and then things went awry . . ." She leaves unsaid what must be a fear that I'd blame her if that advice had proven unwise.

I bring her hand to my lips and kiss it. Then I take her in my arms and tell her all the things that have been worrying me – how much our time here has meant – apologizing, in a way, for having been so self-centered. When I've finished pouring out my soul, she simply nuzzles closer and tells me how much she loves me. Our lovemaking this night is more comfortable and passionate than at any time since before my father's death. I've come home from a long captivity of my mind.

Three days later we take our leave and begin the journey home. As we reach the milepost that marks the border between the kingdoms, Osbert calls to me, "What d'ye think that might be, m'lord?"

I look in the direction he's pointing. It appears to be some sort of camp that wasn't there when we passed this way before. Telling the drivers to follow us at a safe distance, I ride ahead with Osbert to investigate. As we approach, I see that the camp looks as if it's set up for long-term occupancy. I feel for the dagger on my belt just to reassure myself it's there. We slow our horses to a walk. Two armed knights move into the road to block our path. Others take up positions on the verge.

"What's this, Captain?" I ask.

"State your name and your business, sir," he replies.

"Lord Alfred and family returning home. I ask again, Captain, what is this?"

"Border check, sir." By now, the carriages have come up and stopped behind us. Knights move into position beside each. The captain continues, "No one crosses the border without telling us their name and their business and without being searched."

"On whose authority, Captain? We've always had free passage with the Kingdom of Lakes."

"King's orders, sir. Now step down from your horse."

I make no move to dismount and signal to Osbert to do likewise. The captain motions to one of his men to approach the lead carriage. "Search them."

Just as the knight reaches for the handle, the carriage door opens from the inside and my mother descends. Taken aback, the knight retreats to the edge of the road.

"Captain!" calls my mother sharply, startling the captain, who immediately turns his attention from me to her. "What is the meaning of this?"

"Border check, madam. Everything must be searched. Now stand aside, and let my men do their job."

"I'll do no such thing. Move your men back and let us be on our way."

Again the captain motions to his men to get on with whatever they intend. They hesitate, but the one nearest my mother moves tentatively forward. She takes one step in his direction saying, "Stop right there, sir." The poor, befuddled knight stops in his tracks and looks to his captain for help. The captain has no choice but to move away from me and approach this woman who's daring to challenge his orders.

"King's orders, madam. Now stand aside."

"Do you know who I am, Captain?" Without pausing for an answer, she goes on. "I am the dowager queen of this kingdom. You will move your men back and let us pass."

Once again, the captain signals to his men to begin their search. "Captain, were you not listening? If any of your men enters either of these carriages or lays a single hand on any of my family or our belongings, I'll have you drummed out of the knighthood within the week."

The captain turns in my direction. "Sir, can't you —"

I stop him mid-sentence. "Don't look at me, Captain. I can't help you."

"But . . . but . . ." he stammers.

"Captain, if there's anyone in the kingdom who can have you summarily dismissed from your post, it's Lady Alice. I'd pay attention to what she says if I were you." I find this all rather amusing. This feisty side of my mother is something new to me, and I'm enjoying every minute of it.

The captain turns back to my mother and looks directly at her for several moments. She doesn't flinch, meeting his stare with what I imagine is fire in her eyes. Realizing at last that he has no choice but to concede, he says, "Very well, madam," and calls out to his men, "Stand down!" The knights take up positions behind him.

"That's better, Captain, though I believe the proper form of address is 'My Lady' or 'Your Ladyship.' Now," she pauses for effect, "have you completely forgotten all your manners? Do you and your men no longer bend the knee to a queen?"

The captain looks to me in desperation. I hold out my hands, palms up, and shrug, telling him wordlessly that he's on his own. He looks back and meets her gaze once again, still trying to decide what to do. Finally, he slowly goes down on one knee, and his men follow suit.

"Much better," says Mother cheerily. Turning her back on the kneeling men, she calls up to the driver, "Drive on, my good man," and retakes her place inside the carriage. Osbert and I wait beside the road until both carriages and the wagon have passed, then take up position behind them. The poor knights remain on their knees, Mother having cleverly not released them from their obeisance. I glance back and see them finally daring to scramble to their feet. The captain will no doubt be giving orders to his men that they're never to speak of this incident to anyone, ever, and threatening their very lives should they do so.

•　　•　　•　　•

Once back at the castle, we begin planning in earnest for the move. "Mother Alice and I have been talking," says Gwen over supper three days later, with a nod toward Mother. Letty, Osbert, and Nona are taking their meal with us. "We think it would be best not to make it obvious that we intend to leave permanently. We'll put it about that we're going to the country for two or three months. That's long enough that taking most of our things won't seem out of place. When they pack, Letty and Nona will leave a couple of our oldest gowns, some shifts, and a few small things here. Osbert, can you do the same?"

"Aye, m'lady. That I can. His lordship has a pair of old boots I be trying ever so long to get him to throw out. I be leaving those behind fer sure."

"But Osbert," I tease him, "don't you think I'll be needing some old boots for walking around in muddy country fields?"

"Ye be needing *good* boots fer the country, sir," he counters, "not those shoddy old things." Everyone gets a good laugh at my expense.

"We've decided to tell the children only that we're going for a visit," Gwen continues. "You know how they blurt out the most recent thing they've heard to everyone they see. So we won't tell Nurse either . . . that way she won't have to be on her guard around them."

"We'll send the children on ahead," Mother chimes in, "with Nurse, of course, and I'll go with them. That will seem perfectly natural for a visit. After we leave, Nona and Letty can finish packing the nursery. You and Gwen can follow in a couple of days with all the extra baggage."

"It sounds," I remark with a smile, "like you have everything all worked out. What about the other carriage? Gwen and I will have to ride our horses, so I can't see how we'll get a second carriage there."

"Best we leave it here, I think," replies Mother. "A bit more of the subterfuge. Besides, there are at least two nice carriages already at the manor, so we'll have three in any event."

"When we pack," says Gwen somewhat solemnly, "we have to choose a few things to leave behind other than clothing. But we must take everything that's precious to us. Once John realizes we've left for good, he'll most likely order Matthias to burn anything that remains here."

The mood in the room suddenly becomes subdued. This is a big step we're taking . . . but a necessary and important one. It must be done safely.

"My only regret in all this," says Mother quietly, "is leaving the servants." Her eyes glisten with moisture. A single tear escapes and starts to make its way down her cheek. She quickly brushes it away and looks down at her hands, now folded in her lap. "More loyal and kind people I've never known. And once we're in the country, there's nothing more we can do to make their lot better here."

Nona puts her arm around her mistress in a gesture of comfort. "There, there, m'lady. Everybody be knowing what a fine lady you be and how much you look after us."

"I agree, Mother," I add, "though I'm not sure there's much we could do to make their lot better even if we stayed."

"I know, Alfred. It just saddens me to think how much their lives have changed and how uncertain their future may be."

"It's a most excellent plan, ladies," I put a bit of extra enthusiasm into my voice to overcome the momentary sadness. "Wouldn't you agree, Osbert?"

"Aye, m'lord."

"There's just one thing." All eyes turn to me expectantly. "Mother, I'll want Osbert to accompany you and the children. Just a safety precaution."

"Oh, we'll be fine, Alfred. I've made that trip on my own dozens of times. It's less than a day, after all."

"I'm sure you're right, Mother. But these are different times. Think of it as Osbert going along to help you and Nurse with the children if you prefer, but go he will."

"Of course, Alfred. I've no objection if you can manage without him."

"I can certainly try," I reply, "but I wonder, Osbert, if you know someone you can trust who could help me after you leave."

"What about Donal, sir?" he asks.

"Donal? Father's squire?" I ask incredulously. "Does he not have work elsewhere?"

"Nay, m'lord. After Lady Petronilla be gone, he be all at loose ends. No one to serve, nowhere to go."

"Where is he now, Osbert?"

"He be living among the shacks down by the stream. Folks take pity on him . . . let him crowd into a hut with them if it be stormy or too cold to sleep outdoors. They give him bits of food when they can, too, on account of he once be squire to the king."

"Why didn't I know about this before?"

"Donal be swearing me to secrecy, m'lord . . . on the soul of me mother. He be ashamed of how far he be fallen and dinna' want ye to know. He say one day it'll all come right, and I be thinking mayhap this be that day."

"As ever, Osbert, you be thinking rightly. Any chance you could find him and bring him here straightaway?"

"That I could, sir," Osbert smiles broadly as he rises to go in search of his friend.

"And on your way," I add, "stop by the kitchen and find all the spare food you can lay your hands on to take to those people."

When he's gone, Letty and Nona gather up the remains of our meal and leave to take things back to the kitchen. As the door closes behind them, Gwen turns to me, "There's just one more thing, my dear, that I'm afraid we don't know how to solve." I look at her quizzically. "The library. I don't know how you can protect it once we've left."

"I've been giving that some thought," I reply. "One possibility is to simply pack everything up in broad daylight and take it to the monastery for safekeeping. I'd tell John I'm removing a thorn in his side and giving him back the room."

Mother looks doubtful. "That seems risky, Alfred. It could compromise the rest of our plans."

"I agree. And I think there's a better way. We'll take the most valuable volumes with us – the ones that are irreplaceable – packed in the bottom of our trunks. Then I'll lock and bar the door from the inside. To anyone passing by, it will look no different than it has for the past year."

"But how will you get out?" Gwen sounds fearful.

"Magic, my dear," I grin.

"Seriously, Alfred." Her no-nonsense tone.

"Very well. Have you ever looked carefully at that room?"

"It's just a room, isn't it? But with shelves lining the walls."

"Think about it for a moment. It's entirely an interior room – not a single window. The only access is through the door to the corridor – and that door is far thicker and sturdier than any other in the castle. The hinges are enormous . . . and they're on the inside, so they can't be accessed from the corridor. That pole that sits on the hinge side of the door inside the room . . . the one that always holds a replica of the king's banner? It's actually anchored to the wall and pivots down to become an iron bar for the door. That's why the shelves just beside it aren't flush to the wall.

"That room was specially built as a strong room for the king. Originally, it housed the Treasury, but it was always intended as a place where the king could be safe from imminent danger. Grandfather chose it for the library because it's completely surrounded by stone and as safe as possible from a fire in any other part of the castle."

The ladies are sitting in rapt attention. Clearly, not even my mother knew the library's secrets.

"You still haven't told us how you'll get out," says Gwen.

"That's where the magic comes in," I tease her.

"Seriously, Alfred," she says. This time her exasperation is more tempered.

"Very well, but you must never breathe a word of this to anyone. Just inside the fireplace – above the level of the mantle, so it's not visible unless you actually stick your head in there – is a loose stone. Removing it reveals a lever that releases the wooden panel to the right of the fireplace. Inside is a spiral stone staircase that leads up and down from that level, along the side of the chimney.

"At the top, it exits into the king's bed chamber. At the bottom, it comes out at the back of an undercroft where the steward stores candles, spare buckets and cleaning brushes, extra kitchen utensils . . . all sorts of household odds and ends.

"If the king is threatened, he can escape from his bed chamber and move unseen to the strong room until the threat is past. There's a tradition that a set of servants' clothes is kept in the alcove off the staircase at the library level. If the threat is great, the king can change into those clothes and emerge into the undercroft disguised as a servant – and from there make his escape."

"I had no idea!" says Mother in astonishment.

"I don't even know if Father knew, though I'm sure he must have. The passage hasn't been used since before Grandfather's time. His father showed it to him . . . and he showed it to me one day when he was teaching me about the history of the castle."

"Where is the access in the king's bed chamber?" asks my mother.

"Once again, the wooden panel to the right of the fireplace. Those panels were fitted in both rooms by a master craftsman, with all the mechanisms hidden from view."

"Do you think the rest of the volumes will be safe?" asks Gwen.

"For a time. We can get the rest out, though, by the same route. I'll speak to André. Whenever his monks deliver a wagon-load of produce to the kitchens, they can return with a wagon-load of books. They can use the secret stairway to remove the contents from the library – and no one will think twice about a wagon being loaded from an undercroft near the kitchen. I think it will work. In any event, I can't think of another solution."

"How likely is it John knows about the passage?" Gwen asks.

"I'm pretty certain he doesn't."

"How can you be so sure?" from my mother.

"I think if he knew about it, he'd use it to smuggle his women in and out of his bed chamber. You see, he doesn't have a regular mistress." The door opens, and Letty and Nona return. "So when he's in the mood for an evening romp, he has to send for a woman. He puts his squire through an elaborate charade to get them in and out in complete secrecy."

"We be talking about the king's whores?" asks Nona. All eyes turn to her.

"I suppose we are," laughs Mother.

Nona goes on. "See, m'lady, the king thinks it be a big secret. I think he wants to pretend he's loyal to the queen. But all the servants know."

"His poor squire," Letty picks up the thread. "The king threatens to throw him into the dungeon if anyone be seeing one of his harlots coming or going."

"Aye," says Nona. "So when the king wants a woman, the squire puts it about, and we stay out of sight. That way the squire can say in truth that no one saw them in the corridors."

I chuckle. "And the woman can corroborate his truthfulness."

Nona looks at me questioningly. "I dinna' know what 'cor' . . . 'cobor' . . ."

"Corroborate," I help her out.

"That," she continues. "I dinna' know what that means, but the lady . . . though she be *no* lady, ma'am," with a glance to my mother, "she can say she be seeing no one either, so the king believes them and the squire stays out of the dungeon."

Mother and Gwen both laugh softly. "My poor deluded son." Mother shakes her head. "So self-centered he can't see what's going on around him. But I *am* impressed, Nona, with how the servants take care of each other. I can worry just a bit less about their future."

Two hours pass before Osbert returns with Donal. The ladies have gone about their business, and I'm surveying our apartment thinking about how to choose what to leave behind. Donal is thinner than I've ever seen him and looks older, though he's of an age with Osbert. I understand now why they've been so long. Osbert has helped him to get cleaned up and has found him some decent clothes. Donal bows deeply.

"There's no need for that, Donal." I hold out my arms to embrace my father's loyal servant.

"I sorry we be so long, m'lord," he says, "but I not be coming into yer presence in the state I were in."

"It's I who should be sorry, Donal. I had no idea about your situation. We're going to right that wrong from this moment forward. Now, I presume Osbert's told you what we're doing?"

"Aye, m'lord," Donal replies. "And I be honored to serve yer lordship and m'lady Alice again."

"It seems to me the first order of business is to get you some food. And then, if you can put up with sharing quarters with this character," I clap Osbert on the shoulder, "for a few days, you'll be a most welcome addition to our little family."

The next day, we're all surprised when, in midafternoon, two carriages accompanied by two men on horseback, arrive in the courtyard. Engrossed in preparations for our move, I'd forgotten my invitation to Phillip to stop here on his way to visit Addiena's family. Nevertheless, I'm delighted to see him. Gwen summons the steward and lodgings are quickly arranged while the driver and Phillip's squire attend to the horses and carriages.

The dowager – Lady Cecily – is along for the journey as well. "I had no intention of sitting all alone at home like an old lady," she tells us. "Why should the young people have all the fun?"

Phillip rolls his eyes. As we walk up the steps together, I comment, "I'm surprised she agreed to go to the Peaks."

"Agreed? There was no stopping her. Once I mentioned the idea of a journey, she took over the planning entirely. I think it gives her a sense of usefulness. Addiena and I both learned long ago when to just get out of the way and let her do things," he chuckles.

"When you get settled in, come to our rooms and we'll go to the tavern. We're in Rupert's old apartment now. You remember where it is?"

"I do, my friend. I'll be there within the hour. Some ale would go down very nicely after a long day on the road."

Walking to the town – out of earshot of anyone who might be eavesdropping – I ask him, "Can you stay tomorrow night as well?"

"I was hoping that was what you had in mind. A rest and some play with your children would be good for mine."

"Good. Then tomorrow morning, we'll go for a ride . . . perhaps to our old lodge. I have much to tell you that shouldn't be overheard."

In the market square, a crowd has gathered to listen to one of the itinerant priests rail on about sin. Phillip shakes his head. "It seems they're everywhere these days. There's one who's become almost a permanent fixture in Great Woolston. The church priest keeps running him off, but after a few days spreading his poison in the nearby villages, he turns up again. Somehow he always manages to be there on market day, when he can draw the biggest crowd." We stick to the edge of the square, finding our way to the tavern while avoiding the crowd.

Conversation is as easy as if we were just resuming from yesterday, so well do we know each other after all this time. There's much to catch up on, even before we speak of more serious matters tomorrow. We're halfway through our second round when the usual hubbub of the tavern goes suddenly silent. I turn in my seat to see John marching across the room, accompanied by two of the King's Own Guard. He stops at our table.

"Thorssen," he barks.

Phillip bows and says simply, "Your Grace."

"I'm told you and your family are lodging at the castle."

"Alfred was kind enough to permit us to break our journey here, Your Grace. Our children haven't seen each other in over a year, and they were keen to have some time together again. We'll be on our way the day after tomorrow."

"See that you are," he orders. Turning to leave, he seems to think of something else and turns back to us. "What are you two up to here?"

As quick-witted as ever, Phillip answers immediately, "Trying to drink the tavern dry, Sire."

Just at that moment, the ladies arrive to join us for supper. "And we, sir," pronounces Lady Cecily, "are here to see they get safely home after they do. Will you be joining them in their revelry? We'd be happy to see you home as well."

John turns to the new arrivals. "I have better things to do . . . and no need of a gaggle of women to look after me. Good day, Lady Thorssen." And with that, he's gone.

The room remains utterly silent until it's certain the king won't return. Then a rousing cheer goes up for Lady Cecily. She acknowledges the plaudits with a brief nod of her head and plants herself at the table next to Phillip. The innkeeper appears with a glass of wine. "For you, m'lady. On the house. Well done."

When he leaves, she says, "It seems the people also know their king is an idiot." Seeing the looks on our faces, she adds, "Oh, don't look so shocked. When you're my age, you can speak your mind and no one cares."

"Mother, you've been speaking your mind since you uttered your first word," laughs Phillip.

"Why, thank you, Son. That's the nicest compliment I've received in quite a long time. Now what shall we have for supper?"

The rest of the evening is reminiscent of times past when my mates were at court and we often came to town to drink and dine and mingle with the people. Though we don't succeed in emptying the innkeeper's casks, we *are* the last to leave, making our way home by the light of a moon waxing full.

The next morning, Phillip and I make straight for the rundown hut in the woods, where I tell him everything about my conversation with the Lakes king. "When you speak to the King of Peaks, Phillip, hold nothing back. This isn't a mission of diplomacy but of complete candor. The more they know, the better they can help each other . . . and us."

"I thought that's what you'd want."

Then I tell him about the border checks. "I don't know yet if this is some new regulation everywhere, or if the one we encountered was just for my benefit . . . a way for John to remind me that he watches my every move."

"We'll be careful," he says, then adds, "unless Mother decides to give them all a tongue-lashing."

I tell him about my own mother's performance, and he laughs out loud. "*Your* mother? The very proper and demure Lady Alice? I do wish I could have seen that."

He brings me up to date on the most recent gathering of the lords. They still haven't devised the best way to counteract the havoc John is wreaking, but they aren't giving up.

Finally, I tell him about our own plans. "So by the time you return, we should be in residence at the country manor."

He smiles broadly and claps me on the shoulder. "I'm glad to hear it. We've all been hoping you'd get yourself and your family away from here," he says, then adds quickly, in case he may have offended me, "Oh, don't misunderstand. All the lords appreciate what you've tried to do. But we've come to the conclusion that it simply isn't possible in the current circumstances, so we're more concerned now with your being safely out of harm's way."

"Thank you for that, Phillip. With Devereux's concurrence and now yours, I'm no longer tempted even to ask myself if I'm doing the right thing."

They depart the next day, much to the chagrin of the children in both families, who'd been thinking about days and days of playing together. We adults get back to the business of preparing to move. Three days later, my mother and the children leave for the country, Osbert going with them as planned.

While Donal, Nona, and Letty finish the packing, Gwen and I pay a visit to the monastery. Gwen wants to spend some time with Brother Adam, making sure he has what he needs for the kennel. It will be more difficult to visit here from the greater distance of the manor.

I go straight to André's study to talk with him about the plans to secure the remainder of the library. I've prepared it as best I can and have actually brought a few of the more valuable volumes with me.

"I know the passage whereof you speak, Alfred. It's another of those secrets passed quietly from abbot to abbot and never spoken of."

"How can that be?" I ask, truly puzzled. "The next abbot isn't known until weeks or months after his predecessor's death."

André smiles kindly. "That, too, is a secret of which we never speak."

I shake my head in amazement and return to the topic at hand. "There are still stacks of torches in the alcoves of each level . . . and troughs of sand for dousing them. I've no idea how old those torches are. But I've discovered they only need a bit of priming with some fresh oil to get them going again. So I've placed a jug of oil at both the undercroft and library levels. I know that means there's a risk of fire if a spark should get loose, but it's the only solution I could think of. Your brothers will simply have to take great care."

"Perhaps the brothers will carry their own oil in a small flask. We'll sort that out after their first trip . . . once they know better what things are like."

"Of course," I reply. "The wall brackets for the torches are still intact on each level, so I'd recommend they leave a torch burning at the bottom while they make their trips up to the library. The light won't be noticeable if the undercroft entrance is closed. It's darker than deepest hell in that stairwell if the torch goes out."

"I can only imagine," laughs André. "I gather you've experimented?"

"Only once. That was enough," I chuckle. "I don't know if a man's eyes would ever adjust to that kind of blackness. But your brothers should know – in case they have to face that situation – that they can find their way by hugging the outer wall – where the steps are broadest and a man is less likely to lose his footing – and counting the steps. There are thirty-one of them down to the undercroft. I make myself count every time – up or down – even if the torch seems bright and steady."

"Don't fret, Alfred," André says kindly. "We'll protect your treasure and your grandfather's legacy against all harm."

"I haven't sufficient words to thank you, André."

"Be safe and be happy, my son. That is thanks enough."

"There's one other thing that's been troubling me."

"And what might that be?"

"I've only just begun my lessons with Brother Eustace, but I don't want to abandon that project."

"Say no more, Alfred," he replies. "In a week or two – after you're settled in at the manor – I'll send Brother Eustace to you. Perhaps you'd be good enough to let him return to our fold for a week or so here and there, but otherwise he's at your disposal until you've mastered what you want to learn."

"I promise I'll find some way to repay you, André."

"There's no need. Ours is a life of service. And there's no finer reward than to know that we're contributing to a greater good."

The packing is almost finished. Donal and I discuss how to load the wagon. "My strongbox first," I tell him. "That way it should be well-hidden by the other trunks."

"Me and Osbert did some talking about that, m'lord. We be thinking mayhap it be better if ye leave the strongbox here. Ye can put the stuff from it in the bottom of this last trunk. Then I be putting yer boots and extra blankets and such-like on top and no one be knowing what be in the bottom. See, we be thinking if yer strongbox still be here, then it look like ye be coming back. Ye can get a new strongbox in the country."

"And it will be less weight in the wagon as well," I remark. "Good thinking, Donal. I'll transfer the items tonight, and you can finish that trunk tomorrow."

Going through our bed chamber to the sitting room, I overhear Gwen and Letty also dealing with the last of the packing. "Where are my cloaks?" asks Gwen.

"Just here, ma'am. Right on top of this trunk. I thought we'd be leaving your oldest one here and take the others."

"Oh, Letty, I can't bear to part with that one. My mother had it made especially for my marriage. It's far too precious to me. Let's leave the brown one instead."

"Of course, m'lady. Whatever you want. That one was always my favorite on you. I think Lord Alfred be liking it, too. I just thought since you don't wear it much anymore . . ."

"I don't wear it much because I don't want to wear it out."

"That make good sense, m'lady. Mayhap you give it to Miss Juliana one day."

"Perhaps, Letty . . . perhaps."

The next morning, all seems to be in readiness. Donal will load the wagon today, and we'll be away at daybreak tomorrow. My morning ride is nostalgic. I visit the place where my father's accident occurred. I spend a long time in the rundown hut that has been so much a part of my life. I ride to the hidden paddock beside the stream. I want to make sure the opening is still clear so the animals can shelter there from storms. I remember showing it to Amelia and listening to the skylarks high above and wonder if or when I'll see her again.

Finally, I go to the church and visit the tombs of my father and grandfather. As I ponder what they meant to me, a kind of peace settles over me, as if they're somehow giving their approval. The bishop must have been there all along, but stayed in the shadows. As I start for the door, he says softly, "God go with you, Lord Alfred." I smile to myself and step through the church door into the next chapter of my life.

I would be a very rich man indeed if I had a coin for every time over the past months I've asked myself why I waited so long to move to the country. The children are thriving. Gwen and Mother are happier than I've seen either of them in a long time. Donal has regained his fitness and his sense of purpose. And it seems Rupert is as glad of my company as I am of his.

"I can't tell you how pleased I am you've come," Catherine took me aside shortly after we arrived. "Edward's decision to leave us the manor was truly inspired. Rupert's immersed himself in managing the estate . . . he'd have been completely lost without something to do. The estate manager is a genial sort who shows him the ropes and doesn't fret about what Rupert wants to do himself."

"I've no doubt my uncle makes it easy for the estate manager as well, Aunt Catherine."

"Be that as it may . . . and even though he's busy and seems happy . . . I know he misses the company of a man his equal."

Thus begins my education on the management of a noble estate. Rupert teaches me all he's learned about flocks and farms and forests. "The estate really does make a nice profit each year," he says, "despite the fact that we're more generous than many with our tenants and staff."

"I remember always noticing that the people here seem happy and content."

"Actually, I've become convinced that's the very reason we're so successful. They get something as well out of their hard work. It isn't just drudgery for our benefit."

The tenants' rent is modest. They get to keep the entire produce of their kitchen gardens – for their own consumption, to trade with their neighbors, or even to sell in the market if they have a surplus. We share the profit from the sale of our wool – ten percent is always set aside to be divided among the herdsmen. And every lambing season, each herdsman is given one lamb. Some sell or butcher their lambs. Others have raised them and started to build their own small flocks. Those flocks run with our own, and we sell their wool along with ours, to get the best prices, but the herdsman receives all the profit from his own fleeces.

Our farmers share in the profit from the crops. The senior stablemen are allowed to keep a horse of their own if they wish. The house, kitchen, and garden staff all have one afternoon each week to do as they please. And once a year, there's a hunt organized in which all the local population are invited to participate, keeping whatever game they may have snared.

I don't recall that we've ever had to dismiss a servant or evict a tenant. Many of our tenants have been here for three generations or more. In some ways, it seems a model for how the kingdom should be run.

My language lessons progress. Brother Eustace is a patient teacher – which is fortunate because I'm an impatient learner, eager to reach the point where I can speak with Egon in his language as comfortably as he speaks mine. I have a new appreciation for the challenges Gundrea faced in learning our tongue. "Why can't I master this?" I complain to Eustace one day, when I'm having particular difficulties with past tense. "I don't remember it being this hard when I learned Latin as a boy."

"Perhaps," Eustace says kindly, "it's not a failing on your part but simply that we all learn more easily as children."

The shearing is complete, and we're all going to Great Woolston for the annual wool market. Rupert and the estate manager have been pondering their strategy if prices are low, as we fully expect them to be. Get what we can and sell everything or hold something back for next year? The ladies want to visit the dressmaker and shop for ribbons and laces.

Wandering through the market stalls after the wool auction, I'm surprised to discover a strange little man selling books. He doesn't have many – just one box – but I look through all of them. There are a couple of Roman histories – one about Julius Caesar, another telling the story of Romulus and Remus. A biography of Cicero. Two books of poetry by unknown authors. The epic saga of the Kingdom Across the Southern Sea. A treatise on mathematics, rather worn and with several pages missing. And then I find a treasure. Lifting it from the box, I examine it in great detail, inside and out.

"Dinna' know what ye be interested in that 'un fer, m'lord," says the bookseller.

"Where did you get this?" I ask him.

"The man who give it to me . . . he been cleaning out a great house after the owner died. Found it there. He give it to me 'cause he say it be worthless. Must be some kind of code or som'at like that. Ye canna' read it. It not be all proper letters and such."

"Ah, but I think I know someone who can read it." He looks at me curiously. "If this is what I think it is, it's written in Greek, and it's a play, meant to be performed in one of the ancient amphitheaters."

"If ye say so, sir," he says.

"I'm certain enough I'd like to buy it from you." I reach into my purse and hand him a silver coin.

"I canna' take that much from ye, m'lord," he says apologetically. "Ye canna' be sure it not be worthless like I been told."

"I'm willing to take the chance, my good man," I reassure him. "Consider this your lucky day." No doubt this is the most he's ever been paid for a single book.

Approaching the dressmaker's shop, Gwen remarks on a group of people in the square. An itinerant priest is holding forth to any who will listen, and the crowd seems to be slowly growing. My inclination is to steer our little party away, but Gwen and Catherine are adamant. "We've heard so much about these priests," says my aunt. "It seems impossible that what we've heard could be true. Let's just listen for a bit."

So we edge closer, taking care to stay on the fringes and not become engulfed in the crowd. The priest is just hitting his stride with the exhortations I've heard far too often.

"You know in your hearts," he says, "that God is saddened by your sin. That is why He has sent these trials upon you. Like a good father, He must discipline His children when they go astray.

"Repent! Give up your sinful ways! Beg God's forgiveness, and He will take you back to His bosom and reward you with all manner of good things in life. Cast the heathen and non-believers out from your midst! Give up your dancing and singing! Be sober and be modest of dress!"

And then his message takes an unexpected turn. He pauses and drops his voice from its fever pitch. "There is one among you today who may bring more misery upon you. A man selling books." His voice starts to rise again. "Give up your reading of books, for there is only one true book and that is the Bible. There is only one truth and that is God's truth, and the Bible is God's truth writ for mankind. All else is heresy!"

He lowers his voice again. "But this man selling books is more dangerous than you know, for he has books written by non-believers. You must shun such things! Cast him out from your midst! Cast his heresy out with him!" The fever pitch is back.

And I've heard enough. "Donal, take the ladies to the dressmaker's shop. Stay with them there until I come to fetch you. The rest of you come with me."

We return to the bookseller's stall. "Quick, my good man, grab your wares and go with Osbert here to our wagon. The crowd is about to get ugly, and I think *you* will be their target."

The bookseller looks confused, but does as I say. "Osbert, hide him and his books under the wool sacks in the wagon. Then move away to a safe distance so as not to draw attention to the hiding place, but watch that he stays safe. Rupert and I will go find the sheriff or someone to disperse the crowd."

"Rolly, go with them," Rupert tells his squire. "Help make sure he's well hidden."

The three of them scurry off toward the wagon. Just in time, for the priest has finished and the crowd is milling around. At first, it seems they might disperse, but a couple of rough-looking men start to whip them into a frenzy. One carries a truncheon of some sort; the other picks up a loose cobble from the square. "Let's go get him," shouts the one with the truncheon, as he starts to lead people through the market stalls. They seem only too happy to follow.

I've no idea where to find a sheriff or magistrate so we head toward what looks like it might be a meeting hall for the town. There's no one there. By now the crowd has found the bookseller's stall empty and have started tearing it down, haranguing anyone nearby with questions about where he might have gone. When no one seems to know, they start smashing up nearby stalls, throwing the wares onto the ground, ripping down the stall structures. The sellers initially try to protect their property, but soon decide to flee rather than face the raging mob.

The crowd is now completely out of control. We can do nothing on foot. "Let's go get the horses," Rupert suggests.

Faced with men on horseback, the more timid – and the wiser – of the crowd start to disperse. The ringleaders are still wreaking destruction, shouting all the while, "Where's the heretic? Who's hiding him?" We ride back and forth through what's left of the crowd, our daggers drawn, and a few more people begin to wander away. Just when I think we're going to have to confront the most violent ones ourselves, two more men on horseback arrive, one clearly the sheriff. "Grogan!" he shouts at the top of his lungs, trying to be heard over the din. "Drop that truncheon now!"

Surprised, the man with the truncheon pauses and turns to see the sheriff with sword drawn, pointed in his direction. "Now the rest of you," the sheriff shouts. "Stop this instant or I'll have every one of you in chains for a month!"

As the others realize what's happening, they begin to slow their crazed assault on whatever happens to be in front of them. The man accompanying the sheriff, who's also drawn his sword, menaces anyone who isn't showing signs of cooperating. The sheriff turns to us. "Are you two part of this mob?"

"Most definitely not," replies Rupert. "We were doing what little we could to try to break it up." By now, we've sheathed our daggers.

The sheriff looks at Rupert, studying his face. "I've seen you before. You're from the royal manor, right?"

"That's right," answers Rupert.

"Lord Rupert, Prince of the Realm," I supply.

"And him?" asks the sheriff, glancing in my direction.

"My nephew, Lord Alfred, who now lives on the estate."

The sheriff says nothing for several moments. "Very well. Be on your way. I'll deal with these hooligans."

I want to ask what punishment they'll receive, but think better of it. We ride out to the wagon. Osbert and Rolly come up to join us and help the bookseller out of his hiding place. They've all heard the commotion in the market, and the bookseller looks pale and shaken.

"I be grateful, m'lord," he says, bowing repeatedly. "I never be scared like this before."

"I'm afraid, my good man," I tell him, "this place will be dangerous to you for some time to come. My advice is to take your wares to other markets and stay far away from here until the townspeople have had time to forget what happened today."

"I be doing that, m'lord," he keeps bowing for a bit, then slings his box onto his back like a pack and makes for the road away from town. I fear for him no matter where he goes. If these itinerant priests can inflame people so, how can a man like this ever find a safe place to sell his meager wares?

Rupert interrupts my thoughts. "Go get the ladies, Alfred. Osbert and Rolly can bring the carriage round."

At the dressmaker's shop, I find a very nervous Donal and three women who seem more concerned with their purchases. "Donal wouldn't let us near the door," laughs Gwen, "so there was nothing for it but to get on with our selections."

"But we heard all the commotion," adds Catherine. "You must tell us everything that happened." Which I do as we make our way back to where the wagon and carriage await.

"In you go, ladies," says Rupert. Osbert is already perched in the driver's seat of the carriage with Rolly beside him; Donal hops up to drive the wagon. As I mount Sirius, Rupert adds, "Let's go home."

I had thought to feel isolated living in the country – out of touch with events in the rest of the kingdom – almost certain that the chronicle I had begun would remain forever unfinished. Knowing we were well away from prying ears, I broached the topic over supper one night, shortly after our arrival. To my surprise, everyone was overjoyed to learn that somewhere the real truth of what was happening was being recorded. "I'd like to help in whatever way I can," Rupert said.

"The problem, of course," I replied, "lies in knowing what to write, now that I'm no longer observing events at the castle firsthand."

"And why should that be a problem?" asked Mother.

Thinking I'd already explained, I was at a loss for an answer.

"You have friends in the great estates the length and breadth of the kingdom," she continued. "Correspond with them. They'll know what's happening in other parts of the realm."

"In other circumstances, you'd be right, Mother, but all of us have to assume that whatever we write will be read by John's spies." My mother simply sat there, primly sipping her wine. And then it dawned on me. "You, on the other hand . . ."

Her face broke into the broadest smile I think I've ever seen. "I was wondering how long it would take you to figure that out." And then she told the others how she had threatened John in order to ensure the privacy of her personal correspondence.

Thus it was that my mother became our conduit to the rest of the kingdom. She wasted no time establishing a regular correspondence with each of the lords. Her first letters, addressed to the lady of each estate, put things in motion.

Her letters are mostly addressed to the ladies and begin with a few sentences of feminine interests before switching quickly to matters of the business of the kingdom. The replies appear on the outside to come from the ladies and bear the lady's seal, though most of the contents come directly from the lord, with news for Rupert and me. From time to time, she might write to a lord directly, for variety, as a dowager queen would, and receive a direct reply in return. My mates and I stay in touch on important things through postscripts added to Mother's correspondence, though we also exchange the innocuous letters, suitable for spies' eyes, that would be conspicuous by their absence.

And so I embark on the next installment of my history.

The Second Year

As the second year of John's reign began conditions throughout the kingdom continued to deteriorate Increasingly the kings narrow choices on where to focus his attention were taking a toll on both people and places Anyone traveling within the borders of the realm remarked on the deterioration of roads and bridges It became increasingly difficult to get goods to market though farmers herdsmen and traders had no choice but to try There were only two areas in which any funds from the Treasury were expended those being collection of taxes and equipping and feeding the large army that continued to grow month by month By the middle of the second year when there were no more volunteers for either the knighthood or the growing force of infantry and bowmen the king began a program of conscription taking young men away from the farms the flocks and the trades It being impossible to breed in such a short period of time sufficient horses of the type usually chosen for knights ordinary farm animals were bought at cheap prices or confiscated and inferior animals were acquired for the lowest possible cost from abroad The lords refused to accept the paltry sums offered by the Crown for their well bred stock and the Crown refused to pay what the animals were truly worth In any event the lords would have been unable to supply horses sufficient to the needs of the expanded knighthood The result was that knights had inferior mounts and farmers and traders were deprived of their means of cultivation and transportation It appeared the king had no understanding or appreciation for what effect this would have on the availability of food or goods within the realm or on the lives of the people To observers including this chronicler it was obvious he did not care In and around the larger towns the decline in prosperity saw a growth in the number of people whose circumstances gave them no choice but to join the communities living in shoddy shacks and leantos that had become a fixture on the fringes of every town With the passing of months the crowded conditions in these communities grew worse and the people became more and more disheartened as food became increasingly scarce At the port the gangs of dockmen completely took over the running of everything The mayor sheriff and magistrate all left town when they could no longer maintain law and order Each gang claimed a specific patch of territory and required the shop tavern and brothel owners in their district to pay for protection from rival gangs Anyone who failed to pay was fair game for beating robbery or worse from any or all of the gangs Each gang also controlled a section of the docks and extorted payment from ship captains for docking privileges loading and unloading It was not long before the number of captains willing to sail into our port was significantly reduced with the predictable effect on the availability of goods and the livelihood of the traders

Despite the increasingly dangerous conditions in the port town King John continued to insist that the Queen and his children maintain their household there The dowager queen attempted to visit her daughter in law and grandchildren and was rebuffed the queen claiming that it was too dangerous despite the fact that four members of the Kings Own Guard maintained a presence in the house The Queen and her children it seems never venture beyond the garden walls and never receive any visitors Great concern has grown among the royal family and the hereditary lords relative to both the safety and the education of the heir Lord Bauldry as the only hereditary lord remaining on the nominal Council attempted to raise this concern to the king whose reply pointedly instructed him that matters of the heirs welfare present or future were the sole concern of the king and that Bauldry would do well to mind his own business The itinerant priests who first appeared at the end of the preceding year are a continued presence The king could have had them rounded up and expelled from the country had he taken an interest but he paid no attention to the problem Though local clergy attempted to drive them away their persistence was unassailable Their message never wavered and had a growing appeal particularly to those forced to live in the shack villages And it became increasingly common for them to incite a crowd to some sort of violence In Great Woolston a mob rampaged through the market when an itinerant branded a bookseller as a heretic More often the anger is directed at immigrants After a riot against immigrants in Abbeville Market the king decided to take action Once again his peculiar inability to link cause and effect led him to the conclusion that the immigrants were the problem and that the solution was to simply prevent immigration The border checkpoints and searches that had begun earlier in the year became permanent military camps each occupied by a minimum of two troops of knights and every border crossing was guarded by such an outpost Anyone wishing to enter our kingdom had to show proof of their business here Traders with goods bound for the port had all their goods thoroughly searched and were given a token that allowed them passage to the port and back If they were found in any other part of the kingdom or if their business took longer than someone deemed necessary or if they failed to leave by the same route they entered the new law permitted them to be immediately thrown into prison Wagons were even searched as the traders left the kingdom though to what purpose remains a mystery It is unclear if any smuggling of immigrants was ever discovered through these draconian measures It is clear beyond doubt however what impact this had on trade and on passage of ordinary people who had previously been accustomed to free travel **C**ontrolling the border now involved no less than nine troops of knights two or more at each border crossing and one at the north end of the port ferry **T**he western garrison was still manned by three troops and a troop continued to be assigned to guard the reservoir **P**atrols accompanying the tax collectors were a constant presence **T**here was almost nowhere one could go without being in the presence of armed men **T**he lords still refrained from taking any action against the king **L**ord Devereux expressed their collective view when he wrote

> **T**hough the kings neglect of what should be his daily concern for the realm and its people is appalling to us all he has as yet done nothing so egregious as to make action on our part defensible in the context of our laws and the eyes of the world at large **T**hat does not mean however that we are not constantly on watch and constantly evaluating our options

Though the shearing season produced the usual quantities of raw wool there were fewer buyers and lower prices than anyone had seen in living memory **T**he small mill created by the merchants to manufacture woolen cloth within the kingdom bought less than last year its managers fearful that there would not be enough buyers for their finished goods **B**oth the wool merchants and the herdsmen were left with the surplus in their storehouses **T**he slowing of production at the woolen mill resulted in yet more people being displaced from their work **I**t was not a great number of people but even one is one too many in the current circumstances

·   ·   ·   ·   ·

In late summer Mother receives a letter from Lady Ernle. Tensions run high on our side of the border, Lord Ernle reports, but there seems to be no response from the lords of the Territories. He reports little else of note. The interesting part of this correspondence is that, wrapped inside Lady Ernle's letter is a separate letter addressed to me.

Alfred,

I trust this finds you and your family continuing to thrive in the country. I've asked my mother to include this letter to you for I wished you to hear this news from no one but me. I have left the knighthood.

My troops were – and still are, I presume – under orders to hunt down the people who are bypassing the border controls and making their way into our kingdom. Hunt them down, round them up, and take them to the border camp where they're sent back from whence they came.

This is not what I joined the knighthood for, Alfred. There's no honor in hunting down like animals unfortunate people who are merely trying to find a better life for themselves. I found I could no longer do it nor could I order my men to do so. And so I resigned my post and took my retirement.

I'm sorry to disappoint you, Alfred. It's not what we had planned. But I felt it was the only honorable course available to me, and Father agreed. My greatest hope is that you'll understand my motivation and my actions.

Now that I'm at last a gentleman farmer, perhaps you and your family will visit us soon. Tamasine joins me in this invitation and sends her greetings to Gwen, Lady Alice, and Lady Catherine.

Samuel

Over supper, I share the news. Rupert shakes his head sadly. "We were – we should be – a better society – a better people – a better kingdom than this. I'm sad for Samuel that his retirement came in such a manner."

"As am I," I say. "Mother, can you write to Lady Ernle straightaway? I'd like to include a note to Samuel."

"Of course, Alfred."

"A visit with the whole family would be quite an undertaking," says Gwen, "especially if the roads are as bad as we've heard . . . and with Richard and Avelina planning to visit at harvest time. But maybe you should try to make the journey alone, Alfred. Wouldn't that be even better for Samuel than a letter?"

"She's right, you know," says Mother.

I take Gwen's hand and give it a squeeze. "When is she not?" Then turning to Rupert, "If you can spare me, Uncle, I'd like to make the trip."

"What say you, everyone?" asks Rupert. "Can we manage to muddle through for a couple of weeks without this one's august presence?" He grins. Rupert's sense of humor remains intact despite everything that's happening around us.

The roads are indeed in serious disrepair. Passable, of course, for two men on horseback, who can avoid the deepest ruts. But there's no doubt they would pose a challenge in places to a loaded wagon. As we near the garrison and Ernle Manor, however, there's a vast improvement . . . roads equal to the best I've ever seen. I mention it to Samuel as he shows me around the farm. "I rather think I see your fine hand in this."

He chuckles. "Of course! I assigned my men properly, not only to their drills, but also to maintaining the garrison and the roads we'd need to use if we were ever called to action." He pauses, then adds a bit sadly. "At least, that is, until the orders to round up immigrants came down."

"Thankfully, you don't have to worry about that any longer." I clap him on the shoulder. "Don't give it another minute's thought. Your father was right – you took the honorable course. Neither of us can ask any more than that from the other." I watch him visibly relax.

"I was hoping you'd see it that way, Alfred. We've been through too much together to have something like this get in the way."

The week passes swiftly. Samuel seems happy, and there's no doubt that Tamasine is pleased to have him always at home. Ronan Grai continues to reside in the small cottage that was fitted out for him and to help Samuel with the farm. He shares the family's supper most evenings.

"Father's offered Ronan a larger cottage on the manor grounds," Samuel says one evening over supper.

I look at Ronan. "That he has, sir," Ronan replies. "But my lodgings here are quite sufficient to my needs. And I've grown rather fond of this family."

"What he's not telling you, Alfred," Samuel continues with a gleam in his eye, "is that he may soon be taking a wife. That is, if he ever gets up the courage to ask her."

"That's right," chimes in Tamasine. "The eldest daughter of one of Papa Ernle's tenants has been widowed these last five years, and it seems she and Ronan have taken quite a liking to each other."

Ronan looks rather embarrassed. "That's excellent news!" I tell him. "When are you planning to propose to the lady?"

"She's younger than me by a few years, sir, so I'm not so sure she would accept me."

"Don't let that hold you back," I tell him. "If the lady loves you, that won't matter to her at all."

"That's what I keep telling him," says Tamasine. "And I happen to know that Alienor is terribly fond of him and will say yes without hesitation when he finally gets round to asking her."

Ronan looks even more distressed. "Don't let them embarrass you, Sir Ronan," I say. "You propose to Miss Alienor whenever you think it's the right time. But I must say, I hope Tamasine is right and that you two will be very happy together."

"Thank you, Lord Alfred."

"It sounds to me like you might then be in need of the larger cottage."

"Oh, I'm not so sure about that. We're both of an age that we're not likely to be having children, so my little home is probably good enough for us . . . and keeps us close by the people we care about." Samuel does indeed have a good friend in Ronan. I'm happy for that.

One day Samuel and I ride to the manor house to spend time with his father. Osbert comes along to see Lord Ernle's squire. These two squires – Osbert, who's taken care of me since my eighteenth birthday, and Thomas, who took care of me when I returned from captivity and most needed taking care of – have become fast friends, though they rarely get to visit these days.

As we walk in the garden after the midday meal, Lord Ernle waxes eloquent about his fears for the kingdom. "We have our plans, Alfred," he says, referring to the lords' responsibilities. "But we don't think we should act until there's no doubt the people will be with us."

"I agree, sir, and so would have my father. The lords and the people must be united for any action against the king to succeed. It's just that I find it so painful to watch what's happening in the meantime. I can't even contemplate what the aftermath might be like."

"Prepare yourself, Alfred," Ernle says. "You'll be needed. And I hope it's soon, before the kingdom completely disintegrates."

The sun lowering in the afternoon sky is the signal that it's time we should be leaving. Samuel goes in search of a groom to saddle our horses. Walking beside me toward the stable, Lord Ernle stops for a moment. "I'm glad you came, Alfred. It's just what he needed. I tried to reassure him that his choice was the right one, but his fear that you'd be disappointed has weighed heavily on his mind."

"I certainly hope I've relieved him of that burden."

"Of that, there's no doubt. His step is lighter and his mood brighter than I've seen at any time since he retired. It pleases me greatly that the two of you have such a strong bond."

"It pleases me, too, sir. And I can't imagine anything that could ever change that." He claps me on the shoulder, and we resume our walk to the stable.

The next day, we ride to the monastery to see Prior Warin. The number of people there is surprising to me, but seems less so to Samuel. Warin is welcoming as always. "Alfred, my son!" He's as effusive as a man of his calling can muster, and his embrace is one of genuine caring for a fellow human being. "It's always such a delight to see you. Come, let me show you all the changes in our little community."

He takes us first to the monastery garden – an expanse much larger than is often seen in such enclaves – where there are paths for walking and contemplation among the plantings of flowers, shrubs, and herbs that the monks tend for cooking, for medicines, and for selling in the village market. There's a beehive of activity along the back wall. "We're turning the wall into a row of rooms for our immigrant brethren to have shelter and a place to sleep. There are more of them now than we can accommodate in our few extra cells, and the villagers no longer feel safe giving them a place to live."

"I'm rather taken aback by the number of people here," I remark. "It must be a real change from your quiet monastic life."

"It's a change, Alfred, but we have little choice. I can't send them onward with the current mood of suspicion and violence in other parts of the kingdom. And I won't send them back to the life they took such great risk to escape. So they must live the life of refugees for now, and we make accommodations to provide as best we can for them.

"It's not such a hardship. They're eager to work, especially when the fruits of their labor benefit themselves directly. As you can see, a number of them have building skills and have already completed about half of the work on their housing. We'll keep a few more lambs and calves from this year's breeding than we usually do, to augment our stock. And with the extra hands, we can expand our farms to grow more food. So we should be quite self-sufficient if we don't get too many more new arrivals."

"Are you worried about that?" asks Samuel. "I know how many came from the western Territories earlier this year, and I don't think we know yet if the conflict there has ended."

"In normal times, that would be my greatest concern," replies Warin. "But these aren't normal times. The king's border controls are so reprehensible – as you know all too well, Samuel – that fewer actually make it to us anymore. I worry now about those who manage to get across and escape the patrols but then try to fend for themselves in constant fear of being captured. They're surely doomed to misery even if they make it to a village deeper inside the kingdom. I still struggle to understand how people who were once so open-minded and welcoming could have turned so vindictive and violent."

"I'm not sure they would have," I say, "if it hadn't been for those itinerant priests. And the king, as always, can't think beyond the obvious. So the itinerants continue to wander around unchecked, preaching their poison, and things get worse instead of better."

"André has written to me of his dismay over these false priests. I'm grateful we've not yet seen them this far west."

"For your sake, Warin, I hope it stays that way. But know that they tend to spread like vermin, and somehow they seem to multiply, though no one has been able to figure out where they come from."

He takes us next to the orchards, where the new apple trees are thriving. "It looks like they're beginning to produce some fruit this year," says Warin. "Nothing ready to harvest, though, or I would give you some to sample."

"Just as well, Prior," says Samuel. "He'd just give them to his horse."

Warin chuckles. "Horses are God's creatures, too, my son."

Over the midday meal, I venture a suggestion to Warin. "Perhaps I should ask André to send Brother Eustace back to you. I'm sure you could use his language skills with so many people here."

"I won't deny the thought had occurred to me, Alfred. But after due consideration, I've decided the project you've embarked on transcends the day-to-day work we do here." No doubt sensing I'm about to contradict this line of thinking, he continues. "We've all picked up bits and pieces of their tongue over the years, and you can see for yourself that we manage well enough. Eustace simply has a gift for quickly grasping not only vocabulary and grammar, but the cadence and nuances of a language. I've come to believe that gift was given to him so you might succeed in your endeavor. Keep him by your side for now . . . and for as long as you need him."

"Then at least let me contribute some money to help you care for these people."

"I'd prefer to refuse, Alfred, but as you know, building materials aren't cheap. We'll be grateful for any donation, no matter the size or the donor."

As we prepare to mount our horses for the return journey, I take a small purse containing three gold coins from my pocket and press it into Warin's hand. "Thank you, Alfred," he says quietly, his head bowed. He won't examine the contents until after we leave, but I know how much such a sum will help with caring for his refugees. I only wish I could help them in more lasting ways.

Saying our good-byes the next morning is somewhat disconcerting – it's less certain than ever when we'll see each other again. Nevertheless, the time is upon us, and Osbert and I make our departure, promising to bring the family for a visit next year. The following day, as we near the junction with the Great Trunk Road, traveling at a leisurely pace, I tell Osbert, "Lord Ernle described the conditions in Abbéville Market, but as we're so close, I think I'd like to see for myself. What say you to an extra night on the road?"

"Be they having good ale in the tavern?"

"I seem to recall it being better than passable the last time I was there."

"Then I be thinking mayhap we find out if it still be good."

Grinning at him, I add, "And I rather think a bed at the inn might be nicer than camping."

So when we arrive at the junction, we turn our horses' heads northwest and half an hour later, notice what looks like haze on the horizon. We haven't gone much farther when we can make out three great plumes of black smoke. It looks as if parts of the town are on fire. I urge Sirius to a gallop, and Osbert quickly follows my lead.

We arrive to what can only be described as chaos in the midst of hell. Women standing in the middle of the street with babes in arms, staring in disbelief at piles of blackened rubble that used to be their homes. Young children clinging to their mothers' skirts, wailing in fear. A line of people passing buckets of water from the nearby stream to those trying to extinguish the blaze. Older lads grabbing empty buckets to run them down to the stream then rushing back to do it all over again. Men running through the streets shouting for people to help. And over it all, the roar of the flames and the thick black smoke.

The houses and shops in this street, all made of wood, crowd together. Some sharing a common wall. A few with a narrow space in between barely wide enough for a man to pass. Some, just a single story. Most two stories, with a shop below and living quarters upstairs. The fire has already consumed a row of buildings to my left, and several structures on both sides of the street are ablaze. I jump off Sirius, hand the reins to Osbert, and tell him, "Get the horses to safety then come back here and help."

Almost before my feet touch the ground, someone hands me a halberd and points toward a flaming house. "Help pull that building down. We've got to stop the fire spreading." As I join the men already attacking the burning structure, someone shouts, "Pull away from the next house . . . like this. Try to keep the embers from jumping to the next roof." Sparks fly from everything we pull down. Men with axes chop up the charred and smoldering timbers as soon as they're on the ground. The heat is intense. It takes enormous effort to stay out of the way of the flaming pieces being pulled into the street.

Just as it appears we've gotten this structure safely down, there's an explosion of flame on the roof next door as stray embers take hold of the wooden shingles and create a new conflagration. A man and woman come running out, the woman screaming "Nooooooo," the man with a tight grip on her arm, tugging her into the street. "I've got to go back," she wails.

"You can't, Mary. You'll burn."

Somehow, she manages to break free and run back into the burning building. "Maryyyyyyyyyyyyy!" the man screams.

Without even thinking about what I'm about to do, I drop my halberd, grab an axe from the man beside me, and dash in after her. Inside, it's an inferno, the bright flame and the black smoke making it almost impossible to make out where anything is. Much of the floor above is ablaze and two of the supporting beams have caught fire. "Mistress, where are you?" Is that a whimper I hear from somewhere in the back of the house? If it was, it's gone silent. "Mistress, call out so I can find you."

"Here. Help me." I head toward the sound. She's standing there, cradling something in her arms, frozen in her tracks. Dear God, please don't let it be a child. I grab her hand and tug, but she's paralyzed with fear. "Come on. We have to get out of here. Now, Mary," I shout, hoping the sound of her name will jolt her to action, but she won't budge. I drop the axe, scoop her up in my arms, and carry her toward the door. Before we reach it, there's a resounding crack as the front beam splits in two. I put her on her feet and shove her toward the door, intending to follow right behind. And just at that moment, both pieces of the beam crash to the floor, pulling the burning ceiling down with them and trapping me behind a wall of flame.

I look around for another way out. There's no other door and no windows except the one at the front. The only hope is a small corner in the back of the building where the ceiling's not yet ablaze. Dashing back toward where I'd found Mary, I start looking for the axe.

The heat is growing unbearable as the wall of fire moves closer. Even with my shirt pulled up around my mouth and nose, the heat and smoke burn my lungs and cause tears to run from my eyes, making it even harder to see. I drop to my knees, feeling around on the floor, desperate to find the axe. Another beam comes crashing down, and now my frantic searching turns to panic. God in heaven, surely it's not my fate to perish in this raging inferno? What would Osbert tell Gwen? And the children?

Just then, my hand brushes against stone. The hearth! Would its stonework be enough to protect me? I clamber in and huddle as deep inside as I can. But what if the chimney falls? That's what happened in the building next door. Do I have any other choice?

The last beam is blazing away, threatening to fall at any moment. Suddenly, there's a different sound off to the side, a rhythmic chop, chop, chop – the sound of an axe on timber. I dare to stick my head around the edge of the fireplace. A small glimpse of daylight. I have to take the chance. I run toward the small hole in the wall where someone's tugging at the timbers from the outside. I shove against the same timber and, just as the last beam comes crashing down, stumble through into safety, coughing and gasping for breath. Deep gulps of blessed fresh air. Someone shoves a cup of water into my hand. It's Osbert. "M'lord, drink. Dear God, ye give me a fright. What ye think ye be doing going in there?"

"Is Mary safe?" I ask, my voice barely a croak, so parched is my throat.

"Aye, she be, but m'lord . . ."

I sit among the ruins of the building I'd helped pull down, trying to catch my breath and recover my wits. Osbert's right. What was I thinking? At long last, I reach out my hand and Osbert pulls me to my feet. "Where's my halberd? We have to get this house pulled down."

"But m'lord . . ." Osbert protests, certain I've completely taken leave of my senses. I find the discarded tool and we get back to work.

Two hours later, everyone exhausted from the strenuous work and with black sweat pouring down our faces, we finally seem to have subdued this fire. Judging from the fact that the other two columns of smoke have disappeared, it seems the other fires are out as well. The sheriff comes by and posts fresh men to make sure the blackened piles don't flare back into a roaring inferno.

Osbert and I make our way further into the town, headed for the inn. Everything and everyone smells of smoke. The innkeeper's brought a cask of ale into the square and is serving, free of charge, all the thirsty, weary men who've fought the fires. He recognizes me, though how, I don't know, in my current filthy state. "Lord Alfred!" he exclaims, pressing a cup of ale into my hands. I pass it to Osbert, and he hands me another one. "What a sad day fer ye to be coming here."

He turns to his helper. "Fix a bath fer his lordship . . . in the nicest room." Turning back to me, he adds, "Ye be having to wait a bit while he fetch more water from the stream, m'lord."

"I be going along to the stables," Osbert says, "to be sure the horses be settled down good and proper. I be back soon."

"Thank you, Osbert." And he's off with the innkeeper's helper. Turning back to the innkeeper, I ask, "What happened?" just as the mayor walks up.

"Lord Alfred?" he asks tentatively. "Is that indeed you?"

"Aye, sir. I'd shake your hand, but I'm rather sweaty and smoky at the moment. What happened here?"

"What's been happening more and more frequently, sir, but this time it got completely out of hand." He takes a cup of ale from the innkeeper. "That infernal priest. We thought we'd finally seen the last of him. Ran him out of town about a month ago and hadn't seen him since. But today he came back, preaching his vitriol and riling people up against the immigrants. We've always welcomed them here, since we're the closest market town to two borders. But earlier this year he whipped the people into a frenzy, urging them to banish anyone of immigrant background."

"We'd heard you had riots in the spring."

"That we did. And each time this bastard shows up, he manages to get a mob worked up over one thing or another. I wasn't there to hear it myself today, but I've been told he urged the mob to banish the non-believers and purify the town to prove to God they were cleansing themselves of sin.

"So one mob rousted all the immigrants out of their homes and away from their work and drove them out into the fields and woods to fend for themselves – men, women, children – with only the clothes on their backs. And another mob set fire to all their homes. It was more than the sheriff could possibly control.

"I'm sick at heart, Lord Alfred. I simply don't know any more what to do."

"You're not alone. It's happening elsewhere, sir, though not with the degree of violence you saw here today. In fact, I came here on my way home from Ernle Manor hoping to speak with you – certainly not expecting to ride into anything of this sort. Would you do me the honor of having supper with me at the inn this evening?"

"If you'll agree, your lordship, perhaps we should dine in my home instead. I suspect it's going to be quite rowdy in the tavern tonight, with people trying to calm their fears with ale." He turns to the innkeeper. "No offense to your good self, Sewal. It's important they have a chance to find relief and a welcoming place to do it."

"Very well, sir, but I'd like to get cleaned up a bit first. When should I arrive?"

"Just after sundown. Sewal can give you directions."

I arrive at the mayor's home to find Amelia and the magistrate have also been invited. Clearly an impromptu gathering for the supper is plain but tasty. I tell them what I've seen with my own eyes in Great Woolston and the reports we've heard from Devereux about what's happening in Neukirk Market. "Nothing like what happened here though," I acknowledge. "What I saw today tells me I should warn the other mayors to prepare."

"We can't even work out who to charge with lawlessness," opines the magistrate. "All these mobs seem to rise up spontaneously, without any clear leaders. I can't charge half the town."

"And I agree you're right not to do so, sir," I say. "That would likely only make things worse . . . and make you, the sheriff, and the mayor the next targets of the violence. I've been wondering, though . . . is there any legal basis on which the itinerant himself could be charged?"

"There used to be a law against inciting riots, your lordship," he replies. "But these days . . . with all the laws the king has rescinded . . . I don't even know if it's still in force. Worse yet, this creature would likely fall back on his claim that he's a priest and therefore subject to no law but that of the Church."

"What I don't understand," says Amelia, "is why the Church doesn't step in to intervene."

"I posed that very question to the bishop," I reply. "So far, he's been unsuccessful in figuring out who has authority over them. Right now, he believes they're self-proclaimed and thus outside the hierarchy of the Church of Rome. He maintains strict orders to all the local clergy to declare them false prophets and exhort the people to cling to the teachings of the true Church. But it seems fewer and fewer of those who follow the itinerants actually attend services these days, so the bishop's message never reaches the ears of those who most need to hear it."

When I tell them about the lawlessness in the port, Amelia says, "We knew some of this, but not how dangerous it's become. No wonder the traders buy little and have little to sell."

It's hardly the pleasant kind of meal we've shared in the past, but they seem relieved to be able to talk about their worries. At the end of the evening, the mayor says, "I wonder, Lord Alfred, if I might impose upon you to escort Madam Greslet home since it's on your way back to the inn. The magistrate goes in the opposite direction."

"Of course, sir," I reply.

Amelia opens her mouth to say something, and the mayor cuts her off. "Now, Amelia, I know you're about to object that you know your way home and will be perfectly safe, but we don't know who's about tonight. And if the hooligans that caused all the trouble today have been drinking and are back on the streets, God knows what they might get up to. So you'll either let Lord Alfred accompany you or I'll see you home myself."

She smiles. "You're absolutely right, Filbert . . . on both counts. Normally I would object. But I was just about to thank Lord Alfred and tell him I'd welcome the company. I *don't* fancy running into one of those troublemakers on my own."

At the door, we find servants waiting with lanterns. "The moon's not risen yet, so take these. I'll have my man fetch them back tomorrow. But please . . . don't set anything else on fire," Filbert chuckles.

The streets are surprisingly quiet – no drunken revelers or mischief-makers anywhere. Maybe they spent all their fury in the mayhem during the day. But even here in a part of town totally untouched by the violence, the acrid smell of smoke and charred wood is an inescapable reminder of what happened.

Amelia's house is dark – no sign of a candle anywhere. "I sent my servants to take care of their families," she says. "Even the ones whose families weren't harmed know someone else who was."

"Then let me come in and help you get some candles lit."

When we have light in the parlor, I douse the lantern and place it on the table beside the door. "Would you like a brandy?" she asks.

"Perhaps just a small one."

I take a seat on the couch while she pours. She hands me a glass and sits next to me, closer than in the past. We sip the brandy in silence.

"I couldn't tell anyone else this, Alfred," she touches my hand, "but I was truly frightened today – more frightened than I've ever been in my life. The fires . . . they could have consumed the whole town. And then when I heard what you'd done . . . how you almost lost your life saving that woman . . ." I'm uncertain what to say or do.

She edges closer, like a child seeking comfort, and I involuntarily put an arm around her shoulders. And in that moment, the tensions of the day overwhelm me – the realization, hearing her words – that I really *could* have perished inside that building.

She reaches up, caresses my cheek, and gives me a gentle kiss on the lips.

"I have a wife, Amelia."

"Shhhhh," she says putting her finger to my lips. "You're here with me now."

My mind tells me it's time to leave. My body wills me to stay.

She places her glass on the table, then takes my face in both her hands and gives me a long, passionate kiss. As I gently try to break the embrace, I feel her breast against my arm. In spite of myself, I'm beginning to feel a stiffening in my crotch.

She takes my glass and places it on the table, snuggles closer with her head on my shoulder, and begins stroking my chest. The warmth of her, the smell of her hair, the gentleness of her hands . . . the stiffness only increases. My mind tells me to push her away. My body is incapable of obeying. I find myself drawing her closer still.

Her hands explore further but stop just short of the ache in my crotch, and the effect is tantalizing. I will her to reach lower and yet she doesn't. Instead, she rises from the couch and takes my hands in hers, raising me up and drawing me toward her.

"Amelia, I can't," I whisper as she wraps her arms around me and presses her body against mine. The stiffness is becoming unbearable. I'm growing desperate for some relief.

She takes my hand and starts to lead me up the stairs. My mind says I mustn't. My feet follow her.

In her bed chamber, she removes her gown and lets down her hair. Her body is magnificent. "Amelia, we can't," I say again, more feebly this time.

She pulls up my shirt, and her hands on my bare chest are like magic. I'm completely losing control. She leads me to the bed, and I lie there as she climbs up beside me.

She unbuttons my trousers and finally moves her hands to my crotch, and I think I'll explode from the sheer pleasure of it all.

One last time, I whisper, "Amelia, no," but I have no power to move. She pulls me on top of her and guides me inside her. And now I'm a willing participant, thrusting ever faster, eager to finish what she started. At the last minute, I barely come to my senses and withdraw, spending myself in great spasms on her belly. At least I won't be leaving a bastard behind.

Slowly, my rational mind begins to return. I sit up and begin to put my clothing back in order. "Amelia, I never meant for this to happen."

She pulls the sheets around her. "I know that, Alfred. But I thank you nonetheless."

She steps out of the bed, the sheets still wrapped around her, and comes to sit beside me as I pull on my boots. "You could stay. The servants won't return before tomorrow afternoon."

"But Osbert is waiting for me. If I'm not back at the inn by what he considers a reasonable hour, he'll wake the entire town to look for me."

She caresses my cheek again. "At least now I know what it's like to hold the skylark in my hand."

Walking back to the inn gives me a chance to clear my mind – or really, just to muddle it further. How could I lose control so completely like that? Was it the awful things I saw happening today? Did coming so close to dying in the fire make me desperate for a connection with life?

Don't deceive yourself, Alfred. You've been wondering what that would be like since you first laid eyes on her. But now that you know, what are you going to do about it? If I didn't before, I now fully understand why my father kept his secrets – even whether he had any secrets at all. Amelia will never speak of what happened for the same reason she won't take a lover or husband among the men here – she won't relinquish her position of prestige. I'll do the same, though for very different reasons.

But what will I do the next time we meet? The next time we happen to be alone in the same place? A bridge to be crossed only if or when it appears. And with what's happening in the world around us, a bridge I may never see.

In the weeks that follow, between continuing my studies with Brother Eustace and helping Rupert manage the estate, I continue to add bits to the chronicle.

𝕿he riot and fires in Abbeville Market revealed the dark underside of human nature and provided a warning of the discord and destructiveness a demagogue can unleash in the presence of festering frustration and fears 𝕿he magistrate was never able to bring anyone to justice for the events of that day 𝕻erhaps sensing that his own life was in jeopardy the itinerant who incited the Abbeville riots disappeared and was never seen again though others of his ilk came to town from time to time 𝕿he dowager queens correspondence reveals that she wrote to all the lords about the terrible violence urging them to prepare against the possibility of such a thing happening in their domains 𝕬s summer gave way to harvest time an odd sort of calm descended over the kingdom 𝕴t seemed as if there was a growing acceptance of the new regime as the normal way of life 𝕬rmed knights were still seen everywhere 𝕻eople were still thrown into prison for being unable to pay their taxes The itinerants still wandered the land railing against the sinfulness of the kingdom People kept listening to them but the incidents of violence abated at least for a time Though the deterioration of roads and bridges continued and the dangerous conditions in the port persisted the rise in the number of people with no work seemed to taper off Perhaps things were approaching some depth of hell beyond which one could go no deeper and from which a slow emergence could finally begin The harvest would be the next revelation

Richard and his family are visiting earlier than usual this year. He thought it best not to attempt the journey once the winter snows set in. They're due to arrive today and will remain through the harvest and all the festivities that usually accompany it. It remains to be seen how much celebration there'll be this year.

Toward sundown, we catch site of the traveling party coming up the lane. As she descends from the carriage, Avelina fights to keep her composure though she's clearly in distress – and Richard is nowhere to be seen. Rupert opens his mouth, presumably to ask what's afoot, but Avelina silences him before he can utter a word. "Let me get the children settled upstairs, Papa. Then we'll talk."

Half an hour later, she joins us on the terrace overlooking the garden. She manages to remain calm while her mother embraces her, kissing her on both cheeks. But when Rupert attempts the same, she collapses into his arms in a flood of tears. "Oh, Papa," she laments, "it's so dreadful. They've taken him . . . taken him prisoner. And there was nothing we could do."

"There, there," Rupert tries to soothe her. "There's nothing so dreadful we can't find a way to fix it."

When at last her sobs subside, she says, "I'm not so sure this time, Papa."

Rupert guides her to a vacant seat and sits beside her, keeping one of her hands in his. "Now, take your time and tell me what happened." Catherine gives her a handkerchief to dry her eyes.

Finally, she begins. "It was a pleasant enough journey." Then she pauses. "That is, if you don't count the occasional bone-jarring from the ruts and potholes." She smiles. Avelina is Rupert's daughter through and through, even down to her sense of humor. "Pleasant enough until we got to the ferry. There was a camp of knights there. They stopped us on the road. Said everyone and all our belongings had to be searched before we could board the ferry.

"Richard refused. Told the captain he was Lord Devereux's heir traveling with his family and that it was customary for people to have free right of travel within the realm. When the captain signaled his men to approach the carriage, Richard turned back and positioned his horse between the knights and the carriage door. Then the captain said, 'I don't care who you are, sir. My orders are everyone must be searched.' So Richard asked him, 'Whose orders?' And the captain answered, 'King's orders to me. My orders to you. Move away from the carriage and dismount.'

"Richard stood his ground. 'I'll do no such thing,' he said. 'Now stand aside and let us pass.' And the captain said, 'Either you be searched or you turn around and go back the way you came.'

"And that's when things got ugly. By this time, I was watching out the window. His coat open and one hand on the hilt of his dagger, Richard nudged his horse a few steps closer to the captain. 'Stand aside, Captain, and let us pass,' he said. The captain didn't answer . . . just sort of flicked his head . . . and suddenly there were three knights around Richard, their swords drawn and pointing at him.

"The captain said, 'Anyone defies my orders becomes the king's prisoner.' He beckoned to a fourth knight who came over and put shackles on Richard's wrists. 'Now, Gaston,' said the captain, 'take two more men and take this prisoner to the castle to await the king's justice.' The six of them surrounded Richard and rode off . . . and that's the last I saw of him, Papa."

Quiet tears stream down her cheeks once again. She dabs at them with the handkerchief and then resumes. "We'd come so far, it seemed better to come on here than to go back. So I let them search. They made us all climb down from the carriage, and they searched the inside. Then some knights went through all our trunks. They made a right mess of things . . . I just hope nothing is soiled or torn . . . but finally they let us be on our way."

At this point in the telling, she seems to have regained some control over her emotions. "It got worse. The port town was truly frightening –

not at all like the place I grew up. There were men roaming the streets, looking quite menacing, occasionally threatening some poor soul who seemed to be just walking by. I closed the curtains so the children wouldn't see . . . or maybe so they wouldn't see the children . . . I'm really not sure which. But I held a corner open so I could peek out. Twice it seemed as if someone were going to waylay the carriage. But the driver and Richard's squire got us through safely." She pauses briefly. "I can't tell you what a relief it was to finally see the green of the countryside appear in the window."

Rupert puts an arm around his daughter's shoulders. "I'm very proud of you, my dear. Getting the children through all that without unduly upsetting them took courage."

Avelina manages a sardonic little laugh. "Thank you, Papa. But their father is still a prisoner, and I've no idea what to do about *that*."

"You leave that to Alfred and me." Then turning to me, "What say you, Alfred? Shall we ride to the castle tomorrow and prevail upon John to free the prisoner?" I can tell his lighthearted tone is meant more to reassure his daughter than to reflect the formulation of any specific plan.

"Actually," I reply, "I have an idea that just might work. Leave it to me, Avelina. With any luck at all, I'll have him back here the day after tomorrow a free man."

Rupert looks at me quizzically, but I just shake my head slightly. What I have in mind will work best if I go alone.

After supper, I send for Osbert, and we go out into the garden to talk. "It seems we need to free Richard from the king's prison, Osbert. You up for the task?"

"We be helping him escape, m'lord?" he asks querulously.

"Better than that, my friend. We're going to convince the king to void the charge against Richard and send him away with us a free man."

"That be a bit more to me liking, sir." I can hear the relief in Osbert's voice.

"I don't want to take much . . . just the minimum we need for an overnight stay. But we'll need some special things. Pack a small flask of oil and my tinderbox."

"Ye be going to set fire to the castle, m'lord?"

"As much as it might be amusing to watch all those knights running around trying to put out a fire, I actually have something quite different in mind. To that end, I'd like to go dressed as a squire rather than as a gentleman. Do you think you could manage that?"

"Whatever ye say, sir."

"We need to arrive just at midday without overtaxing the horses, so let's leave a bit before dawn. The moon is just past full, so it should still be high and bright from midnight to sunrise. And Osbert . . . saddle one of Rupert's horses for me . . . not Sirius or Star Dancer. I don't want someone recognizing my horse before I'm ready to make my presence known."

Osbert wakes me before dawn, and we're on our way. I forego a bath and shaving in an effort to make my disguise a bit more credible. When we arrive, we stay outside the town and steer our horses in a very slow walk toward the castle. There's little activity, and the sentries don't seem particularly alert. "Just as I'd hoped, but I need you to be my scout, Osbert. Pull up your hood so it's not so easy to recognize you. But don't worry if someone does. If anyone asks, you're on an errand from Rupert's steward to Matthias, alright?"

"Right, m'lord."

"What I need to know is if the king is away and when he's expected back. It would also be nice to know if his squire is with him. Don't be in a rush. Get some food from the kitchen, just as you would if you were heading back to the manor. Then ride slowly out and head toward the town. I'll meet you about here."

"I be back as quick as can be, sir," he says.

"Quickly as you can, Osbert, but don't look like you're in any sort of hurry. Off with you then. I'll watch for you to ride out of the gate."

When he's gone, I ride a short distance away from town to a spot where I can watch without being too conspicuous from either the town or the castle. I've never fully understood why time seems to move so slowly when waiting for something to happen. It seems as if Osbert is gone for half a lifetime, though in point of fact it's probably no more than half an hour from the time he rides through the gate until he emerges again. Mounting my horse, I ride slowly to meet him.

"The king be away," he says, "like every day, on exercises with the knights. They say he never be back until two hours afore sundown. Mayhap it be later if the knights not be getting things right."

I glance up at the position of the sun. Plenty of time to accomplish what I need to.

"And his squire?"

"He be with the king. They say that poor man have to be wherever the king be, day or night, and the king always keep him running doing this and that."

"Good. Now, when you entered and left the castle, did the sentries stop you or ask your business?"

"Nary a word, m'lord. Not sure they even noticed."

"Even better. Now take my pack. I want to look like I'm just coming and going on ordinary business." I hand him a small purse with a few coins in it. "Stay out of sight for a while. Then, as it gets closer to sundown, go to the tavern and have a mug of ale. Richard and I should join you for supper. If we don't, stay for the night, and if we haven't arrived by morning, go back to Lord Rupert and tell him he has two prisoners to rescue." I laugh, trying to reassure Osbert there's really nothing to worry about.

"I dinna' know what ye be up to, but best ye take care, m'lord. I be having mugs of ale waiting fer ye both in the tavern."

And with that, we part company once again. I pull my hood over my head and ride slowly toward the castle gate. No one challenges me, and, once inside the outer bailey, I dismount and lead my horse around to the kitchen where I tether him to the rail beside the drinking trough. Two other horses are tethered there, so a third won't be conspicuous. Just as I'd hoped, no one is about in the yard, the servants taking a short respite before getting ready to feed the hordes of knights their supper. I make my way around the kitchen to the undercrofts unnoticed.

The steward seems to have more supplies than ever stored here, so I have to pick my way over and between crates and baskets to get to the back. Once there, I trigger the hidden latch that opens the door. Leaving the door ajar just enough to see what I'm doing, I take the flask and tinderbox out of my pocket and prime a torch. It's been years since I've had the need to start a fire this way, so I'm a bit apprehensive about my skill. The fresh oil, however, reacts to even the smallest spark, and the first torch springs to light. Placing it in the holder, I close and latch the door, and light a second torch from the flame of the first. My tools back in my pockets, I take both torches in hand and start to climb the stairs, instinctively beginning the count . . . one, two, three, . . .

Reaching the landing at the level of the library, I place one of the torches in the holder and trigger the latch to open the door. As I step inside and hold the torch aloft, I'm momentarily taken aback. Though it's what I'd hoped to see, it's nevertheless a breathtaking sight. The room is completely empty . . . the shelves bare . . . not a book or scroll anywhere to be seen. André's monks have succeeded in their mission; Grandfather's treasure is safe. Crossing the room, I raise the iron pole to its vertical position and unlock the door. Let anyone who wishes come in now. There's nothing here they can harm. I take one last look around before exiting and latching the secret panel securely behind me.

Not wanting to take any risk that both torches should go out, I douse one in the sand box and prepare a fresh one for the rest of the way. It blazes quickly to light and I resume my climb, counting once again. Thirty-seven steps to reach the top. On the landing, I take several deep breaths. This is the most dangerous part of what I'm doing, for there's no way to know what I'll find on the other side of the door. I douse one of the torches, keeping the fresher one. The latch is in the same location and identical to its twin on the landing below. Holding my breath . . . and holding the torch both for light and to use as a weapon should I be attacked from the other side . . . I trigger the latch and gently ease open the door. Hearing nothing on the other side, I open it a bit wider and peek around the edge. I see no one and hear nothing. Quickly, I douse the torch, enter the king's bed chamber, and close the panel firmly behind me. I stand perfectly still, glancing around and listening for any sound or movement. There's nothing but silence.

Relaxing just a bit, I take a seat in a chair beside the fireplace. There's nothing to do now but wait. The last time I was in this room was the day my father died. Memories start to flood back, but I push them away. I need all my wits focused on the task at hand. When finally the light through the window shows signs of weakening, I hear bootsteps from far away, coming in this direction. Time to be alert.

The door is thrown open, and John marches in. I catch myself wondering, "Does he have no other gait?" He starts to cross the room, initially unaware of my presence, then suddenly stops short. "You!" he exclaims. "What are you doing here? More to the point, how did you get in here?"

"Just like your women, Your Grace," I reply in my most cordial tone, "unseen by anyone in the corridors."

"I'm in no mood for your jests, Alfred." Then he shouts, "Guard!" and two guards rush in from the outer chamber.

I stand slowly and equally slowly open my coat to reveal that I'm unarmed. Extending my hands to the side, palms outward, I say, "There's no need for guards, Your Grace. I would never come armed into the king's bed chamber."

"You shouldn't be here in the first place," he barks, but waves the guards to step back. "Now what do you want?"

"I believe, Sire, that the heir to the first lord of the realm is being held unjustly in your prison."

"Nonsense!" he scoffs.

"Perhaps you haven't yet been informed, Sire. He was detained at the ferry crossing yesterday and brought here."

"I didn't say he wasn't here – only that it's nonsense he would be held unjustly."

"Have you looked into the matter yourself, Your Grace?"

"He's not been brought before me for the king's justice."

"Then I suggest you have him brought before you now, Sire."

"What makes you think you can barge in here and tell me how to conduct my court?"

"That's not my intention at all, Sire. I merely hope to save you the embarrassment of having this matter come up in your public court."

"What makes you think it would be an embarrassment?"

I hold my tongue.

"Well, what?" he persists, growing impatient.

"Perhaps we should have him brought before you . . . along with the knight who brought him in."

John glares at me for a very long time, finally realizing, I think, that I have no intention of leaving until this matter is settled. At last he turns to one of the guards in the room. "Fetch the prisoner Devereux and the knight who brought him." When the guard hesitates before making his way to the door, the king shouts, "Now, man!"

Then he turns back to me. "This better be good, Alfred, else you'll find yourself sharing a cell with your friend." Nothing more passes between us while we wait for Richard and the knight named Gaston.

When they're escorted into the king's presence, Richard's eyes grow as big as saucers. I shake my head slightly, indicating he should say nothing. The knight clicks his heels together, bows his head sharply, and says, "Sir Gaston, at your service, Your Grace. With the prisoner, as ordered."

"What's the charge, Sir Gaston?" asks the king. "Or did you just haul this man in for no reason, as Lord Alfred seems to think?"

"Failing to respect my captain and refusing a search, Your Grace."

John turns to me. "There you have it, Alfred. Satisfied?"

"Not at all, Your Grace," I answer politely. John glares again. "I believe it's customary in our kingdom for the nobility to be shown respect by those of the lower classes. I seem to recall Your Grace having made this point on more than one occasion. Is there some new law of which I'm unaware that changes what Your Grace has more than once described as 'the natural order of things'?"

"Of course there's no such law," John snaps.

"Then it seems to me, Your Grace," I'm careful to remain properly formal, knowing John will never perceive it as the implicit mockery I intend, "that there can be no charge of failure of a noble to respect a knight captain. No law has been violated."

"Hmph," the king snorts. Sir Gaston stiffens his posture.

"As for the charge of refusing a search," I continue calmly, "it was my understanding that your people have the right of free travel within your kingdom. Once again, Your Grace, if there is some new law of which I'm not aware, then I'm sure you'll enlighten me."

"There's no new law, Lord Alfred. However, you yourself know there are new controls for crossing the borders . . . controls I ordered to stop the influx of immigrants."

"I wasn't aware that the ferry crossing constituted a border, Your Grace. I'd always believed it to be much like our roads, except that it provides a way to cross the river at a place where there's no bridge."

"We have to control what comes into the kingdom from the port on that side of the river."

"Ah, but the Devereux party was not arriving from the port, Your Grace. They were traveling from Devereux Castle to the home of Lady Avelina's parents. I believe that constitutes travel within your kingdom."

"Gaston!" shouts the king.

The knight is now ramrod straight, both arms held stiffly at his sides, doing his best not even to blink. "Your Grace," he replies.

"Unshackle that man's wrists and then get out of my sight. Tell your captain he'd best think twice before sending a prisoner to me again just because he thinks he's been insulted. And tell him to read his orders again."

The knight walks stiffly to Richard, takes out a key, and unlocks and removes the shackles. Richard shakes out his hands and rubs his wrists.

"Now get out of here," barks the king. Sir Gaston can't leave quickly enough.

"As for the two of you," continues John, pointing at Richard and me, "I'd best hear no more of this nonsense. Get your horses and be gone from here immediately."

"Not so fast, Your Grace," I say quietly.

"What now, Alfred?" he's getting impatient.

"I'd like for you to sign and seal a safe passage document for Richard Devereux and his family."

John glares at me again. "I thought you just proved such a thing isn't necessary."

"Of course it's not necessary in your presence, Your Grace. But it seems that some of your captains don't have the same appreciation for the customs you value so highly. A safe passage document, if you please."

John stands there in stony silence, and I begin to worry I may have pushed him too far. At last he turns to the remaining guard and says, "Fetch my secretary." He follows the guard into the private reception room, and we follow behind. When the secretary arrives, John says curtly, "Tell him what to write."

So I dictate to the clerk. "This document provides safe passage throughout this kingdom for Richard Devereux, his wife and children, and any near relatives, servants, or attendants traveling in their company. They may pass through any checkpoint at will, and neither they nor their belongings shall be subject to detention or search." When the clerk finishes, John signs and seals the document.

"While we're at it, a similar document for me, if you please."

"Why? Are you planning on traveling somewhere?" asks John sarcastically.

"Not particularly, Your Grace. Only between here and the manor. I simply prefer not to run afoul of your orders not to bother you with such a matter in future."

"Oh, very well," he huffs. And to the clerk, "Write it out."

With the documents in my hands, I bow and ask, "Permission to leave, Your Grace?"

John waves his hand toward the door. "Go, go, go." And then, as an afterthought, "I *still* don't understand how you got in here."

"Like I said, Sire. Just like your women. Unseen by anyone in the corridors." And before he can rail at us further, I make my way out the door, Richard hot on my heels, across the public reception room, and into the corridor.

Richard has the good sense to keep a sober look on his face and not utter a single word until we've collected our horses and ridden out through the gate. About halfway to the town, he finally bursts into laughter, bringing a big grin to my face. "Alfred, thank all the gods you're my friend. What a performance!"

I make a mock bow in my saddle.

"All that your-grace-ing. Weren't you afraid he was going to figure out you were making fun of him?"

"John's opinion of himself is far too grand for him ever to consider that possibility," I chuckle.

"And that safe passage document. A stroke of pure genius."

"I wish I could get them for all my friends, but I rather suspect I wouldn't get away with this twice."

"By the way, how *did* you get into his bed chamber?"

"Like I said . . ."

He cuts me off. "I know, I know. Like his women. Perhaps one day you'll tell me."

"Perhaps."

Once in the town, we stable our horses for the night and make our way to the tavern on foot. Despite my rather scruffy appearance, a few people recognize me and stop to ask after my family. The streets are not nearly so busy as they were in my father's time. True to his word, Osbert has a table staked out for us and two mugs of ale at the ready, in addition to his own. He's overjoyed to see us safe.

"I tell the innkeeper we be needing his two best rooms tonight and a good supper, so all be ready, m'lord. But I be telling ye, I not be liking *at all* this waiting and not knowing if ye be in danger."

Sitting down, Richard takes a great long gulp of ale, then raises his mug, "To friends in need!" I raise my mug in response; Osbert demurs. "You, too, Osbert," says Richard.

"Absolutely," I chime in. "You were a very important player in this little adventure."

Osbert beams and raises his mug. "Friends!" says Richard again, and we all drink the toast.

Osbert and I have had a very long day, and I'm sure Richard slept not at all the previous night, so after a delicious meal, we all find our beds. Not wanting to keep Avelina in suspense any longer than necessary, we set out for the manor just after sunrise. The weather is pleasantly cool, so we let the horses run whenever they seem to want to stretch their legs. We're back home by midafternoon. Avelina must have been keeping watch at the window, for she's out the door and running down the steps before we can stop the horses and dismount. Osbert gathers the reins to lead our mounts to the stable.

Avelina has Richard locked in an embrace from which I don't know if she'll ever release him when Rupert comes through the front door. "You have to let him breathe at some point, my dear," he chides his daughter playfully. When she releases her embrace, he claps Richard on the shoulder and says, "Welcome home, Richard. Everyone's on the terrace eager to hear the rest of the story."

I shout to Osbert. "You, too, Osbert. Give the horses to the grooms and come back straightaway. They'll want to hear your part of the adventure too." Even though he's walking the other way, I know there's a big grin on Osbert's face.

Avelina locks arms with Richard and leads the way. Rupert puts a hand on my arm to hold me back for a moment. "Thank you, Alfred. I don't know what you did, but I'm grateful."

I chuckle. "I'm sure you'll hear soon enough. Let's go reassure Gwen that I didn't have to swap my freedom for Richard's."

And so the story is told. The only part I have to supply is John's surprise when he found me sitting in his bed chamber – I carefully omit how I got there – and how I convinced him to bring Richard up from his cell. Richard's imitation of my extreme formality draws howls of laughter. "If I didn't know better," says Rupert, "I'd say you've been taking lessons from Alice."

"A poor imitation, at best," I reply, which draws an admiring smile from my mother.

"I still don't understand," says Catherine, looking puzzled, "how you got into his bed chamber."

"All he'll say, Lady Catherine," Richard supplies, "is 'Like the king's women. Unseen by anyone in the corridors.'"

"But," Catherine persists innocently, "wouldn't that involve servants somehow?" . . . providing just the opening my mother and Gwen need to relate the servants' gossip about the king's squire and his women.

Throughout the telling, Rupert has been watching me with an odd expression on his face. As the women launch into their gossip, that expression changes to an approving smile. He catches my eye and nods almost imperceptibly. My uncle, too, it seems, knows the secrets of the castle.

The harvest is average at best, but that has turned out to be a good thing. Though prices are no higher than last year, the farmers are able to sell everything they take to market. The satisfaction of seeing all their hard work turned to profit rather than rotting in a storehouse raises their spirits in a way I'm not sure I could have predicted. The estate once again turns a profit, even after our taxes are paid, though it's decidedly less than in previous years.

In the week following the big harvest markets, the tax collectors are everywhere, accompanied by their armed escorts. Despite the fact that we continue to hear how the tax burden on the people weighs heavier every year, the taxes for our own estate were actually lower than the previous year – lower, says Rupert, than at any time since my grandfather's reign. I find this puzzling. Logic would argue that the great estates should pay in proportion to their wealth.

"Your brother is pandering to the nobles," says Rupert. "Trying to buy their favor as a misguided attempt to forestall any action against him. It's short-sighted."

"I'm sure that doesn't surprise you," I chuckle.

"Hardly."

"Does he think the lords will now pay for the things he's not doing in the kingdom?"

"Nothing that goes on in my nephew's head would surprise me, Alfred."

"What surprises *me* is that they're letting him get away with it. Are they really so venal that they'd rather have the money than confront the king?"

"I think it's more likely they see it as a way to deny him money to spend without their having any voice in how it's spent."

"I'm still scratching my head over why they haven't acted yet. Surely John's actions could be described as egregious. Is there something else in it for them to let things continue to deteriorate? Or if not for all of them, at least for some? I've no doubt Devereux would prefer they all be in agreement rather than take unilateral action. But what if he can't get unanimity?"

"My guess?"

"Please, Uncle."

"If I were in Devereux's shoes, I'd temporize until John breaks *all* of the lords' hereditary rights. And I'd let the people's anger escalate to the boiling point – to where they're ready to revolt on their own. Then, whatever they do, they'll have the people on their side. The best you and I can do for now is continue to take care of our people here and let John push the lords to the breaking point."

So we all pitch in to help make the village harvest festival just a little nicer than the people could do on their own. The estate provides all the ale and wine, and Richard provides small prizes for the friendly contests organized by the village men. Mother organizes a spinning contest for the women, to see who can spin the most wool in half an hour. The winner will receive a length of fine cloth and some lace – enough to make a nice dress – and the next best two will each get a length of cloth.

This festival feels like the celebrations I remember from years past. The villagers set aside their worries for a day and truly enjoy themselves. Everyone gets into the spirit of the contests, and the winners are roundly celebrated. In our little village, at least, the troubles besetting the kingdom are, for a short time, forgotten.

The big autumn hunt is another opportunity for the villagers to feel good about their lives. They have meat to eat now and to cure for the winter months. Richard generously donated his kill to the town of Great Woolston to feed the people there who have no work.

Richard and his family take their leave in time to complete the return journey before the snows set in. Mounting his horse to depart, he holds up the safe passage document and waves it at me. "I'm deeply indebted to you for this, Alfred. It should make the return trip much easier."

"I just hope that captain can read," I laugh as he stows the document back inside his coat.

He laughs too. "Well, if Sir Gaston is there, I'm pretty sure no one will attempt to lay a finger on us." And with that, they're on their way.

Life settles into a familiar autumn pattern. The winter solstice will soon be upon us and preparations are underway for the Christmas celebration. It will be a quiet Christmas this year – well, as quiet as Christmas can be with three young children in the house. Rupert and Catherine, Gwen and I, and my mother all make three Christmas offerings this year: one to the village church; one to the church in the castle town – the traditional offering from the royal family; and one to the monastery. All are designated to help care for the people whose lives have been changed by the new king's rule. I send a bit extra to André along with a short note that says only, "In thanks for your special favor." He'll understand my intent to help him to protect the library that's now in his care.

Mother writes to Gundrea, inviting the queen and her children to keep Christmas with us. There's no reply. Despite John's claim that he has sole responsibility for the rearing of his children, the lords and the senior royals have a duty to the kingdom to ensure the safety and welfare of the heir. Concern for the well-being of the king's children is growing.

𝕾oon after Christmas winter settled like a pall over the kingdom colder than anyone remembered for dozens of years past 𝕬 heavy snow ushered in the new year with a deep blanket of white over villages towns and fields 𝖀ninterrupted grey skies for an entire month did nothing to alleviate either the bleak mood or the bone-chilling temperatures 𝕿he occasional sunny days in the month that followed merely taunted with their promise of warmth and cheer for each was followed by yet another snowfall and more grey skies 𝕿hose with a sturdy house and a fire to warm it were the lucky ones 𝕿he hundreds who huddled together in makeshift shacks suffered dreadfully 𝕱rom time to time there would be reports of a shack catching fire as a result of people desperately trying to find warmth 𝖂inter took its toll in other ways 𝖂ith little to eat and with what few blankets or cloaks people may have had already threadbare from use the weaker began to die As is so often the case the very old and the very young were sadly among the first to go The frozen ground was impenetrable making burials impossible The bodies of the dead were taken to the edges of the encampments and left there to await the thaw Such misery had not been known here since before the time the kingdom as we know it today was formed The sickness first appeared in late February It showed up initially in the shacks of the castle town and was then reported in the port It would start with a fever that came on suddenly laying its victims low within a day They would then suffer chills sweats coughing often cough up blood difficulty swallowing making it hard or impossible to eat drink or even breathe Most who contracted it succumbed and their bodies were laid alongside the others awaiting burial after the spring thaw As the days grew warmer the burials could at last begin but the deep ground was still frozen and most of the graves were very shallow However the sickness seemed to abate with fewer cases being reported and more people actually recovering Unlike the previous year the arrival of spring did not signal the return of frequent patrols At first this seemed a welcome relief from the constant presence of armed knights No one could guess that this was a portent of events that were about to unfold

·   ·   ·   ·   ·

The Paschal Moon comes just after the equinox this year, meaning Easter will be earlier than usual. Nevertheless, the early spring flowers are already beginning to appear, and the farmers have started preparing their implements for the first plowing. The sheep all have massive coats as a result of the harsh winter; there will be an abundance of fleece from this year's shearing. I only hope there's a good market.

The early calves have already arrived, and the mares Gwen bred last year have produced early foals. Lambing season will soon be upon us. Normally this would all induce feelings of rebirth and anticipation of the summer to come. Events of the past two years have, however, left us all just a bit wary.

A week after Easter, we're astonished to see a large mounted troop coming up the lane . . . more astonished when the king's banner comes into view as the troop draws closer . . . more astonished still when they halt in front of the house and the king himself is the first to dismount. As always with John, there are no pleasantries and only the most cursory acknowledgment of the formal obeisances that he expects. Marching past us all, he announces, "A word with you, Alfred. Rupert, you should hear this as well," leaving us to follow in his wake. Continuing his march into the study, he stops abruptly and turns to face us. My uncle and I both almost stumble in our efforts to stop quickly enough to avoid running into the king.

"My army marches on the Territories one week hence. I require a commander for my rear guard. That, Lord Alfred, will be you."

It takes every ounce of self-control I possess to keep my face expressionless and take a deep breath before venturing a response. Finally I say, "Despite the honor I'm sure you intend, Your Grace, I'm not a knight and I've never been a troop captain, so I wonder—"

He cuts me off short. "Precisely! It's tradition in our family that an heir must have experience in command of knights in the field. You have none, despite being second in line of succession. It's high time that failing was remedied. Do you really want to be the one who shatters more than a hundred years of family tradition?"

At first, I'm speechless. He's kept Harold's words festering in his mind all this time. And he's finally found a way to take his revenge for that and any number of other perceived offenses. I doubt I'll be able to escape this, but I have to try. "Actually, it wouldn't concern me in the least, Your Grace. Truth be known, I have absolutely no expectations of remaining second in line for very long and even fewer of ever being king. I know full well you're likely to have more sons." Much as I would like to add "sons who aren't bastards, that is," I say instead, "In fact, you may be intending to return home by way of the port to attend to that very matter."

"That's none of your business," he retorts. "We march in one week. You will command my rear guard. Report to Sir Louve in three days."

Before I can muster any sort of reply – even a "yes, Your Grace" – he's out of the room and on his way out of the house. And just as quickly, we hear the sound of hoofbeats making a rapid departure up the lane.

Rupert walks to my side and puts a hand on my shoulder. "I'm sorry, Alfred. I never saw that coming."

"Nor I, Uncle."

"The others will be in here in a minute."

"I know. But there's something I have to do first. Take them to the drawing room, and I'll join you as quickly as I can." He looks at me curiously. "It's important, Uncle . . . please." So he heads off to gather the others.

I find Brother Eustace and return with him to the study, sending a servant in search of Osbert. "Eustace, I need your help to write a letter to Egon. What I need to say is far beyond my abilities so far. Will you do it for me?"

"Of course," he replies, taking a seat at the table.

"Very well," I say, "here's what you should write.

"Lord Egon, I write to you in your own language so my words cannot be read if my messenger is intercepted. Lest you believe this is a forgery, know that it is written with the assistance of the monk who is my tutor. I am learning, but my abilities are not yet sufficient to convey the full scope and gravity of what I must tell you. Do not concern yourself about anyone revealing the contents of this letter. My tutor is loyal to me and to his god and would never reveal what is written here even though his life be threatened."

Eustace hesitates before he writes these last words. "Don't concern yourself, Eustace," I assure him. "Your life won't be in danger. I use those words only because I don't know if Egon follows our religion. If he doesn't, then a reference to the sanctity of the confessional would have no meaning for him." Eustace visibly relaxes, so I resume my dictation.

"I have this moment learned that King John intends to march his great army to invade the Territories. He intends to depart from the king's castle one week from today. My messenger will be able to tell you how many days have passed since I write these words.

"I've been commanded to take up the role of captain of the rear guard. For a brief moment, I considered refusing, but that would only have resulted in the king's declaring me a traitor and having me executed before leaving on his great campaign. I hope you agree that would serve no purpose.

"I firmly believe that our lords know nothing of the king's plans. And by making me a part of his army, the king has removed any opportunity I might have had to influence them to act. I believe equally firmly that the lords will be appalled by the king's actions. While they won't be able to act directly on your behalf, I can say with confidence that none of them will find fault with any action you take to defend your lands and your people.

"I believe I can also assure you there will be no threat from the Kingdom of Peaks. The western lords can be confident that the Peaks king will keep his army at home, their swords sheathed.

"Though I can't fully know his mind, it's my assumption that the king has assigned me the rear guard to ensure I have no opportunity to share in what he believes will be the glory of leading a conquest. That's the best I can hope for now and must work out a way to extricate myself from this situation while events are unfolding around us.

"Know this. You have my oath that I will never raise my sword against you or your son nor will I order troops under my command to engage with troops under yours.

"May our gods watch over us and bring us safely through whatever is to come."

When Eustace finishes, I sign the letter in my own hand, fold it into a small packet, and affix my seal. "Thank you, Eustace. You've done this kingdom a very great service today. Pray that there'll be a good outcome."

"I'll pray for you as well, Alfred," he says.

"And Eustace?"

"Yes?"

"There's one person to whom you may reveal the contents of this letter if he asks and that is Lord Rupert. He won't even know to ask until many days hence . . . after the army has marched . . . but if he asks you directly, you have my permission to tell him what I wrote.

"Now, I suspect you'll find Osbert waiting outside the door. Send him in to me, if you will."

Osbert is distraught. He knows something is up but not what, so I take the time to tell him everything about the turmoil the king has just created. As I expected, he's now even more distraught.

"Osbert, there's something of the greatest importance I need you to do for me. Do you remember when we were at the reservoir and I asked you to take a message to the king?"

"Aye, m'lord, that I do."

"Then I'm sure you remember how I asked you to carry the message inside your stocking and get to the king as fast as could be."

"Aye, m'lord."

"Osbert, this may be even more important than that message to my grandfather. I need you to travel in the same way – quick as you can. But this time, you must be careful not to be seen by any knight or anyone who might be the king's man. If they see you, it's very likely they would conscript you into the army, and that would *not* serve our purposes."

"I can do that, m'lord."

"Take the message to Samuel. Tell him the king's army marches one week from today. Tell him to get my letter to Lord Egon as quickly as he can. Can you do that for me, Osbert?"

"I can, m'lord, and I will. But how I be going to get back to ride with ye when the army marches?"

"That's the other part of the favor I need to ask you, Osbert. I want you to come back here as soon as you deliver the letter to Samuel. I want you to take care of my family while I'm away and whatever happens."

"But, sir, Lord Rupert be here to do that. And what ye be doing fer a squire?" He's truly worried.

"Don't fret, Osbert. I'll ask Donal to go with me. It won't be the same as having you to look after me. But it's more important that my family have you to look out for them. Gwen and Lord Rupert will need things and will need your help with my sons. There's no one on this earth I trust more with their safety, Osbert. I'm deeply honored that you want to look after me. But they are the most important things in the world to me, and taking care of them is the best way you can serve me.

"And Osbert?"

"Aye, m'lord?"

"You must keep this mission a secret from everyone except Lord Rupert – even Gwen and my mother. Do you understand? We could all be hanged as traitors if anyone ever found out."

"Aye, m'lord." He's very solemn.

I embrace my loyal squire. Then I hand him the letter and a purse with some coins. "Money for food and enough you can buy a fresh horse if you need to. Osbert, the future of our kingdom may depend on this. It is truly that important."

"I not be letting ye down, m'lord," he says. His eyes are gleaming with moisture, but he stiffens his posture in an air of importance. "I not be letting ye down," he repeats. For fear of letting my own emotions overtake me, I clap him on the shoulder and head out to join the others in the drawing room.

The mood there is somber. Rupert has poured brandy for everyone, and I down mine in one gulp as I take a seat next to Gwen. She's angry and hurt. "What could you *possibly* have had to do that was more important than coming to me . . . coming to us . . . with this news?" she demands.

"Saving the future of the kingdom, I hope," I reply quietly, hoping by my demeanor to defuse some of her anger.

"Don't jest with me, Alfred. Now's not the time."

I take both of her hands in mine, draw them to my lips, and cover them with kisses. "I'm not jesting, my dear. I'm deadly serious. But it's best I say no more just now. When the danger has passed . . . I promise."

She realizes now that I'm not being callous or unfeeling. "What can you do, Alfred? Surely there's some way you can get out of this."

"I don't see one, my dear. But if anyone has any ideas?" I look around to the others.

It's Gwen, though, who speaks up. "Leave the kingdom, Alfred. Go somewhere else. I know my parents would welcome you, and the King of Lakes would protect you."

"That's the first thing that occurred to me, but then I realized it's impossible. Aside from the fact that most of the borders are too far away to reach in three days, there are the knights guarding the crossings. And in any event, I'd have to pass in the vicinity of the castle to get there. John would have people on the lookout for me."

"What if you go north? Cross over from somewhere on the Devereux estate?"

"There's that small matter of the knights camped at the ferry crossing."

"Alright, then. Go to Phillip's. Hide out there for a bit, then find a boat to take you across the Southern Sea. We could follow you later."

I take her hands again. "My love, I know you're only trying to keep me safe. And I wish with all my heart that any of these schemes would work. I think, though, should I attempt to flee, John has already put things in train such that I'd be captured, charged with treason for failure to obey the king's direct order, and executed . . . before the army marches."

"I agree, Alfred," says Rupert quietly.

"I know my brother," I continue, keeping my tone subdued. "He rarely thinks beyond the end of his nose, but when it comes to me . . . The one thing he doesn't want to risk while he's off on his grand campaign is that I should remain here stirring up trouble against him. So as he sees it, that leaves him with two choices: either I'm dead or imprisoned . . . or I'm with him in a capacity where I have no choice but to obey his orders."

Gwen's eyes are glistening with moisture, but she fights to hold back the tears. "If I go with him, then I can somehow find a way to get myself out of this. I think that's the best I can do."

Mother, who has sat stoically silent, shakes her head sadly. "I had hoped never to see the day when one of my sons would be plotting the destruction of the other."

Trying to allay her sadness, Rupert says, "At least one of your sons has his wits about him and can find a way out of this mess. I can think of no other way than to trust Alfred to act when the right opportunity presents itself."

Gwen reaches for my hand again, not totally in command of herself. "We should go tell the children. They must hear it from us."

After supper, I see Rupert sitting alone on the terrace and join him. He has a decanter of brandy and two glasses sitting on a low table between two chairs. Hearing my footsteps, he fills the glasses. I sit quietly and sip brandy with him as the first stars begin to sparkle in the night sky.

"We knew he was plotting something," says Rupert. "Just not what."

"Perhaps," I reply, "this will give the lords the pretext they need to act."

"Perhaps. But what if his campaign is gloriously successful, and he comes back as the conqueror of the Territories?"

I take another sip of brandy and look up at the night sky. When I speak, I don't answer his question directly. "I'll be taking Donal with me as my squire. Osbert is away on an errand for me and won't be back in time. He'll return here to help look after my family while I'm away."

It's Rupert's turn to ponder the stars before replying. "What sort of errand?"

"As much as it pains me to keep anything from you, Uncle, I think it's safest you not know until Osbert's return. By then, the army will have marched."

"I take no offense, Alfred. I trust your judgment." And I trust that he understands he's to question Osbert and then decide how to use what he learns.

We sit for a long time in silent communion with each other, our brandy, and the stars. At last, Rupert says, "You should go to Gwendolyn." I rise and slip quietly away, leaving him alone with his thoughts.

Two nights later . . . the night before I'm to leave . . . Gwen and I are silent as we sit in bed together . . . the time when we usually talk at length. There's little more to say. I've entrusted her with the safe passage document and the key to my strongbox. I've given her all the advice I think may matter, mostly boiling down to trust Rupert and trust your own instincts. I take her hand and kiss it softly. "I *will* be back. Of that you can be sure."

She comes into my arms. Our lovemaking has a desperation born of fear and uncertainty, and we fall into an exhausted sleep. Sometime in the middle of the night, I wake to her stroking my chest and we make love again . . . this time with a tenderness that hearkens back to the first days of our marriage. I fall asleep praying to every god man has ever imagined for the safety of this woman whom I love more than life itself.

The army began its march at dawn this morning. It's a massive train with hundreds of knights and more hundreds of foot soldiers and archers; countless wagons laden with food for men and horses, tents, cooking implements, casks of ale and small ale, armaments, equipment, and supplies to repair things in the field; dozens of spare horses for knights and wagons; squires and others to attend the needs of the army; and two priests. The bishop was called upon to bless the undertaking and pray for the army to return home victorious. And then it took most of the day to get the full column on the move.

The king leads the procession with his knight commander and senior captains riding alongside, banners flying. Each troop proudly displays its own banner as well. The two troops of the rear guard under my command ride behind the other knights and just ahead of the supply wagons. John ordered that my personal banner *must* be flown in addition to the banners of the troops.

As the sun begins to set, a halt is called and tents are set up for the king and his entourage. The rest of us are left to camp as best we can in whatever dry spots we can find beside the road. This first night, men eat from the bread and cheese they carry in their packs while the attendants fill enormous pitchers from a cask of ale and walk up and down the line filling cups held out by thirsty men. It's all a bit haphazard – no doubt it will take awhile for this to become a smooth and practiced operation.

Our progress is slow. At least once a day – more often, twice or three times – a wagon gets mired in a mudhole. The entire column has to be halted while men and extra horses push and pull to free the wagon from its sticky trap. In the first week, three wagons suffer broken wheels from the strain of moving such heavy loads over rough roads with deep ruts and an abundance of small potholes. Thankfully, someone had the good sense to include spare wheels among the vast quantities of supplies. The broken ones are abandoned on the roadside as the army marches on.

At last we arrive at the junction east of Abbéville. What should have taken no more than four days, even at the pace of the foot soldiers, has taken a full week. Thankfully, the king has the good sense to make camp early and give his weary army a bit of rest. The next morning, we turn southwest and move on.

The following day, well before the sun reaches its noon-time zenith, we come to a quagmire on the road that's completely unpassable for the wagons. The knights' horses and the foot soldiers have obviously gone around, but the hundreds of hooves and boots have churned up the verges so badly that the mudhole now extends well off the road on both sides. My own troops have to maneuver much wider than those ahead of us to find a safe path.

The column stops while the drivers and three of the knight captains who claim to have some engineering skills debate what to do. Over the drivers' objections, the knights decide to try to build a bridge over the morass using boards from the sides of one of the wagons. Declaring themselves satisfied with their contrivance, they urge the driver of the first wagon to attempt the crossing. Unconvinced, he refuses to try it until his load is removed. The captains eventually get impatient with how long this is taking and force the poor man to drive on with half his load still in the wagon. Midway across, at the deepest part of the hole, the boards give way and the back of the wagon sinks up to its axle in mud. The driver halts his horses, who've made it most of the way across and throws up his hands in frustration.

The road is now completely blocked by a disabled wagon that's still carrying half its contents and is practically inaccessible for off-loading. Plus, we're burdened with a second wagon that now has no sides. Its load will have to be exchanged with other wagons for items that can be lashed in place with ropes for the remainder of the journey. One of the captains shouts at the drivers, "Figure something out!" before they all ride forward to report on the fiasco. I've no doubt *they* will come off blameless in the telling.

The drivers quickly unhitch the four horses from the disabled wagon. Four men get a leg up onto the backs of the big draft horses and ride off to explore the fields on either side of the road, looking for a way around that's firm enough to support the wagons. They return in a bit and start to confer with their fellow drivers. They've found a reasonably dry path, but the heaviest wagons will still have to be partially unloaded to avoid a repeat of the earlier disaster. That means some will have to make the trip twice, with four unloadings and reloadings, before everything can be taken round. It takes the rest of the day to get the remainder of the column a hundred yards up the road. The knight captains order a detail of foot soldiers to offload the goods on the stranded wagon. But when the first few men attempting to reach it sink up to their knees in mud, common sense finally prevails and the order is given to abandon the crippled wagon entirely.

Four days later, just at midday, we finally reach the western garrison. The king orders camp to be made and summons all the captains to his tent. "We'll add to our strength, leaving only one troop at the garrison," he announces, pacing back and forth in front of us. For a brief moment, I dare to hope that, as commander of the rear guard, I'll be left with the troop here. My hopes are dashed as John continues, "Louve, review the garrison troops and choose the best two to join us. Leave the weakest one behind."

He goes on. "The roads here seem better, so we march to the border tomorrow. There we'll set up camp and assess the enemy. When I've planned our tactics, you'll receive your orders. Until then, keep your men alert and ready to march at any moment. That is all."

Thus it is that some two weeks after we departed the castle, the massive army arrives at the border . . . which is deserted except for the border-control post. John orders a sumptuous camp to be set up. Huge tents for himself and Louve. Individual tents in close proximity for each of his senior commanders. Smaller tents for the troop captains, to be shared by two captains and their squires. As a show of force, he orders the camp to be as wide as possible, with the wagons and paddocks close behind, and orders the cook fires to be lit early so the smoke can be seen from a distance. None of his dispositions make any sense from a tactical perspective. Perhaps all he intends to achieve is intimidation.

He summons the captains at dawn the next morning. "I have this hour sent out scouts to find and survey the enemy's location. I've ordered them to report back to me by midday." The scouts won't get very far before they have to turn back, especially if they're to scout widely on either side of the main road. "I'll base my plans on their reports. Be ready to be summoned for orders before sundown. That is all." Hardly a necessary assembly, but John clearly enjoys strutting around in the role of field commander.

The afternoon comes and goes, the sun goes down, and there's no further summons nor are there any orders. The next morning, we see two troops ride out under the king's banner. Rumors fly through the camp that the king was dissatisfied with the previous day's reports and decided to reconnoiter the enemy himself. It's hardly a covert scouting party. They're back by midday.

Donal finds me early in the afternoon as I'm wandering around the camp to relieve the tedium of waiting. "There be a monk back there on the road asking to speak to ye, m'lord."

"Bring him to my tent, Donal. "

"He say he be lame, m'lord, and need to rest his ankle. He say can ye be going to him?"

"Why not? I've nothing else to do. Show me to this fellow."

We find the monk sitting on a low stone wall beside the road, well back of the camp, his hood pulled up on his head as he huddles over, rubbing his ankle. Once we're close he looks up and then slowly pushes back his hood. I stop in my tracks. "Samuel?" I ask hesitantly. "Is that really you?"

"Brother Samuel, my son," he answers with a mischievous grin. "Sit with me if you will, for my ankle needs rest."

"What on earth?" I ask, keeping my voice low but still astonished at the look of my good friend.

"Returning home from your errand. I decided this was the best way to avoid drawing attention to myself. The habit and haircut are courtesy of Prior Warin. No doubt Tamasine is going to have a raging fit when she sees my hair - or lack of it - but the ruse worked. I must tell you, though, I have a new respect for these men who walk everywhere they go."

"How bad's the ankle?"

"Not as bad as I've been making it look, but a horse to get the rest of the way home would not be unwelcome."

My mind is racing. This is the perfect opportunity to do something I've been plotting for days. "Donal, fetch Sirius and bring him here."

"Sirius, m'lord?"

"Yes, Donal. You know that trick he has of pretending to be lame when he wants to stop and graze for a while?"

"Aye, m'lord. But I thought ye be trying to break him of that habit."

"Actually, Donal, he'll do it on command now. Just touch the toe of your boot to his left fetlock as you lead him out, and he'll limp along as if he's in terrible pain. Make sure lots of people see him limping as you lead him through the camp."

"Aye, m'lord. I be back with Sirius."

When he leaves, Samuel says, "I can't take your horse, Alfred."

"You'd be doing me a favor. I couldn't leave him behind from the outset. John would've noticed and asked too many questions. But I'd never be able to make good an escape on so recognizable a horse, so I've been teaching him this trick. I'd feared having to simply abandon him somewhere to fend for himself, but now you can take him. He's perfectly sound. I just need a reason to ride nondescript horses. Now tell me what you can before Donal gets back."

"Egon was away on a hunt when I got there, so I had to wait a day and a half for his return. He told me what was in your letter. There must be an enormous amount of trust between the two of you."

"It's growing."

"I stayed a few extra days. Told Egon everything about how I thought John would order his forces and conduct a campaign. God help us, Alfred. We're both traitors now and doomed if anyone should find out."

"Traitors to a king, perhaps, my friend, but not traitors to the kingdom. We're merely being forced into unconventional means to try to preserve the realm."

"By the time I left, I feared the army would already be here, so I took the long way back using the trails to the reservoir."

"Sometime when this is all over, remind me to tell you how it can take an army an entire day to cover a single mile," I laugh.

Donal is coming down the road with Sirius following behind, still pretending lameness. Samuel pulls his hood up and reaches for my hand to help him stand, though we both know that's not really necessary. "Don't let him keep that up for very long else he really will strain a muscle and go lame," I say, giving him a leg up onto the horse. I stroke Sirius's nose and tell him, "You're safe now, my friend."

"I should be on my way," says Samuel. "It's probably not wise for you to linger here."

"And Tamasine is probably beside herself with worry. Get yourself home and grow your hair." They ride off slowly.

Walking back to camp, I tell Donal, "Find me the most ordinary looking horse you can from the paddock. In fact, once we're on the move again, get me a different horse every day or two, as if I'm having trouble finding one that suits me."

"Ye be up to something, I be thinking, sir."

"Just being prepared, Donal."

"Ye can count on me, m'lord."

"Of that, I've no doubt." We walk on a bit before I add, "And Donal?"

"Aye, m'lord?"

"Not a word of what just happened to anyone. Do you understand?"

"We just be helping a poor lame monk who need to get back to the monastery. And we give him a lame horse to do it."

I clap him on the shoulder. "Donal, you are indeed a squire fit for a king."

The next morning, another dawn summons . . . another chance for the king to show off as field commander. "Neither my scouts nor my own troops have seen any sign of the enemy. Either they are unaware we are here or they've fled to the west. It's my belief they've fled as it would be difficult to be unaware of an army of this size.

"We must therefore pursue them. We march tomorrow morning at first light. Lord Alfred, your rear guard will remain here. Secure the border. Protect the reserve supplies. If and when you're to move forward, a courier will bring my orders. The rest of you, get your men ready. My commanders will organize the supply train and advise you of the order of march. That is all."

The day is a beehive of activity for all but the two troops under my command. And it takes the entire morning of the next day before the final elements of the column are underway. What's left behind is an unorganized hodge-podge of half-empty wagons, piles of off-loaded supplies, discarded tents, half the paddock horses, a couple dozen camp attendants, and two troops of knights. Much as I would like to give them the time to rest, maintaining discipline requires that I issue orders to occupy the afternoon. I assign Mordyce, the captain of my other troop, to reorganize the camp, making it more compact and better suited to action should we be called on to defend our position. I take half the men from my troop and assign them to help the attendants reorganize the supplies in the wagons so we can be ready to advance when the orders come, for I have no doubt they will.

As we settle in to wait, I give Mordyce responsibility for organizing the knights' daily drills, knowing he has more experience in such things. Three days later, as we're starting the midday meal, the messenger arrives. He's ridden hard, his horse lathered with sweat. Desperate to complete his mission, he breathlessly blurts his orders. "Lord Alfred, sir. You're to march as soon as you can, sir, to join the army." Panting, he adds, "With all the supplies, sir."

I turn to the nearest attendant, who's serving small ale. "Get a cup and some food for this man. He's had a hard ride." Turning back to the courier, I bid him to sit and catch his breath. Once he seems to have recovered his wits, I call Mordyce over. "Now, my good man, eat . . . drink . . . and tell us everything that's happened since the army left here."

He gobbles down half a bowl of pottage and drains his cup before he begins. "We marched the whole first day, m'lord, with nary a sight of the enemy. Same thing the next day. But the day after, we come up over a little rise and there they are. A huge force massed across the road at the bottom of the hill. The king calls a halt and makes camp on the high ground. That night, he sends for me and orders me to ride at top speed to give you your instructions. I rode all night and this morning to get here."

The courier tucks into the rest of his meal, and Mordyce asks, "If we left this afternoon, man, how far could we get?"

"If it be just your knights, Captain, maybe halfway." Then he gestures around the camp. "But with all this – what with having to break camp and all – no more than a quarter of the way there, if that far."

Mordyce turns to me. "What say you, Lord Alfred?"

I rub my chin. "It sounds like if we leave in the morning, we can get there in a day and a half with our smaller force. Let's spend the afternoon getting properly organized and be ready to leave at sunrise. Mordyce, you're in charge of the order of march." Leaving him to sort out all the tasks that need to be done, I walk back through the wagons and toward the spot where I had spoken with Samuel. I need some time to think about what awaits us.

Egon's tactics are nothing short of brilliant. By not assembling his force on the border, he's forced John to invade, removing any doubt that John is the aggressor. His choice of where to deploy his force is equally impressive. I know that spot well. The westbound traveler is aware of a rise in the terrain, but it's gentle and deceiving. Coming over the ridge, the land drops away suddenly to what appears to be a valley below. This is where Egon has positioned his troops.

John will no doubt be confident, being in possession of the high ground. What he won't know, since he's not using his scouts effectively, is what lies beyond. What from the top of the ridge looks like a small valley extending westward with high ground on all sides is actually just a narrow flat that falls off again to a much wider plain below. I have no doubt that the rest of Egon's men are deployed on the plain and that the other lords are bringing up their own forces to join him there. With Egon's deployments obscuring the view of the terrain to his rear and John focused on the army arrayed directly in front of him, I have no doubt who really holds the advantage.

My own situation now becomes much trickier. Tomorrow I'll set foot on foreign soil as a captain in an aggressor army. Though this is not of my choosing, it's still not to my liking. Keeping my promise to Egon will be a narrow and difficult path to walk, but walk it I must.

Tonight, while Mordyce is away from the tent checking that all his dispositions are in place for the morning, I tell Donal, "Fold my banner and stow it away."

"Ye be sure of that, m'lord?"

"Aye, Donal. There's no reason to draw attention to where in the army we might be."

"What about the king's orders, sir?"

"Leave that to me, Donal. From now on, we ride only under the banner of the troop." One more preparation achieved.

But naturally, it's the first thing Mordyce notices as we prepare to move out at sunrise. "Your banner, Lord Alfred," he remarks. "It seems we've forgotten it."

"Not at all, Mordyce. It's still with us. But I want our men to take pride in their troop, just as the knights of the other troops do. They'll be a better fighting unit that way." He looks at me curiously but can think of no good objection. Not for the first time, I wonder if he's the one keeping an eye on me. But then I've wondered that about every man under my command at one time or another.

By early afternoon of the following day, the king's camp is in sight on the top of the ridge. It takes our column another hour to reach it. I order our camp to be set up at the rear and assign Mordyce to find out what's to be done with the wagons and to organize their deployment. I take time to observe that everything is being taken care of properly and to check with Donal on my personal arrangements, before setting out on foot for the king's tent, where his sentry admits me immediately.

John looks up from some sort of drawings he's poring over with Louve and the senior captains. I bow slightly and say, "Lord Alfred reporting as ordered, Your Grace."

"About time you got here," he says. I make no reply.

"Very well," he continues, "set up your camp at the rear. Your men are to be on watch for any action that might come from the rear or our rear flanks."

"Yes, Your Grace." There's no need to agitate him by telling him I've already given those orders.

"Then that is all."

I'm on my way out the tent opening when he calls me back. "One more thing, Alfred."

"Yes, Your Grace?"

"Your banner wasn't seen when you rode into camp. Are you defying my orders?"

"I hope not, Your Grace. However, I've been observing – as Sir Louve suggested – how the more experienced captains run their troops. It seems to me, Your Grace, that the best captains make sure their men take pride in their troop and fight for the glory of their king. I want my men to be loyal to you above all else."

"Hmph." Thankfully, John isn't quick-witted, so he can't come up with a retort in the moment that would force me to fly my banner without somehow diminishing his own stature. So he changes the subject.

"Where's that horse of yours?" Proof that he has someone watching me, for he wouldn't himself have seen us ride in.

"He came up lame, Your Grace."

"Lame?" he asks, as if not believing me.

"I removed a stone from his hoof the day we arrived at the garrison and thought he was improving. But he got worse. I'm sure many people in camp saw how badly he was limping."

"Hmph. Where is he now?"

"There was a monk passing in the rear of the camp while I was assessing the injury. Said he thought he could heal him but it might take several weeks. So I gave him to the monk."

"What was a monk doing loitering behind our camp?"

"It wasn't unusual for people to wander up near the rear while we were camped at the border, Your Grace. Mostly, it was lads from the village – likely wanting to watch the grand army and imagine being knights themselves one day. This fellow was just making his way to the monastery from who knows where and sat down to rest on a stone wall."

"Hmph. So why would you give him a horse you set such store by?"

"An army on the march can't be held back by men or animals that can't keep up, Your Grace. I preferred to give him away rather than see him slaughtered."

"Hmph. Sounds like maybe you're actually getting some military sense. Very well, get on with it. I have work to do here." And he waves me out.

Two more dangerous hurdles cleared.

The next morning, another dawn summons for the captains. "I've consulted with my commanders. They agree we hold the position of advantage on the high ground. The enemy will have to attack uphill to engage us. So we wait. Eventually, they won't be able to brook invaders in their territory and will have no choice but to attack. We wait. Keep your men alert and at the ready. That is all."

If John could think beyond what was staring him in the face, he might be a formidable opponent. As it is, the only thing his strategy is achieving is buying Egon time for all the western lords to gather on the plain. John, however, is confident in his assessment and so, like a siege army, we sit in camp and wait. Unlike a siege army, I see no indication he intends to do anything to harass his opponents or challenge them to begin the fight.

Two days later, I'm contemplating writing a letter to Gwen when the king's squire bursts into my tent. "The king be wanting to see ye now, Lord Alfred," he says breathlessly. It's obvious the man's been running as fast as he can. "He be right angry and say get ye to him quick as can be, m'lord."

I rise. "Calm yourself, man. You've done your job. I'll hurry along to the king's tent." In fact, I walk at my usual brisk pace but with no added sense of urgency. The sentry doesn't even bother to tell me I can enter . . . just quickly steps aside.

John is pacing about, a piece of paper in his hand. He stops the instant he sees me. "What's this all about, Alfred?" he demands, clearly enraged.

"With respect, Your Grace, I have no idea what you're talking about."

"This!" he shouts, waving the paper above his head.

"Again with respect, Your Grace, all I can discern is that it appears you've received a message of some sort."

He thrusts the paper at me. "Read!" I take the page from his hand and begin to read.

Your Grace,

As from the moment of writing this letter, I withdraw my oath of loyalty to Your Grace and reclaim the Devereux lands as a fiefdom distinct and separate from your kingdom. My messengers will inform the knights among your army who hail from the Devereux domain that their loyalty is now owed only to Devereux and that they are free to return to their homes if they choose to do so. I will not punish or seek to force the return of any man who chooses to remain in your service.

May God be with Your Grace and your kingdom. May God be with the domain of Devereux.

Given under my hand and seal in the third year of the reign of John, 15th king.

Lord Devereux

It takes every ounce of will I can muster to remain silent and keep my face free of expression as I hand the missive back to John, who's resumed his furious pacing. He jerks the page from my hand. "I ask you again, Alfred. What's this all about?"

"It seems, Your Grace, that Lord Devereux has chosen to exercise his ancient right to withdraw from the pact that created the kingdom."

"He can't do that!" shouts the king.

"On the contrary, Sire, he has that right. The oath freely given can be freely withdrawn."

"For what reason?" John is still shouting in rage.

"No reason is required, Your Grace. Those who willingly joined with our ancestor to form the kingdom did so with certain rights guaranteed in perpetuity. Withdrawal was one of those rights. It provided the assurances necessary for the ancient lords to agree to cede some of their power to the king in return for the advantages of a larger and stronger realm."

John continues pacing for several minutes without saying another word. I have no need to interrupt the silence. Finally, he stops, apparently having reached some decision, and slams the paper down on the table in front of him.

"Very well. Let him go," he says angrily. "He's no use to me here, anyway. Now get out and get back to drilling your men."

Once out of sight of the king's tent, I slow my pace. I need time to think. The lords have acted. As first lord of the realm, Devereux had to go first. But I know – as certainly as I know the sun rises in the east – that messengers will begin arriving from all the others. They've chosen to dissolve the kingdom rather than be part of John's madness. A bold move. One that's unlikely to be reversed in John's lifetime, for he would never acquiesce to their demands. One that may be irreversible if John Gundar is raised to be of like mind to his father. Of one thing, I'm certain. It was not a decision taken lightly. And as I think more about it, I must admire the path they've chosen, for it avoids the violent and bloody revolt that I've no doubt would have come on the heels of this war.

For myself, it means that I'm likely in greater danger than ever before, being isolated in what's left of John's realm. But it also means there are more and closer places where I could take refuge with my family should I decide to flee.

The next morning, two more messengers arrive and rumors fly through the camp that the king is raging mad, though no one seems to know the cause.

Tonight, I take the first watch. I've observed a few of the captains sharing watch duties with their men, so my following suit raises no eyebrows. After the stars begin to appear, with the camp settling into a quiet slumber, I walk our section of the perimeter. As I reach the point farthest away from any tent, three men approach from behind a wagon. One of them whispers, "A word with you, Lord Alfred?"

"How can I help you?"

"Well, sir, we just want to know if it's true," says the one who spoke first.

One of his mates adds, "You see, sir, we hail from Neukirk Market, sir. And the man who was here yesterday . . . he said we're free to go home."

The third man says, "He said we only owe loyalty to Lord Devereux now, and we could go serve our lord. How could that be, sir?"

Whispering as well, I reply, "The explanation is long and complicated, but the simple answer is that it's true. Your loyalty is bound only to Lord Devereux now, so you may stay or go as you choose."

The first man speaks again. "If it's true as you say, your lordship, then what should we do?"

"I can't tell you what to do, my friends. You must each make that decision for yourself. But I'll give you this advice. If you speak with your mates, do so quietly and in secret. You don't want your captains or the king getting wind of it. And if you choose to go, leave quietly in the night. The king has no right to pursue you or detain you, but it will be easier for you if you just slip away quietly and not draw attention to yourselves."

"Thank you, Lord Alfred," whispers the first man. "God go with you." They disappear behind the wagon, back to their units, and I continue my patrol. This could get very interesting indeed.

The remaining four messengers arrive throughout the following morning. Word passes quickly through the camp that the king is raging at anyone and everyone who comes into his sight. Yet when the captains are summoned at midafternoon, there's no sign of fury – only the pompous field commander that has become the familiar centerpiece of these assemblies.

"I've been assessing the enemy over these past days as we've prepared for an attack. We hold the advantage in both position and numbers – an enormous advantage in numbers." My poor deluded brother. I almost feel sorry for him.

"There's no need for us to delay here any longer. We attack tomorrow – when the sun is at its zenith and they're distracted by their midday meal." Even I can work out there would be better times to attack, but apparently the commanders have little influence over their king. "We'll dispense with the force that's blocking our path, and on the day after, we'll resume our march to clear out and take control of the Territories once and for all. Sir Louve will give you your orders. That is all."

As the others leave the tent, I hang back. Perhaps I owe it to the men, if not to John himself, to try to prevent a complete slaughter. "Are you waiting for something, Alfred?" John growls. "I said you were dismissed."

"With all due respect, Your Grace, do you know what's beyond that blocking force?"

"What business is that of yours?"

"If you recall, Your Grace, I've been on this road before. I know something about the terrain."

"Ah, yes. When you came back from your captivity," he wrinkles his nose on the last word, as if he really doesn't believe I was ever held captive. "Tell me, why should I put any stock in the supposed memories of a man who was half out of his mind with starvation when last he was here? Now get back to your troops and obey your orders before I bring you up on charges."

His mood and manner leave no doubt that anything further from me would do no more than put myself and others at risk. I'll have to assuage my conscience with the fact that I tried.

It's to be a full frontal assault down the hill onto the flat. Thankfully, my orders are to maintain position as rear guard, out of sight behind the crest of the ridge. We're not to engage or change our position unless the army is outflanked and assaulted from the rear. I'm confident my men will see no action tomorrow.

Tonight, I've elected to take the second watch, mixing things up to be sure no one can detect a pattern in my behavior. As I make my rounds, I notice the occasional stealthy movement of men among the wagons. From time to time, I see shadowy figures, hunched over to minimize the risk of being seen, hurrying away from the camp, back toward the border. "God go with you, my friends," I think to myself. "You've made a very wise decision." In all, I see three dozen or so making good their escape. Their numbers are no more than the number of deserters that would typically be expected on the eve of a big battle, so there will as yet be no cause for concern.

The day dawns fair, and the captains begin assembling their troops. At midday, the horns sound and the downhill charge begins. Archers have been positioned on the ridge with orders to take out any of the enemy who might get past our troops. Leaving Mordyce in charge at the rear, I edge up to the top of the ridge, ostensibly to keep an eye on our flanks, but also to observe the battle.

Egon has prepared well. Our lead elements are cut down immediately by ceaseless volleys of arrows from his archers. He then quickly moves his knights in to engage with our next wave. In the narrow space, what John had perceived as an advantage in numbers becomes our biggest disadvantage as the advancing troops ride into the backs of those ahead of them. With our army compressed into a solid mass, our archers can do little to help them, for fear of killing our own men. We have no long-bowmen, who could easily shoot into the back ranks of Egon's forces – only the standard bows with their limited range – another tactical mistake.

The melée below is ear-shattering. Swords and armor clashing. Men shouting battle cries or orders. Horses and men screaming in agony as they're taken down. Blood everywhere, turning the ground to bloody mud under the churning of scores of hooves.

Realizing that his men are being slaughtered for no gain, John calls an end to the attack. There's massive confusion as our tightly compressed forces try to get turned around to come back up the hill, and more men are lost as Egon takes advantage of the chaos.

By midafternoon, it's all over. The white flags are flown and men from both sides move into the field to retrieve the dead and wounded. Even this is a brutal affair. The wounded who are deemed unlikely to survive . . . or who would be too much of a burden to drag along with the army . . . are ruthlessly dispatched by their fellow knights, screaming as they're slaughtered. Those with wounds that can be quickly patched up are helped back into the ranks. The dead are then carried from the field. Ours is the more arduous task, as our dead have to be carried up the hill.

Someone decides this is a waste of effort and orders all the bodies to be piled up halfway up the hill. One of the empty wagons is broken up and the wood placed around the bodies. Then the whole thing is set ablaze in an enormous, horrific funeral pyre. The stench of burning flesh pervades the air, and I wonder if I'll ever smell anything else again.

I take the second watch again tonight, knowing I won't be able to sleep after what I've witnessed today. As the camp slumbers, more shadowy figures steal away into the night. I try to get inside Egon's mind. Most likely he's spending this night bringing fresh troops up from the plain, allowing today's fighters to retreat to rest and recoup their strength for another day. Will his fellow lords leave him in overall command? Or will we face a different commander in the next battle?

The next day dawns cloudy, and soon after daylight, the rain begins, dousing the smoldering remains of the pyre and helping to cleanse the air. John calls another assembly of captains. "The enemy is more capable than we credited them to be. We must therefore change our tactics. We will attack with a smaller force, allowing more room to maneuver and engage. The remainder of our army will be held in reserve to finish them off once the lead force has reduced their numbers.

"Report your losses to the senior commanders. They'll reorganize so the remaining troops are at full strength. Then the lead attack force will receive their orders. We attack once it's dry enough to avoid the risk of breaking the horses' legs. That is all."

The rain stops and the sun appears just after midday, but the hillside and battleground are a morass of mud. There'll be no attack today. Much to Mordyce's dismay, I invite the senior knights from both our troops to share the dry ground inside our tent for the night. Ten men in a space usually occupied by four is crowded by any standard, but the men are grateful, and even those not so lucky as to be invited inside seem to appreciate that their captains are doing what they can to take care of the troops. Tonight, I don't share the watch.

The next day, the smaller force attacks after sunrise. Watching from my position at the top of the ridge, I can see they're having more success in maneuvering, but the smaller number of men in the narrow space helps the enemy as well. After a flurry of fighting, our attack force turns and rides back up the hill.

In the early afternoon, another, different force is sent down the hill. It seems the commanders have convinced John to change his tactics. Short, harassing attacks to wear the enemy down seem to be the new approach.

This keeps up for the next two days. I've been watching carefully. Egon and his fellow lords are not fully replenishing the blocking force each night. They want to be seen to be losing numbers as well, in an effort to convince John that he's making progress, wearing him down while enticing him to further action. As our commanders tally our own losses, the realization hasn't yet dawned on the king that an increasing portion of those losses is due to the growing number of men who are quietly walking away each night to go home to their lords.

On the following day, it seems John has prevailed over the commanders, for an all-out frontal assault is ordered once again. This time, the following elements aren't allowed to follow so closely behind those ahead, so the density of men and horses in the small valley is better managed. But the outcome is the same, and the attack is quickly halted.

As the sun is lowering in the west, I'm summoned to report to Sir Louve. He wastes no time. "Another attack is planned for tomorrow. I need fresh troops to lead it. You'll move your men to the front at dawn. You'll get your orders then. Dismissed."

This is the moment I've been dreading . . . dreading and planning for over all these past weeks. I *will* keep my promise to Egon. And so I must put the last bits of my plan into action tonight. Fortunately, it's a new moon.

I go in search of Mordyce. "So those are our orders."

"Finally," he says. "A chance to be part of the action."

"I've assigned myself the third watch so the men can be fully rested for the fight tomorrow. Assemble them at the front at dawn and collect our orders. I'll turn things over to the day watch, collect my gear, and join you quick as can be. Now let's get the men together and tell them what's afoot."

After supper, I ask Donal to walk with me, and we wander as far away as I dare from prying ears. He already knows what tomorrow's orders are, having been present when we briefed the men, so he's quite distressed. "Here's what we're going to do, Donal," I tell him, speaking in a whisper. "Before you wake me for the third watch, I want you to saddle your horse and get one from the paddock saddled for me – one I haven't ridden before. Tether them to a wagon somewhere out of sight of the watch, and put feedbags on them so they'll be quiet.

"Once you wake me, stay in the tent like always. Then when the others are again asleep, sneak out and come find me. I want to be away as many hours before dawn as we can manage."

"Aye, m'lord. What do we bring with us?"

"Nothing, Donal. Leave everything. I want things to look perfectly normal when Mordyce and his squire awake in the morning."

"Aye, m'lord."

"Everything except my banner, that is. I don't want to risk anyone deciding to march under that banner once we're gone."

"I be putting it under yer saddle like an extra blanket, sir."

"Perfect, Donal. Now let's get back. We don't need anyone getting suspicious."

I return to the tent and join Mordyce in attending to all the things any knight would do in preparing for battle. I check my sword and dagger. Our squires lay out armor and the rest of our gear for the morrow, and we check the gear. Everyone is quiet, filled with anticipation and trepidation. With nothing more to do and dark settling in, we go to bed. Pulling my blanket over me, I say, "I don't know what tomorrow will bring, Mordyce, but you're a good captain. I know you'll bring your men through." It's all I can do for those I'm leaving behind.

I feign sleep, for actual sleep eludes me entirely. The others snore softly. No one stirs when Donal rises. It's a peculiar thing I've noticed with soldiers – they seem to be able to sleep soundly through anything whenever they have the chance. There's a bit of snorting and snuffling and shifting position when Donal wakes me, but that's normal.

I take over from the second watch and begin a regular patrol as the man I've relieved heads off to his bed. Midway through my second pass, Donal appears with the horses . . . sooner than I'd dared to hope. I take the reins of mine, and we begin to walk as quietly as possible through the field, avoiding the clatter of hooves on the road and hoping desperately to avoid stepping on big sticks in the dark and alerting the watch with the noise. My eyes have already adjusted to the starlight, so I can see at least some of what's underfoot. The horses seem to sense the need for silence – neither of them has uttered so much as a low nicker, and they're taking care where they step. The night is clear, meaning sound will carry, but there's a slight westerly breeze that will help to carry it away from the camp.

After what I judge to be about half an hour – when we've long since lost the ability to make out the silhouette of the camp on the ridge and we're likely more than a mile away – we mount and begin to ride at a slow walk up the slight rise ahead of us. Once over that rise, as the land slopes downhill, we urge the horses to a trot and angle toward the road. The horses easily clear the low stone wall beside the road, and we're on a metaled surface once again. Knowing that the horses can see far better in the low light than we can, I urge mine to a gentle canter and Donal follows suit. By the time the sun is fully above the horizon, I estimate we must be nearly a third of the way to the border.

It's a long, nerve-wracking day, but we dare not stop. My ears are alert to every little sound. Several times I turn to look back, fearing to see riders galloping in pursuit. We have to rest the horses from time to time and let them graze. The little streams are running full, so there's water for us and our horses. But we push on as soon as we can. As sundown approaches, we come to a dilapidated hut . . . the sort so familiar to me on my long walk home from captivity. We spend the night there, both of us so exhausted we sleep soundly all night.

At the first hint of light, we saddle the horses and are on our way. Nearing the border, we take to the fields again to avoid the border controls. When I can see the village in the distance, I know we're safely across. I want to avoid the village, knowing I'll be recognized, but we need food.

"Ye keep on, m'lord," says Donal. "They not be knowing me in the village, so I get us some food and meet ye between here and the garrison." I give him a small purse with a few coins, and he's on his way. We still have to be careful not to meet a patrol from the garrison looking for immigrants, but since they're down to a single troop, I judge the risk to be much reduced.

When we meet back up, Donal has managed some bread, cheese, and small ale for us and oats for the horses. We stay in the fields until we're well past the garrison then turn south. Knowing we're safe on Ernle's land, we stop in a little grove by a stream. The food and ale go down well. Donal puts the oats in the feedbags for the horses, and they munch contentedly.

I've been debating all day whether to divert to Ernle Manor for a day or to continue home. I'd like to express my gratitude to the lords and get word to them what's happening in the Territories. But I also know that my family is at risk if John decides to do something like order their detention once he discovers my desertion. We've not seen any fast couriers, but we've also taken diversions off the main road. In the end, I decide I can't risk my family's safety, and we press on.

We stay on or near the road as much as we can. I want to know if any fast riders go by. I avoid the villages; Donal continues to buy our food; we camp in the open at night.

Rejoining me beyond the village just before the junction with the Great Trunk Road, Donal says, "There be talk in the village of a great sickness, m'lord. At first they be fearful of me, but when I say I come from the west, they agree to sell me some food. They tell me best I go back west – there be a plague in the east, and people be dying from it."

Now I have a new worry for my family. We pick up our pace. The next day, when Donal goes into a village along the way, he comes back with a very worried expression on his face. "There be sick people there, m'lord. Lots of 'em. I think mayhap it not be safe for us to eat their food, so I just get some oats for the horses."

"We have a bit of bread and cheese left and two and a half days' ride ahead of us. We can make it," I tell him. "Just a few bites of bread and cheese a day for each of us."

"A bit of ale left, too, sir."

"Save that for tomorrow. And let's not drink from any stream that's close to a village."

We keep moving as fast as the horses can manage. Tonight they only get half the oats Donal has bought. I don't want to risk going into another village.

As we ride on, there's more and more evidence of the sickness. Even though we stay clear of the villages, we sometimes pick up a terrible stench as of bodies rotting in the sun. We skirt the castle town and turn south toward the manor. The sun sets, but we press on. I can't wait a moment longer to know if those I love are safe.

It's an hour or so before midnight when we arrive. My banging on the door eventually brings a servant with a candle. In his sleepy state, he doesn't recognize me at first. I push on the door saying, "Let us in," and finally recognition dawns. "Oh, my God, Lord Alfred!" And then he shouts for Rupert.

I push past him and head up the stairs where Rupert intercepts me. "Calm down, Alfred. It's the middle of the night. How did you get here?"

"Later, Uncle. I want to see Gwen and the children."

I try to go past him, but he says, "Come downstairs with me, Alfred."

"Whatever it is can wait," I reply curtly. "I need to know my family's safe." And again I start up the stairs.

Rupert puts a hand on my arm and stops me. "Alfred."

Fear grips my heart. I can tell by his tone that something's terribly wrong. I turn to face him.

"Alfred, they've gone."

In the drawing room, Rupert pours me a brandy, which I down in a single gulp. He refills my glass and motions me to the couch. The servants have been awakened, and one of them is kindling a fire in the hearth, for though it's nearly summer, there's still a chill in the night air. Rupert has sent for my mother. I'm trying to get my wits about me despite being exhausted, hungry, and frightened for my family's safety.

The door opens, and Mother hurries across the room to embrace me. "Thank God you're safe, Alfred." Her mere presence helps to calm me, as my uncle knew it would.

Taking one more sip of brandy, I say with as much calm as I can muster, "Tell me everything."

"She never wavered," begins Rupert, "in her belief that you'd find a way out and come home before the war ended. It looks like she was right." The door opens again and Catherine crosses to sit beside Rupert.

"She began preparing just as soon as Osbert returned," Rupert continues, "convinced somehow that you wouldn't have sent him back here unless you were planning to return soon yourself. She knew it wouldn't be safe for you to stay here if you'd deserted the king. So she wanted to be ready to leave as soon as you arrived."

"We can talk about that later," I say, trying not to sound impatient. "Just tell me why and where they've gone."

"It was the sickness she was afraid of, Alfred," says Catherine.

"Everyone thought it was gone with the warm days of spring," Rupert picks up the thread again. "Then the rains came. Some of the loose soil washed away from the shallow graves near the castle town. No one paid much attention at first, but then people started seeing rats and such nosing around the graves, preying on whatever bits of corpses were exposed. And the sickness started again. Among the shacks, at first, but it quickly spread to the town. It wasn't long before we heard it was rampant in the port as well. People dying in great numbers."

"There's a rumor that the queen and her children have all been taken ill," says Catherine. "No one knows for sure. Alice wrote to her, but as usual, there was no reply."

Rupert resumes. "Gwen thought we were safe here, being far enough away and in the open air of the country. But then we heard there were sick people in Great Woolston. That's when she decided she could wait no longer."

My mother reaches out and touches my hand. "She's with child, Alfred. She wouldn't risk the children or the baby."

I bury my face in my hands, and Mother puts an arm around my shoulders. "As much as it broke my heart for her to leave before you returned, Son, I knew her decision was the right one."

"Why didn't I know?" is all I can think to say.

"She was about to tell you when all this madness with John began. But she held back, not wanting to add to your worries while you were in his clutches," Mother replies softly.

Gathering my wits, I ask, "When did they leave? And where have they gone?"

"They left a week ago," replies my uncle, "with your safe passage document to get them through any checkpoints. She knew once she was on Devereux's lands they were safe from harassment by the king's men. Her plan was to wait three days for you at Devereux Castle before going on – to where, she wouldn't say."

"So you know about the lords' action?"

"Aye," answers Rupert. "I was in the room when they took the decision. They were having one of their usual gatherings at Montfort's when the news came that the army was on the march. Devereux called a formal meeting of the lords in Council and sent word to me to be there. Three days after the army marched, they met in the Council chamber at the castle and held a proper vote. There was some cursory discussion as part of the formality, but it was clear they were all resolved. The messengers accompanied Ernle when he went home and were sent out from there after the last elements of the army crossed the border and were gone a full day with no sign of returning. It was all very legally and properly done."

While my uncle was talking, my mind has been racing. "You say she left a week ago?" I'm up and pacing the room.

"That's right," replies my mother.

"That means I've only a day – two at the most – to get to them. I've got to leave now." I make for the door.

"Alfred," calls my uncle, somewhat sternly. "Sit down. You're exhausted and hungry. You need sleep and food. Stay the rest of the night. Get yourself some clean clothes and a pack with food and water from here that we know is safe. You can ride out in the morning."

Then it dawns on me. "You said she was going to Devereux's. That means they had to go through the port. But the sickness is rampant there. How could she take such a chance?"

Mother's voice is quiet and calm, trying to allay my fear. "They left at dawn, Alfred, so they wouldn't have to stop anywhere until after they'd crossed the river and cleared the houses around the ferry. She insisted everyone wear kerchiefs over their noses and mouths. Once back in the countryside, she planned to burn the kerchiefs.

"She took enough food and water for the whole journey. We don't know if there's sickness in Neukirk Market or not. And she planned to sleep in the carriage at night . . . said she wouldn't risk staying in an inn where she didn't know who'd been there the night before."

"Where do you think she's going?" I ask again, somewhat plaintively.

"As Rupert said, dear," Mother replies, "she wouldn't tell us. But if I were to venture a guess, I would say it's most likely she would go to her parents."

Exhaustion is finally taking its toll on me, and I collapse back into my seat. I finish my brandy.

"Go to bed," says Rupert. "I'll have the servants pack for you and get a groom to saddle you a horse in the morning."

"Star Dancer," I tell him.

"Star Dancer it will be. Then you and Donal can be on your way as soon as you've eaten."

"No, Uncle. I'm going alone. A man alone can travel even faster than two, and I won't subject Donal to the risks I may have to take."

"Are you sure?" asks Rupert

"Absolutely, Uncle."

"Very well, now get some sleep."

The brandy has done its work, and I'm asleep as soon as my head hits the pillow. I'd expected to sleep fitfully, but I stir not even once until the early light streaming around the edges of the draperies brings me suddenly alert. Donal has a hot bath ready, and, as he helps me bathe and dress, he protests my decision to go alone. "What if something happen, m'lord? What if ye get hurt or sick? Ye'd have no one to look after ye."

"I'm grateful for what you want to do, Donal. But if I don't get to my family . . . if I lose them somehow . . . then it matters little if I'm hurt or sick or dead. Stay here and look out for Lady Alice. Then I'll know I don't have to worry about her."

"It make me sad to see ye go off on yer own, sir, but if it be what ye want . . ."

"It's the best thing you could do for me, Donal."

My pack is ready, Star Dancer is saddled, and I'm on my way while the early morning sun is still casting long shadows of the trees and buildings. Though departure is poignant – I've no idea when I'll see these people again – I can think of little other than how quickly I can cover the distance between here and my family. Urging Star Dancer to a canter, I tell him, "Take me to them, old friend."

We arrive at the edge of the port town before midday. I slow Star Dancer to a walk, and we begin to make our way through the town to the ferry dock. The smell of sickness is pervasive. Looking down one side alley, I see the undertaker's wagon collecting bodies from a house and move quickly on. There are few people about and no sign of the gangs that once roamed the streets and alleyways.

At the dock, disappointment. The ferry is on the other side. I ring the bell to call for it to cross. Many minutes pass with no sign of activity on the other side. I ring again. Behind me, I hear a voice, "Ye be wasting yer time. They all be dead on t'other side . . . dead or so sick they be a'most dead."

I turn to see a shabby figure shuffling up the dock. He looks sick himself. He sits down on the dock and leans against the wall of the warehouse.

How am I going to get across? The current here isn't swift – that's why this spot was chosen for the ferry crossing. Star Dancer could probably swim it, but not with me on his back. Could I swim it alongside him? Of that, I'm much less certain. And how would I keep the food in my pack dry?

Seeming to read my thoughts, the old man – even though he's probably not much older than me, the effect of the sickness makes him seem old – the old man says, "Ye be needing a boat."

"That would help, but there's none in sight," I tell him.

"I know where there be a boat . . . my boat."

"Would you let me use it?"

"Aye. But I have to sell it to ye as it not be coming back."

"Show me the boat."

"It be round the corner." He points in the direction from which he'd come. "Ye go look at it if ye want. I be too tired to go back."

I lead Star Dancer down the dock and around the corner of the warehouse. There, tied to a post is a small boat, big enough for two people at most, with a couple of oars in the bottom. It's floating and dry inside, so presumably it's not leaky. I return to the old man.

"I'll buy your boat. How much?"

"Two gold coins," he says.

"It's not worth that much. Why would I pay you that when I could just go back and take it?"

He grins a toothless grin. "Ye be a fine gentlemen, but ye not be a dumb one. And I think ye not be a thief either. It be a sound boat. And I not be having any food these last two days."

"Very well. Half a silver coin and no more."

He holds out his hand, which shakes slightly from hunger or fever or both. I drop the half-coin into it, taking care not to touch him. He bites the coin to be sure it's real, then closes his hand tightly around it. I wonder if he'll survive long enough to buy something to eat.

Returning to my boat, I realize I have another dilemma. I'll need both hands to row so how to keep hold of Star Dancer? I could tether his reins to the iron ring on the bow of the boat but what if the bit gets pulled out of his mouth? Farther up the dock, I find a long rope line lying abandoned. I tie it around Star Dancer's chest, just behind his forelegs, and am relieved when there's enough left over to easily secure him to the boat.

I climb the three steps down the ladder, step in, and secure my pack in the bow – only to realize I have another problem. The river is deep here where the trading ships come in, but the docks are at least three feet above the surface. Where can I find a lower spot where my horse can more easily enter the water?

As if he senses my dilemma, Star Dancer starts prancing about on the dock above me. Before I realize what's about to happen, he leaps and lands with a giant splash in the river just beyond the boat. Thankfully, I've held onto his rope. I immediately secure it to the bow ring and then shake myself dry of the river water that splashed onto me. Releasing the mooring, I grab the oars and we start to make our way across, aiming for the shallow bank just west of the ferry.

Climbing out of the water and onto dry land, Star Dancer gives a massive shake to rid his coat of the river water. I let him pull the boat up onto the bank to a point where I can disembark without getting my boots soaked. Slinging my pack on my back and releasing my horse from his rope, I mount up and we're on our way.

I push on even after sundown trying to reach Neukirk Market. We camp in the open before we get to the town. I'll follow Gwen's example and not risk the inns. Dawn breaks fair, and I know if we push hard we can make Devereux Castle sometime after nightfall. Star Dancer is willing, and we cover the distance as quickly as I could hope.

The last rays of the sun have long vanished and the stars are growing brilliant in the night sky when we come upon a village and I can make out the silhouette of the castle in the distance. As we draw closer, lights in the castle windows heighten my sense of urgency, and I press Star Dancer to a gallop. The sentry makes me wait at the gate for what seems like an interminable time until Lord Devereux's squire arrives to vouch for me. Walking across the outer bailey and through into the inner courtyard, he keeps up a running babble. "Lord Alfred, sir. Lord Richard, he be going to be so glad to see ye. Yer lady wife, she be here and now she be gone. And Lord Richard, he say he not know where ye be and why ye not come and he think ye be with the army way off in the west somewhere. Lord Richard, he be going to be ever so glad ye be here, sir."

As we approach the steps to the main door, he adds, "Ye be giving me yer horse, m'lord, and I take him to the stable and see the grooms take good care of him and feed him and settle him down for the night." I stroke Star Dancer's neck and say, "Thank you, friend," before handing the reins to the squire just as Richard bursts through the door. He scrambles down the steps and embraces me as if it's been years since we last saw each other. "Thank God you're here, Alfred. Come inside."

Following him up the steps, I ask, "Are they still here, Richard? Please tell me they're still here."

Stopping in the doorway, he says quietly, "I'm sorry, Alfred. She said she couldn't wait any longer."

"Then I'm sorry, Richard, I have to go on. I have to find them before they get too far away."

He takes my arm and gently guides me inside. "Not tonight, my friend. Your horse needs rest. You need rest. You can travel faster when you're both refreshed." Reluctantly, I let him lead me inside and upstairs to the second-floor study where he and his father had been finishing the last of the wine from the evening meal. Lord Devereux – usually not one for displays of emotion – rushes across the room and embraces me in a great bear hug. "Thank God you're safe, Alfred. Come here and tell us how you got away from that madman that is your brother. Richard, pour us all a brandy."

"In good time, sir," I tell him. "First I have to know about my family and what you know about where they've gone."

"Of course, son, of course." He gestures for me to sit.

Richard hands around the glasses. "She stayed here three days, Alfred, just as she told your mother she would. Then, night before last, as we were finishing supper, she announced that she had no choice. They had to go the next day. Sometime in the night . . . long before dawn . . . long before anyone was awake . . . they left. To all intents and purposes, vanished in the night."

"Where are they going, Richard? She wouldn't tell Rupert or Mother. Did she give you any clue?"

"She was just as secretive with us," he replies. "And she'd sworn Osbert to secrecy as well. He wouldn't answer any of my questions, though I tried every trick I could think of to wheedle something out of him."

I can't help but smile. Richard looks at me quizzically. "That's exactly why I'd wanted Osbert to look out for them. And now it's working against my finding them."

"He wouldn't answer any questions, that much is for sure. But the evening before they left, he somehow managed to find me alone in the corridor, on the pretext of looking for my squire. As he turned and walked away, he said, as if talking to himself, 'I do hope the track north be passable.' I think he was leaving you a clue, Alfred. If I were a betting man, I'd say they're going to her parents."

"That's what Mother thought as well." I take a sip of brandy. "She's with child. Did she tell you that?"

"No. I don't think she told Avelina either, else I would have heard it from her."

"I didn't know it myself until two days ago.

"What is it with you two?" asks Richard with a chuckle. "She always seems to wind up in that condition when you're about to be in some kind of danger."

I can't help but laugh with him. "Does seem to work out that way, doesn't it?"

Lord Devereux, who's been quietly nursing his brandy, finally speaks. "Your Gwendolyn is a remarkable woman, Alfred. She understands how important your sons are for the future of the realm, despite how uncertain that future may look at the moment. It takes great courage to do what she's doing."

"I never forget, sir, what a lucky man I am. I only hope my luck and whatever wits I may have will reunite us soon."

"Now tell us what's happening in the west. How did John react to the dissolution of the kingdom?"

"He raged in a fury for two days, as the first three messengers arrived. Then he decided he had no need of any of you anyway and turned his attention back to conquering the Territories. You know how short-sighted he is. At the moment, I think he's rather pleased that seven pesky lords are out of his hair. I don't think he's fully grasped the vast reduction in the size of the territory over which he reigns.

"I must tell you, sir, how much I admire the courage you and your fellow lords showed. To split asunder something you and your forebears had worked so diligently to build . . . I'm grateful that my grandfather and father aren't here to see it. And yet I believe they would heartily approve of the path you chose. I only hope that when John is defeated in the Territories and has to come home with his tail between his legs that he'll have had enough of war for a while and can just settle in to be the autocrat he wants to be over the small kingdom that's left to him."

"You seem sure he'll be defeated," Richard remarks.

"John is convinced he'll prevail by numbers and the force of his own will. We know he can't think strategically, and from what I saw, his tactics leave much to be desired as well. Only once did he defer to the recommendations of his commanders, and when that didn't immediately succeed, he took over issuing the orders again.

"The Territorial lords are already out-thinking and out-maneuvering him. They allowed him to cross the border unimpeded, making him the obvious aggressor. And their tactics are worthy of Harold's best. The place they chose to first engage him and the disposition and management of their forces . . . I really don't think John quite knows what he's up against. Either they'll drive him out of their lands – and God only knows if they would cross the border in pursuit – or he'll bull-headedly march into certain defeat and get himself and whatever's left of his army killed. The number of men quietly deserting to return to their homes was growing daily before I left."

"All we can do is wait and see," says Lord Devereux. "Now tell us how you escaped his clutches."

By the time I've finished recounting my plotting and planning – careful to omit Samuel's role – and our eventual escape and journey home, it's grown late. "I think I should get some of that rest everyone keeps telling me I need. I want to be off at daybreak."

"Come," says Richard. "I'll show you to your room."

The day dawns grey and sullen, but I can't let the weather deter me. Richard shows me where the track leads north from behind the stables. Not half an hour later, the rain begins. It never lets up throughout the day. The going is slow, for the track is just that – not a proper road at all but more of a wagon track with well used ruts that would be passable in dry weather but form endless parallel lakes in the ceaseless rain. I keep Star Dancer to the higher ground between the ruts, but even that is uneven and becoming increasingly muddy.

I've no idea how far it might be to the border of the Kingdom of Lakes. By late afternoon, even my rain cloak is soaked and useless. With the heavy cloud, the light disappears early, and no matter how much I might want to go on, there's no choice in this unfamiliar place but to try to find a spot that might provide even a modicum of shelter for the night. I venture off the road and into the woods on one side and eventually find a thicket of shrubs over which I can drape my rain cloak as a sort of poor roof. I hobble Star Dancer, remove his saddle, and give him his feedbag with a ration of oats. Huddled inside the thicket, I try to sleep. But even though the tree canopy and the cloak provide some protection, I'm still miserably wet and uncomfortable.

I must have finally dozed for I wake in grey light to soft whinnies from Star Dancer. It's still raining. I feel even more miserable than the previous night. Attributing that to the fact that I'm soaked to the skin, I munch on a bit of bread, saddle my horse, and head back to the track.

By midday, I'm feeling feverish but know I have to press on. Thinking I must surely have crossed the border by now, I begin looking for a road or even a track that heads west, knowing Lord Godwin's home is far west of here, near the middle of the kingdom. The rain keeps falling, and I see nothing on either side of the road but forest.

Later in the afternoon, I stop at a stream for water. My knees almost give way beneath me as I dismount, and I realize that I really am ill. My forehead is on fire, and my thirst must surely be from fever, for there's certainly no shortage of water all around me. I must go on, though; the fever will pass, I'm sure. It takes more effort than usual to get back in the saddle, but once there, I cluck to Star Dancer and he walks on. I give him his head and let him choose his pace and his ground. Still, there's no sign of a track or even a narrow path leading west through the forest.

As the light begins to fade, I'm feeling more feverish than ever. It occurs to me that perhaps we should stop for the night. But I wonder, if I dismount, would I ever be able to climb back onto my horse's back. I tie the reins together and let them droop over Star Dancer's neck. He walks on as the rain continues to fall and the night closes in around us.

I must have dozed in the saddle for I'm jarred awake by my head falling forward on my chest. Thirsty again, I lean my head back and open my mouth to catch some rainwater. It isn't much, but it takes the edge off my thirst for the moment. The night is black – no stars – no hint of a moon – just the heavy low clouds and the endless rain. It's getting harder to stay in the saddle, so I lean forward and rest on Star Dancer's neck. He keeps his pace slow and steady, making no sudden movement that would jar me from my perch. I hear the voices of children at play but know this is just my feverish mind playing tricks on me.

I'm vaguely aware of Star Dancer taking a detour and rouse myself to see what it is he's trying to go around. There's a fallen limb across the track that, at any other time, we'd have easily jumped. I see what looks like light and some sort of building far in the distance, but I'm sure it's the fever once again playing tricks on my mind. I lay back down on Star Dancer's neck and he plods slowly on. I doze again.

In my dreams, it seems Star Dancer is slowing his pace and coming at last to a stop. I hear a whinny as if he's calling me. Then there are hands . . . someone trying to take me from my horse and calling out. I cling to my horse's neck. Then more hands come and help me down. I hear voices. "Careful . . . let's carry him inside."

And then there's light and there's no more rain. The light is so bright, I dare not open my eyes. I hear more voices and to my fevered brain, one of them sounds like Osbert. And then shouting, "M'lady . . . m'lady . . . come quick!"

I'm being lifted by my shoulders and feet, and it seems as if I'm being carried up some stairs. The light is dimmer at first. Then a door opens, and it's oh so bright again. So many voices . . . drifting in and out. "Put him here." Softness beneath as the hands release me. "Soaked clear through." My head pounding. "Need a fire." Shivering, even under blankets. "Burning with fever. Best ye wait." So many people. I want only to sleep, but there's so much light. Then from somewhere nearby, a different voice, "Alfred . . . my love." And the world goes black.

Author's Notes

Reading medieval and Renaissance documents can be challenging for the modern reader. Paleographers tell us that the written word developed slowly as a poor imitation of speech. Early writings would be sounded out by the reader, often aloud, to determine the words of a text.

Parchment, and later paper, were expensive, so writing was tightly compressed, often with very little space between words. Conventions were used such as well understood abbreviations (for example, .M. instead of writing out the word "Majesty"), superscript letters (w^t for "with"), the use of dashes or wavy lines to indicate omitted letters (such as "demād" for "demand"). (Examples are given for the English reader; different languages had their own conventions.) The "minim," or single downstroke, was used to form several letters, including i, m, n, and u. Words containing numerous of these letters could often be difficult to decipher.

Spelling was not standardized, and the meaning of a particular spelling often had to be deduced from context. In a document describing the architecture of a church or castle, the word "belhaus" was most likely a reference to a "bell house" or "bell tower." In an inventory of kitchen equipment, however, the same spelling very likely meant "bellows."

Punctuation developed slowly. The use of an initial capital at the beginning of a sentence and a large capital at the beginning of a paragraph helped to organize the text into complete thoughts. Later additions included various combinations of dots to indicate separation of words or sentences, slashes to show where the reader should pause for breath, and evolving techniques for indicating that the writer was conveying a question.

Creating Alfred's recorded history of John's reign accurately for the time period would prove challenging for both writer and reader. However, in an attempt to achieve a modicum of authenticity, I've chosen to present the chronicle devoid of modern punctuation, using only the initial capitals and large capitals to delineate sentences and paragraphs. It's my hope this will give the modern reader a glimpse into the nature of early texts without trying his or her patience too severely. In the interest of readability, I've stuck to modern spellings.

Readers interested in pursuing this topic further might consider starting with the website of the National Archives, (Kew, London, Surrey, UK), which provides an informative tutorial on paleography. (http://www.nationalarchives.gov.uk/palaeography/default.htm).

Many authors of historical fiction choose to eschew the use of contractions in favor of more formal dialogue and narrative. In fact, many people believe that written and spoken language in medieval and Renaissance times was more stilted and formal than it is today.

A bit of research, however, reveals that contractions have been with us for many centuries and by Shakespeare's time, were widespread. I've therefore made the decision to use contractions liberally in both the narrative and dialogue within this series. I find it provides a more natural flow and allows my readers to more easily identify with the characters and feel a deeper sense of immersion in the story.

I've tried to be diligent about avoiding linguistic anachronisms (well, anachronisms in general), such as references to someone "going off half-cocked" before guns were even invented. In some cases, however, I've made the conscious choice to use a more modern word to preclude my readers' having to scurry to the dictionary over and over (or worse yet, give up on the book altogether). Use of the word "wagon" is an example of such a choice. In Alfred's time, people would have used "wain" to refer to such a conveyance; but since "wagon" came into common usage in the mid-1500s, I've opted to make the reader's life easier by using the more recognizable word.

On the other hand, I've explicitly chosen to use some period-appropriate words—including slang—for authenticity and for "flavor."

One example is "paindemaine," the term for the finest bread, made with flour that had been sifted multiple times to eliminate as many of the husks and stones from grinding as possible. In later centuries, words such as "manchet" and "wastel" came into use for this fine bread, but since any of the three might require a trip to the dictionary, I chose the most period-appropriate one (and besides, it just sounds fun). Wherever I've used period slang, I don't think the reader will have much difficulty working out the meaning.

Occasionally, there just isn't a period-appropriate word or phrase that is "fit for purpose" for the modern reader. One set of such words: "diplomat," "diplomatic," and "diplomacy." They came into the language much later than Alfred's time – (nineteenth century for the first two, slightly earlier for the last). I simply could not find suitable synonyms that instantly convey all the nuances we understand today from these terms; and writing an elaborate, period-appropriate explanation seemed an unnecessary distraction from the narrative.

Names of characters (both forenames and surnames) are all authentic for the period.

This novel is a work of fiction that tells the story of what might have been in a world that doesn't precisely correspond to the one we know. Readers will note similarities with northern Europe, but my decision to fictionalize the setting was a matter of practicality for my characters. European history from this period and its major actors are too well known for it to be plausible that a different set of kings and nobility might actually have existed. The fictional setting also gave me the freedom to embed the allegory of our own times within Alfred's story. *Pestilence* explores demagoguery, xenophobia, authoritarianism, organized crime, pandemic, and the real human toll of the absence of social responsibility.

For those who prefer to read the Second Son Chronicles solely as entertainment, I hope you get as much enjoyment from immersing yourself in Alfred's world as I've had in bringing his tale to life.

COMING SOON

Upon This Throne

Will Alfred survive? Will his determination to find his family give him the strength of mind and body to endure? Or will rain and fever conspire to achieve what Ralf was unable to?

Where is Gwen taking the children? Is there anywhere she can go that's truly out of John's reach?

What about the war? Will the Territorial lords prevail? Or has John finally listened to his commanders and changed tactics?

And what of the kingdom? Is there any hope of restoring it to its former glory? Or is the dissolution just a prelude to the various fiefdoms joining with the Lakes, Peaks, or other kingdoms, leaving the dreams of Alfred's ancestors just a forlorn memory?

Note from the Author

Word-of-mouth is crucial for any author to succeed. If you enjoyed the book, please leave a review online—anywhere you are able. Even if it's just a sentence or two. It would make all the difference and would be very much appreciated.

Thanks!
Pamela

About the Author

Pamela Taylor brings her love of history to the art of storytelling in the *Second Son Chronicles*. An avid reader of historical fact and fiction, she finds the past offers rich sources for character, ambiance, and plot that allow readers to escape into a world totally unlike their daily lives. She shares her home with two Corgis who remind her frequently that a dog walk is the best way to find inspiration for that next chapter.

Thank you so much for reading one of Pamela Taylor's novels.
If you enjoyed the experience, please check out our recommended
title for your next great read!

Volume 1 of the Second Son Chronicles
Second Son by Pamela Taylor

It is the dawn of the Renaissance, a time when new ideas are just beginning to emerge. Alfred — the eponymous second son — comes of age in the enlightened court of his grandfather. Alfred is convinced that his life will be unremarkable, spent in diligent but mundane service to king and kingdom. His grandfather, however, foresees for him a special destiny.

It is also a time when peace and stability are tenuous, and threats can arise from unexpected quarters. Taken captive while on a mission for the king, Alfred is held for ransom and taken ever farther away from his home. With his prospects dwindling, he must find a way to survive if he is ever to fulfill that mysterious destiny.